Spring Into SciFi 2025 Edition

A Cloaked Press Anthology

All Stories contained in this book are the creations of the authors' minds. Any resemblance to persons/places/events – living or dead – is purely coincidental or used in a fictitious manner.

Published by: Cloaked Press, LLC
P. O. Box 341
Suring, WI 54174
https://www.cloakedpress.com

Cover Design by:
Carmilla M. Ravensworth
https://carmillacreates.carrd.co/

Copyright 2025, Cloaked Press, LLC
ISBN: 978-1-952796-52-4

With Stories From

Duncan Shepard
Barend Nieuwstraten III
Charles Walter
Andrew Akers
K.P.S. Plaha
G.C. Collins
Cliff Aliperti
Hugo Glinn
Steven R. Southard
MR Wells
Mathew Austin
Petina Strohmer
Anthony Boulanger
Matthew McKiernan

Contents

A Mile Beyond Sanity By Duncan Shepard 1
Titans' Gravebelt By Barend Nieuwstraten III 11
The Universe is a Capricious Place By Charles Walter 43
Purgatorium By Andrew Akers 57
There is No Place Like Home By K. P. S. Plaha 91
Assassins By G. C. Collins 105
Obedience Training By Cliff Aliperti 119
Sierran Paradise By Hugo Glinn 133
Its Tender Metal Hand By Steven R. Southard 151
The Alpha Centauri Shuffle By MR Wells 169
Three Bullets for a Glass of Chardonnay By Mathew Austin . 185
The Pied Pipers By Petina Strohmer 207
For a Few $ollars More By Anthony Boulanger 217
The Last Actor By Matthew McKiernan 239
Thank you… 251

A Mile Beyond Sanity

By Duncan Shepard

New Detroit – September 2043 C.E.

Prime Casino's bells would start the race like they always did, ringing between life and death. Brigitte recognized the familiar vibration of the engine building, begging to be unleashed. She glanced at the crowd of humans and androids before pulling her clear full-faced visor down. Even though years had passed since she was last in the driver's seat of a Solar Rocket car, she was confident.

Brigitte tapped a button on her helmet and the dashboard interface lit up as her grip tightened on the sidestick. Her navigator Cliff's twitching eyebrows caught her attention for a split second.

"Cliff, run a system check," Brigitte said in a soft voice.

His anxious energy funneled into his fingers, tapping through a myriad of buttons. *Cliff's mannerisms are just like his father's*, she thought, letting out a sigh.

She blinked her tired eyes, trying to focus them before the inevitable surge of adrenaline hit and electrified all the nerve endings in her body. Competitiveness raged like a fever that could only be extinguished by proving she could beat the AI champion, Vanth. A one-off race, she thought, excusing the abandonment of her rational decision to remain retired.

Vanth's shimmering black Solar Rocket car revved its engine. The machine had soundly beaten all her protégés. In the jungle of lights and wires, deep in the cockpit where the driver and navigator usually sat, there was a competitor unlike anything she faced before. No doubt it had run the race through hundreds of simulations, deciding every inch of tarmac it would use beforehand, an unfair advantage against human competitors.

"Citizens organic and synthetic," the announcer's voice boomed through the streets and radios. "The race between champions will start in two minutes. Both cars will have their wheels engaged for an old-fashioned street duel. Four to one odds in favor of Vanth. As always, the choice of route is up to the competitor. Place your bets and follow along on the V.R. livestream!"

Brigitte ran her hand down her seven-point harness and reconfirmed everything was buckled. "Cliff, I don't think I should tell you, but this race isn't just for glory… I've bet my savings on the win."

He turned his head toward her and raised his index finger over the center of his mouth, contemplating. "That's reckless, foolish even. Why jeopardize yourself?"

She completed her ritual of unzipping her fire suit down to her chest and then back up to her neck before answering. The fire suit was more of an inane gesture than anything else; a heavy crash would mean their immediate deaths.

"I grew up on these streets…" her gaze turned to the row of buildings with flickering lights along old Woodward Ave. "Pilgrim Charity Hospital, the one I'm director at, is out of funds and the Advanced Intelligence senators don't want to help people that can't afford care. Our aid is deadlocked," she said, punctuating it with a nervous chuckle.

He gave a shallow nod. "Damn it Brigitte, I wish you hadn't told me that." He turned his focus back to the interface. "Everything is good to go with our systems; the solar cells are fully charged," Cliff said. He chewed his lower lip.

The solid-state sulfide electrolyte battery in the Solar Rocket car meant it could run faster than any streetcar, as long as there was sun. The hard afternoon light silhouetted the car, and Brigette's hopes, against the road as the early smell of autumn's approach provided a false sense of calm.

The bells rang, and Brigitte slammed the accelerator to the floor.

Nothing happened; they were still idling. Vanth rocketed away, its precise logic ensuring the perfect getaway. Frustration boiled in Brigitte.

"Trouble for the organics!" The announcer yelled.

"No kidding," Brigitte said under her breath as she studied the car's dash. Her cinnamon eyes widened. "Cliff, we're still engaged in system check!"

He winced as he punched a green button on the side of the cockpit. They were hurled into their seats as Brigitte stomped the accelerator and the acrid smell of burning rubber filled the air. The crowd became a mere blur and the LCD billboards affixed to buildings were just flashes of light as their speed increased.

Not the way to start the race…, Brigitte thought.

She zeroed in on getting her tires up to temperature and her head back in the game. Their Solar Rocket car sped toward the strange place between seconds on a clock. A place where a single breath felt like eternity, and exhaling at the wrong moment could spell disaster. The skyline was painted with a kaleidoscope of camera drones and advertisements.

"Toward the Wall of Desolation. Next right, then a sharp left," Cliff choked out.

Their car arced around the empty gray streets. Brigitte's eyes narrowed on the road ahead, acting more like a huntress than a competitor. Up ahead the faint outline of Vanth took a sudden right-hand turn and entered a rusty warehouse's parking lot. Brigitte kept her foot pressed down as they continued straight.

"What are you doing? We're going the wrong way," Cliff strained.

"I know a shortcut to the Wall, an alleyway I always walked through as a girl," Brigitte said, and then gave a bold white smile. "Bet Vanth didn't consider that in its probabilities, our little advantage."

Brigitte guided the car across sections of broken pavement. The concrete walls of buildings flanked the car, leaving only inches to spare. They bounced as she fought the car's urge to dart left and right over the potholes, before reemerging on two-lane Warren Avenue. In an instant, Brigitte swerved as a pair of young kids wandered into the street. Her heart was in her throat as her adrenaline pumped even harder.

"There hasn't been a pedestrian accident in years… glad I didn't break that streak," she said.

They drove by an old speed limit sign: 30 MILES PER HOUR

She glanced down at the interface speedometer, "208 miles per hour."

Red and green lights in the cockpit began flashing as they slowed to make a left turn onto a street with derelict houses. "We've got minor suspension damage," Cliff said. "Shouldn't impact the handling but avoid potholes." He switched the lights off and resumed searching the nav map.

Brigitte's neck stiffened and a warm pulsating pain crept in. Years out of the car left her susceptible to the strain of G-forces. Something the AI driver doesn't have to worry about. She wrestled the car through turns, passing under streetlights that swayed.

Brigitte gritted her teeth as the remnants of deserted dreams in the form of abandoned homes bordered the road. The musky smell of rotting wood filled the car as they passed the decaying houses.

"This place was so beautiful… before organic tech workers were obsolete," Brigitte muttered. A city park buried in overgrown shrubs and trees flew by.

"Ah! I see where we are now, we'll be back on the designated route shortly," Cliff said.

Brigitte caressed the brake pedal as they entered a 90-degree corner. Her motion on the sidestick was smooth; the car effortlessly sweeping into the corner before she accelerated back to the outside of the road.

There was Vanth. The engine looked like the burning torch of an underworld goddess as it sped along.

"An update on our race! Brigitte Nice and Cliff Wheldon have rejoined our leader, Vanth. The racers are approaching half distance."

The two cars swapped places back and forth as they zipped past an empty university.

Brigitte's mind was unusually adrift, a real danger for a racer. Brain fade. She was in the heat of battle but fatigue crept in. Vanth pulled ahead and maintained a two-car length lead. The illusion of relative speed urged Brigitte to go faster to make another pass, but Vanth was simply too quick. Its decisions were governed by mathematics and the lines it took were perfect. The sun was beginning to set, and the ghosts of the night were ready to emerge.

"Your dad was the best…" Brigitte said under her breath, almost resigning to being runner-up.

Cliff shot her a wide-eyed look.

"He didn't deserve that swift end. I should've done things differently." A lump formed in her throat as truth and emotion wrestled within her chest.

"Now's not the time, Brigitte. The accident wasn't your fault," Cliff said.

Droplets of water struck the glass windshield and painted it with opportunity. Brigitte knew Vanth hadn't raced in the rain, but she had. The black Solar Rocket car slowed down, and Brigitte maneuvered around the righthand side.

Gloomy clouds covered the orange sky as the race cars' lights illuminated the way forward. Brigitte sensed the wheels struggling to grip the pavement as the moisture darkened the road.

"You're going to get us killed!" Cliff exclaimed.

The rear tires undulated back and forth, fighting the amount of power Brigitte was putting into the throttle. The rain washed away her self-doubt and the champion reemerged. She chose lines that gave little room for error but maximized speed, improvising her decisions. Their car hugged the very edge of the yellow painted curb as they sped toward the Wall of Desolation.

"Citizens, we're witnessing something special here. The Queen of Solar Rocket Racing is reclaiming her throne. We've received approval from the United Northern Corporation to continue the race in the rain based on the number of bets that have been placed, though there's a chance the cars will run out of battery," the announcer barked.

Brigitte ignored it; her concentration was razor sharp. The Wall wasn't far now, and the car dipped and bumped as she braked and maneuvered.

"Vanth's closing," Cliff said, looking into their rearview mirror.

"It's learning," Brigitte said. She responded with even more speed as the street signs whipped around in the piercing wind. Her movements inside the cockpit blended into a syncopated symphony of braking, turning, and accelerating.

Vanth crept alongside and made its move past them. Brigitte's fingers hurt from her tight grip on the sidestick, which rattled around from the turbulence of Vanth's wake. On intuition, she guided their car behind Vanth.

In a flash their car felt like it was floating. Brigitte watched as Vanth slid with precipitous speed into the curb.

Aquaplaning.

Brigitte lifted her foot from the accelerator and jabbed the brake. The tires bit back into the pavement that glistened with water. Vanth continued spinning its tires, fruitlessly trying to gain traction with power.

"Solar energy is down, we're going to lose interface shortly," Cliff said.

The Wall of Desolation stood like an ominous foe against the dark horizon.

"Just give me five minutes, Cliff. I can run without the interface."

"Affirmative."

The lights illuminating Brigitte's visor dimmed and then disappeared. She would be driving on instinct alone now, something she hadn't done since she raced go-karts 20 years ago.

Vanth regained control and blew past them as the rain began dying down. The heavy cloud cover remained but Brigitte was determined to finish the race, even if it was second to the AI champion.

"I'm disconnecting nav from the car completely," Cliff said. "We're running blind now."

Brigitte's mind flashed back to her last podium four years ago. The sweet taste of Neo-Stroh's beer, the smell of the fireworks, and the roar of the crowd. The memory spiraled out of her psyche as Vanth approached the finish line at the Wall of Desolation.

Without warning, Vanth slowed and then came to a standstill. Brigitte swung the car to the left. The sickening sound of metal twisting and scratching filled the cockpit as the side of their car scraped along Vanth. The front right wheel ripped off and went hurtling into a building. Brigitte jerked the stick to the right and activated the handbrake, catapulting the rear end of the car into a sharp turn to avoid the wall, allowing the laws of kinetic energy to decide if they'd smash.

She scrambled to straighten the car and released the handbrake. "Old bootleg turn," she said, fighting with all her strength to keep the car going straight.

"In an unbelievable change of events, it appears that Vanth has run out of solar energy… it can't run," the announcer blared.

This is it. Brigitte's heart pounded with anxiety and excitement. Renewed hope. The unmistakable mix of feelings that meant she'd staved off the shadow of death once again.

Their Solar Rocket car crossed the finish line as the engine grumbled and shut down. A cacophony of cheers and yells erupted from the spectators gathered.

Cliff couldn't contain his excitement. "You've done it, Brigitte. The car held out just long enough!"

Brigitte lifted the clear visor and used her gloves to remove the beads of perspiration from her forehead. She looked into Cliff's eyes and a swell of pride, sadness, and unabashed jubilation washed over her in waves.

"Wish your dad could've seen this," she said, her voice picking up volume.

"Me too," Cliff replied.

They both let out a yelp of victory.

Brigitte unbuckled her harness and removed her helmet. Drones swarmed around their car like piranhas on a struggling animal. She lifted the gull-wing door and stepped out.

The announcer ran up to Brigitte and stuck a microphone in her face with its metallic hand. "How'd you beat Vanth?"

"Vanth can't drive on instinct; it needs a stream of data from its sensors to determine its decisions. That wasn't possible when the battery lost charge with all this cloud cover. That's the only way we beat it. Well, that, and human spontaneity, our unfair advantage, the thing that edged us over the competition," Brigitte said, catching her breath at the end of her statement. Her nose twitched from the smell of the smoke now emanating from the burned-out brakes.

The announcer showed no emotions which was not unusual for a synthetic. "A lot of people bet the AI would beat you. What do you say to them?"

Brigitte removed her gloves and grimaced as she massaged a set of blisters on her fingers. "It was by far the toughest race I've ever finished. Androids sure know how to build a racecar and Vanth was fierce. Pilgrim Charity Hospital is going to have some much-needed funds," the edges of her lips formed into a wry smile. "A special thanks to my navigator, Cliff, for his quick reactions when we started losing energy."

Cliff stumbled over to the two of them, in awe of the feat he had just accomplished with Brigitte. She put her arm around him.

"You heard it here first on U.N.C. sports stream. Vanth was the toughest competitor that 38-year-old retired champion Brigitte Nice has ever faced. We'll be certain the next time Vanth encounters these circumstances it won't lose; it'll know what to do," the announcer said.

"Compassion. You put yourself in jeopardy because of compassion, Brigitte. Something the Advanced Intelligence doesn't have. It paid off," Cliff said, hugging Brigitte.

As darkness settled across the celebration, the bells of New Detroit rang out once more. This time the bells didn't signal the dawn of Brigitte's race. The pendulous motion tolled the sunset of Brigitte's racing career and she felt peace.

Duncan Shepard is a writer and musician living in Hartford, Connecticut, USA. He began writing short stories in 2022 as a way to connect with his late father, George V. Shepard. When not writing, Duncan is creating music with his wife, Chantelle, in their psychedelic rock group The Striped Bananas.

Titans' Gravebelt
By Barend Nieuwstraten III

There were stories, barely beyond rumour that sounded like monumental exaggerations, but they didn't do the sight justice. Whatever words Kellan had heard describing this place, fell substantially short. A belt of ruin orbiting a small sun between its second and third planets. Rocks and shrapnel, floating in a scattered belt of both planetary debris rich in minable minerals and the corpses of metal titans. Each a colossus or the remains of one. Most seemed bipedal in nature. At least those sufficiently intact to tell.

"Giant robots, just floating about in space," Kellan marvelled, leaning forward to see as much as he could from the passenger section.

"Cyborgs, to be precise," another man on the shuttle said. A thin man whose white coveralls precluded the likelihood of any physical mining. "There is an organic component to them. Very dead and frozen. A stretched membrane of some kind, or so I've heard. Whatever they originally were, they were organic underneath. Like shellfish but far better at making shells."

"Yeah," another passenger said, dressed in the same coveralls as Kellan but with a different logo on his chest and arm. "I heard they look like snot inside. Like someone sneezed in something and then tried to open it. But it's all gone hard."

The thinner man frowned and nodded. "Crude but, from what I've been told, apt."

Kellan shrugged. "Well, I'm just here to pull ore from rock. I wasn't really briefed on giant robots with snot for brains. But it doesn't mean I'm not impressed to see them."

The thin man nodded and smiled. "Well, the three main branches are represented here. Miners, scrappers, and reverse engineers," he said, pointing to Kellan, the other man, then himself. He then pointed to the shuttle's forward starboard window where a giant mechanical hand lay open as if reaching for something. It could easily have gripped the shuttle in its bronzy fingers if it was still active. "Guess we won't being seeing much of each other to compare notes." He shrugged and leaned back in his seat.

Kellan tilted his head, noticing long dark globules of something stretching across megameters of the belt, barely catching the sunlight as it turned. "What's that?"

The thin man looked for a while before he seemed to realise what Kellan was talking about. "Oh, iron and nickel, mostly. Once part of the planetary core of the world that became this debris belt. I thought most of it had been-"

***

That was the last thing Kellan could remember when he woke on the rocky floor of the asteroid cave. He blinked himself awake, staring up at green-grey rock and elements of buried architecture and piping protruding from it. He spat out grains of dirt and coughed, confused and lost. His right leg was numb, and he soon realised it was because something was laying on top of it. The e-drill. He leant up and pushed it off only to see his headgear rocking on the ground. There was a hole in the visor with blood sprayed on the inside of it.

He suddenly remembered disembarking from the shuttle onto the main station, with brief flashes of his induction and tutorial. He then remembered visiting a park as a boy with his parents, playing with some old man's dog. Then, after the unrelated interlude, he recalled arriving at the sleeping quarters of the mining facility on the asteroid and unpacking his things. He flashed back to kissing Toshiko in the supply cabinet in high school. Next, he was strapping on the e-drill and commencing work, cutting through rock with a flickering beam of red, emitting a digital snapping sound as it eliminated portions of rock.

Between each flash of memory, he realised he was seeing far more than the focal points to which he was paying attention. It was as if two people were driving a terrain buggy down memory lane and fighting over the steering wheel. Instead of recalling all the fun times he had, he was seeing himself in class. Moments in different years, learning English, maths, science, and struggling with it all. At least, he remembered struggling.

He looked again to his helmet, rocking on the ground, and the blood-spattered about forehead height and off to one side. He squinted at it, concerned.

He remembered approaching the debris ring on the shuttle and talking to the other two. He flashed back to taking the job and signing a contract. The words didn't mean much to him at the time when he skimmed over it, but he remembered every word now, and was less than keen on some of the clauses. Children's learning programs flashed past his eyes from his earliest education, with colouring games, connecting dots, puzzles, tests. He saw himself writing down answers he now knew were terribly wrong. He winced, embarrassed at questions he asked, now understanding why the other children laughed. He saw the sympathy in some teachers' eyes. He grimaced at the ones who were disappointed, and squinted at those who seemed to delight in humiliating him. Only now did he recognise them for what they truly were: educators failing at their task and taking their insecurities out on him. It was so frustrating, but as he found himself back in each classroom, looking at the displays, it all seemed rather simple now. Every word every teacher ever said finally sank in. All the things he never understood were now unlocking, compiling in his mind, and finally broadening his knowledge base.

He picked the helmet off the ground and stuck his gloved finger through the hole. Pulling off the glove, he then felt the right side of his forehead. Something hard stuck to his flesh. Something metal. His finger came away wet. His eyes bulged at the blood on his fingertips.

"Interface established," a voice in his head said. "Language and developmental programming extrapolated from soft storage data. Cerebral functionality optimised. Hello, Kellan Mathew Reed."

"Uh… hi?" Kellan said, back.

"Colloquial familiarity," it said again. "Hi… Kellan."

Kellan looked around. "Sorry, who's this?"

"Interface bridging unit."

Kellan looked around. Technically the question was answered but he'd need a lot more. "Who… or what… deployed you?" he asked, surprising himself. It seemed a very out of character thing to say.

"Self-launch to assess and contextualise circumstance."

Kellan suddenly remembered something flying out of the rock and hitting him in the head. He recalled ripping off his helmet, and staggering. There had been a terrible noise vibrating in his skull and the brassy object that launched at him was longer than what he had just felt outside his head. "You drilled a hole in my head to find out what was happening?"

"Correct."

Though it was a shock, he was surprisingly calm. "So, now what?"

"Acquire more data on expired civilisation."

"This is just a mining rock. The station might have more information, but…" he let his memories catch up to him. "I've only been here three days. I don't have clearance."

"Contact station," the voice suggested.

"And talk to who?" Kellan asked. "The only way I'm getting over there is if I tell them what you are. I don't think that'll work out well for either of us."

"No other access method available. Probability of data core component present on station: high. Interface."

"I don't know if they'll let us near any of the salvaged tech."

"Interface."

"I don't think you understand."

"Interface with contact," the voice clarified and flashed an image of the skinny man from the shuttle ride. "Katano."

Kellan pulled his head back. "Where did you get that name from?"

A memory of boarding the shuttle asserted itself in his mind. The skinny man in white boarded just before him. Kellan was distracted by a young woman operating a nearby loader when he heard Katano say his name to the dockmaster.

"Report to medic," the device said. "Request contact with Katano, using medical clearance."

"Alright…" Kellan stood up, collecting his gear and made his way back down the tunnel.

"You're back a little early, aren't you?" the equipment management officer said, as Kellan returned the e-drill.

Kellan handed him the helmet, tapping his finger above the hole in the visor. "Going to see the medic. Got shot in the head with a rivet or something."

The officer looked up to Kellan's forehead and jumped back with bulging eyes. "Ah… yeah. Go, go."

***

The medic's waiting room had about five people already sitting there, nursing arm wounds, a burn, and other issues. Kellan walked past and wrapped a knuckle on the reception desk. "I need to see a doctor."

"Swipe your thumb to queue," she said.

Kellan coughed to get her attention. "Triage might dictate a more urgent approach."

She looked up and reacted in much the same way the equipment officer had. She hit the comm. "Doctor Thorpe, I think we have an emergency."

The doctor came out and quickly ushered Kellan in. "Good god, man," he said, leading him to his surgery.

"Listen, doctor, I need you contact the station. There's someone new there named Katano. He's going to want to be involved in this."

"How are you feeling? Are you dizzy, nauseated? Can you-"

"Doctor, please listen. Call Katano on the station. It's not a rivet. Its tech."

"Listen, you're probably in shock, you need to-"

"Doctor," Kellan said, grabbing his arm. "The damage to the cerebellum has been compensated for by the interface. You need to use your clearance to call the research department on the station for immediate collection. The medical emergency has passed. But the need to communicate with those examining this precise technology is paramount." Kellan pulled his own head back, having consciously planned to say none of those things. "Damage?" he asked the interface.

"Irreversible but no longer of concern," the device in his head said, internally. "Net gain achieved for neurological functionality."

"I see…" Kellan said, wincing.

"You see what?" the medic asked.

"The call. Station. Katano."

The medic nodded and made the call.

"Sorry, was there an issue with my physical?" a familiar voice asked.

Kellan turned the monitor around.

"Oh," Katano said, looking closer. "I know you."

"Yes, good to see you again. Just letting you know, a piece of tech drilled into my skull. Thought you might want to send for me so you can take a close look." Kellan angled the point of entry towards the screen.

"What's it doing?" Katano asked, pressing buttons near his console as he stared intrigued.

"Internal communication, mostly. It's an interface to bridge organics with the mechanical tech, you're researching. It's in a rush to learn what you have."

"Me? I've only been here a few days."

"Didn't know who else to ask for."

"Fair enough. I'll see what I can do. Expect… a lot of security."

"Don't think it means to put up a fight. Just wants to determine how long it's been out of service. Along with everything else, I suppose."

Katano nodded. "Protocol. These great mechs were built for combat, so command's going to take every precaution."

Kellan nodded. "See you soon."

"In the meantime, doctor, if you're there…" Katano said. "Some scans would be helpful."

"Oh, uh, of course," the medic agreed, turning the console back towards himself.

***

After a series of medical scans primarily focusing on his head, Kellan boarded a shuttle at the docking bay. There, as promised, a team of security personnel supplemented the mining facility guards and had him restrained.

"That's really not necessary," Kellan assured them. "I'm the one who called you guys. You haven't captured me, I'm a willing participant in this relocation."

"Just a precaution," one of the senior guards said. "Nothing personal."

Kellan sat quietly in the shuttle as they took him to the central research station. Once more, he was given a view of the Titan's Gravebelt. Flying across it instead of towards it gave him a closer look at some of the giant mechs frozen in their final poses as they slowly turned in their orbital ring. Some were partially covered in white or light grey as the unfiltered sun had bleached their colour. Between blockier armoured parts and mounted weapons, thick metal cables formed a structure like a network of great copper and silver muscles. Shuttles docked at platforms erected onto them for on-site research.

The group of security officers accompanying Kellan were watching him instead of the wonders outside. The shuttle soon docked at the station and brought him to the office where Katano worked. When he saw the man he'd shared a shuttle with a few days earlier, he raised his cuffed hands together to give him an awkward wave.

"Yes, I am sorry about that," Katano said, but after reviewing the scans, the senior science officers thought it necessary." He gestured to two men with him. "This is Dixon and Singh, in charge of the research sector of the station, here."

They both walked past Katano and stared at Kellan's head, barely acknowledging him on a personal level.

"Seems to have just drilled its way in, sealed the entry point, and cauterized the soft tissue, as well as locally anesthetising the area, omitting any pain to the subject," Singh said.

Dixon hummed in agreement. "Yes, let's get him into the lab." He signalled the guards to bring him.

As the guards grabbed Kellan's upper arms, he sighed and rolled his eyes. "Ah, good. I'd forgotten how to follow people."

Powerless to intervein, Katano gave an apologetic look.

"Sarcasm is viewed as resistance in functionaries with minimal intellectual capacity," the device in Kellan's brain warned him. "Compliance has a higher probability of yielding a later opportunity for escape."

Escape, Kellan thought. Is that the plan here?

"Ultimately, but acquisition of data is primary," it responded.

Wait, you can hear my thoughts? So, I don't need to talk out loud to communicate with you?

"Correct."

Well, that will look less crazy at least.

"And lower the perceived threat level."

Before long, Kellan was sitting in a lab while the two senior science officers were probing his implant with hand held-scanners and readers. The interface device remained silent during their investigation.

"The intrusion into the forward lobe seems irreparable yet somehow unimpactful," Dixon said. "The patient exhibits no discomfort or inebriety-like symptoms."

They continued to share their assessment with each other without consulting Kellan himself. He waited patiently, with his bound hands in his lap and security guards standing nearby, watching for any sudden movements.

"How are you doing?" Katano asked Kellan.

"I feel fine, all things considered," Kellan said, with a shrug. "Though, considering all things, as I recently have, I can't help but feel I sold myself short getting into physical labour. I think, perhaps I might be better suited to something that exercises a little more cognitive functionality. I'm confident that if were to stay here I could probably aid in the understanding of these dormant giants."

Katano looked at him, curiously. "You believe you have something to bring to this operation?"

"More than anyone else, I should imagine."

Dixon and Singh looked to each other cynically.

"I don't see any major activity taking place, but then we don't know how this thing operates," Dixon said. "For now, it doesn't seem to be doing much more than maintaining functionality it otherwise would have severely diminished with its intrusive entry."

"Along with mitigating a potential fatality," Singh added.

When they stopped scanning his head, Kellan sighed with exaggerated boredom and held up his hands. "If you're going to have armed guards watching me at all times, they probably don't need me to be constrained to improve their aim."

Katano nodded. "I don't think he's a threat."

Dixon shook his head. "He has alien tech embedded in his brain; we can't really be sure."

At the device's prompt, Kellan spoke. "Run into this trouble before, have you?"

Dixon and Singh looked at each other again.

"Much of your tech carries the digital hallmarks of another civilisation familiar to the one over whose ruins you hover. There is no direct translation for their name that would really suit, at least not one I'm willing to volunteer while constrained. But presumably you're familiar with the source data. A quadrupedal cephalopodic aquatic species cybernetically augmented. Aggressively xenophobic, especially towards gas breathers. Unlikely to have shared technology willingly. Most likely scenario... salvage. Similar to what you're hoping to achieve here." Kellan found himself thinking back on every bit of technology in his lifetime with an additional perspective provided by the device attached to him. "Oh... well before my lifetime it seems. Were your predecessors able to establish a timeline? I'm not facilitated to approximate the time elapsed since they made the mess outside, but I'd be curious to know."

"You know about the ship?" Singh asked.

Kellan smiled. "I do now. How long ago was that?"

"That's classified."

Kellan huffed with disappointment and looked away. "Have it your way."

"But it was a few centuries ago," Singh reluctantly admitted. "Even then, it was believed at the time to be positively ancient. Yet, it brought humanity forwards, leaps and bounds. Artificial gravity, energy weaponry, cybernetics, diagnostic tech, propulsion, manoeuvrability in astronautics, forcefields, containment barriers, holography, and so many other areas all stemmed from that discovery. Launching us out of our native solar system, it was the single most significant discovery in human history."

"Not that it's in any history texts," Kellan mused. "They certainly don't teach us about this catalyst for our technological renaissance in school."

"A second renaissance spawned by technology that predates our first," Dixon said. "Hardly encouraging to the innovative department of the human spirit to admit we stole progress only to catch up to where someone else was a millennium earlier. An alarming admission to announce we're so far behind the only other example of interstellar life we've discovered."

"Two fought to mutual extinction," Kellan reminded them. "Had they survived and continued to progress, what would that make us in their eyes?"

"Beneath contempt if they set sights on our civilisation," Dixon said.

"It's a substantial galaxy," Kellan said. "Our nearest neighbours wiped themselves out some time ago and no one else has tried to contact us or managed to cross our path. Maybe they're just as far behind as we are. Perhaps more. Only time will tell." Kellan held up his hands again. "Far less time if you let me help you."

Dixon and Singh seemed to consider it.

"We're on the same side here," Kellan said. "The third renaissance awaits, immortalising us in the secret pages of history."

Singh gave a reluctant nod to a security officer who unfastened Kellan's wrists.

Kellan rubbed his wrists and pointed to the component in his head. "Now, this is not the first time you've seen one of these, is it? The organics in the mechs, would each have one implanted in the nucleus of the membrane into which they were engineered."

Dixon tightened his brow with intrigue. "Ah, so that's not an evolved state?"

"Not a natural one, no," Kellan instructed him as the need for internal conversation had in turn evolved within him. He was now practically one with the interface. "The titans were originally designed to be piloted by the planet's dominant species who walked the world, when all these asteroids were assembled, but a subspecies was instead bread for longer term inhabitation able to bypass the threat of physical atrophy and not require nutrition from materials subject to spoilage. Something that could live on a combined diet of chemicals, radiation, energy emissions, and refined substances of extraordinary longevity. They were afforded limited sentience making them less prone to biochemical urges and speculative neurology. Single minded, obedient, and entirely focused on tactical operations and objectives. Of course… the other benefit was that life support systems would be easier to maintain over extended periods in emergency scenarios. Whatever catastrophic event took place here, seemingly extended its effects beyond those systems' capacity to preserve and protect. That is why I need to interface with another neural node. I wish to determine precisely what took place here."

"Wasn't your... node here for that event?" Katano asked.

"In the vicinity, perhaps," Kellan explained. "But not integrated into a living witness. This unit was inactive at the time. Part of what preserved it."

The three lead Kellan to another room where large chambers were set up with clear viewing windows. Within, there were petrified segments of stretched membrane, frosted and hard with nerves stretching across them. There were segments broken with stretched viscous film still connecting them from within.

"It's a strange consistency," Singh said. "It has lost its elasticity, petrified even at room temperature, but only a few centimetres in. I'm impressed that it didn't congeal completely solid."

Dixon nodded. "Yes, the chambers and conduits it inhabited, did quite the impressive job of preserving the organic tissue, even after all other systems failed."

"We removed one of the neural interface components like the one in your head," Singh explained. "We don't know the technology well, but it seemed some of its internal components were fused. The result of an electromagnetic pulse or some similar discharged shockwave that-"

"How much of it did you leave intact?"

"We managed to remove the outer casing, then relied solely on scans to study the rest," Singh explained. "We want to be precise when we eventually perform a complete disassemble."

Kellan looked around. "If I might view those scans, I could design some replacement parts, if you have the facilities to manufacture them."

"We mostly use the ones in here for medical tools, as our primary research here is focused on the biological aspects," Dixon explained. "The labs attached to the giant mechs are more engineering based. But… that terminal will access the engineering hub."

Kellan went to the terminal. His whole adult life he'd never really interacted with one before. He'd swiped his hand over terminals, the odd pass, or connected his datapad, but it never went beyond that. Not since school, and he didn't really pay attention there. Now, however, everything said in those classes swam fresh in his head along with everything done in front of him, typically after an annoyed sigh from his teacher or fellow student. He began investigating the computer and exploring beyond the direct interface, looking at files and systems, he'd never thought to look for before. Still logged in under Singh's access, he opened the system up to remote access and found connections to all other terminals on the network, throughout the facility.

"What are you doing?" Katano asked.

"Looking to see how this network connects and transmits so I can access all stored data faster," Kellan found himself saying. "I want to be able to link with it to establish an overview to gage limitations and parameters. Ah, here we go." He felt the neural interface take over as the screen displayed a turning cog. Information and knowledge flooded in and Kellan suddenly understood a variety of mechanical devices for both mining equipment, medical tools, wiring, circuitry, processors, even how to build the terminal before him from all its separate components.

"What's happening?" Singh asked, concerned.

"I appear to be educating myself on the next step in replacing the parts in the damaged neural interface."

"But... you're just sitting there."

Kellan smiled and accessed the module design application, developing first a tool to operate on the device, then the replacement parts. The others watched intrigued, as the interface provided data exponentially faster than Kellan could hope to enter it manually.

A hatch opened in the wall nearby, offering the parts he'd programmed into it. He took them and commenced work on the piece of ancient technology, identical to the one burrowed into his head.

When he was done, the two units communicated and Kellan saw the life of the organic augment from the moment it was connected. Born and educated in a glass cage, fed knowledge like a battery animal, flooded with hormones and steroids to accelerate its initial life cycle. Genetically adapted and unrecognisable from the species from which it was extracted, it slowly developed a consciousness within an extremely limited scope. It knew nothing of life as its progenitors did. Born to be a functionary with little to no understanding of what else there was before military tactics, strategies, historic campaigns, sieges, and invasions were dumped into it, just as they were with Kellan. He saw a whole life, spent in a chamber to support it, viewing its world and the surrounding systems with only military objectives in mind, reserving only some secret corner of its consciousness to admire the wonder, beauty, and majesty of how the galaxy around it worked.

Kellan looked to the congealed broken body of the bioengineered membrane sitting in pieces in another glass cage. It looked like nothing more than biological resin; stretched, frozen, and hardened with translucent organs that had failed over a millennium ago. Physically, it looked like mucus, as the other man on the shuttle had said, but now he knew its mind intimately. He remembered its life in addition to his own. Proud to serve. The titans stood guarding cities of their world while others orbited it, patrolling their system and moving between others to defend their colonies as the aquatic species invaded. A great interstellar war of the mechanical titans fighting against enormous destructive fleets of their enemy. It took a lot to bring a titan down, but the enemy's sheer numbers were their strength. He saw the great hands of the titans tearing apart the ships and watching their enemy's breathing fluid escape into space, expanding quickly, boiling then freezing as the hostile four-tentacled creatures within either slipped out into the vacuum of space flailing or caught in the suddenly solidified spreading water. Missiles and beams of energy fired in both directions, and Kellan knew the pleasure of exacting revenge on the creatures. As cruel as the titan pilots' lives were, they were proud and dedicated to fight and fall for their progenitors.

"There was a war," he told them as soon as he digested the years of memories thrust upon him. "Between the people of this world who made these great mechanical constructs and the swarm of the aquatics in their fighters; the originators of humanity's great technological renaissances." He smiled in wonder. "It was terrible, but… I've never seen anything like it. It was beyond anything I would have thought to imagine. The aquatics didn't have colonies of their own, requiring very specific conditions for a fluidic atmosphere. Not unlike the sea water of our aquariums. But they had designs on the colonies of those titans' creators. Worlds with oceans and seas that could be terraformed to suit their needs. Worlds they could have shared, needing nothing of the land and those who dwelt upon it, but they instead chose to attack. And when all the colonies were lost, the titans were sent to the aquatics' home world and they released a deadly pathogen into their ocean world's water that killed everything. Everything. All terrestrial life was lost in retaliation. So, the remaining fleet sent everything against this world. I'm not certain what precisely happened but the world was broken. Not in some great cataclysmic explosion but torn apart in some painfully slow catastrophe, engineered by the aquatics. Few escaped, as some nova spread, knocking out all technology. The titan pilots survived but the titans themselves did not. Frozen as they were while the organic pilots must have been trapped for months in their small chambers. Left to watch the planet they were created to defend break apart. The enemy ships had to sacrifice themselves to pull off the cataclysm and the rest were destroyed in battle. A few they disabled and sent hurtling off while their own pilots must have eventually suffocated on stale water." Kellan sat despondent as he felt the dead soldier's sorrow of failure and imagined its months of torture, trapped inside the disabled mechanical warrior it inhabited. He looked back to the terminal. "I could design you the replacement parts for all of these locked giants. They could all potentially work again. In exchange, I'll need to claim one for myself."

"Why would you need one?" Katano asked.

"I need to seek out and survey the colonies to see if they are safe for human habitation. There may also be remaining dormant tech there I could repair."

"I'm not sure we could authorise that," Dixon said. "Certainly, they wouldn't want us to let an... asset like you free."

"I wouldn't be free, I'd be working for humanity. I have no allegiance to an extinct civilisation. I certainly can't run away and join them. If they had survived and managed to rebuild, you'd probably know about it by now. Either way, the neural interface wasn't designed to dominate a mind but augment it to communicate with technology. Technology I thought you had an interest in acquiring and learning more about. I'll show you what I can, here, but I need to acquire more data. There may be a terminal or datahub somewhere that I can access or bring back online. One way or another, one of these titans, or at least the head of one of the broken ones will need to be adapted for a human pilot." He looked back to the terminal. "I suppose I could design something that would work in them. Though, it would be missing a lot of the benefits that came with housing genetically modified pilots." He pointed to the remains of the semi-petrified membrane from which the other neural interface was removed. "But I could give you what you need to get the rest of these titans all back up and running again, refitted for human pilots."

"I'd have to check in with our superiors," Dixon said.

"I have to assume that what I'm offering precisely matches their objectives but of course they'll want to facilitate my assistance in such a way that it would exclusively benefit them," Kellan explained. "It will slow down everything I want to show you, and ultimately, they'd prefer to have someone they already own interfacing, so I'd more likely be kept as a subject of experimentation and study while one you would be nominated for the interface unit I've restored. Are you sure that will satisfy your scientific and academic curiosity that aligns with all your own professional goals or would you prefer to opt for something more mutually beneficial?"

"I don't think you understand," Singh said. "We answer to people. We don't get to make decisions like that. The way they want to do things is exactly how things are going to get done. That's just how it works."

"I'm afraid that's not acceptable," Kellan said, picking up the other restored neural interface node. There were several clamping sounds about the room as it was put into lockdown, followed by high pitch sounds coming from the security officers' earpieces before they collapsed unconscious. "Of the two of you, Dixon and Singh, who has seniority?"

Katano subtly pointed to Singh without his colleges seeing.

Kellan held up the small device as it powered up and let it launch at the scientist's head. It let out a high-pitched whirring sound as it shot into his forehead, drilling at high speed, burrowing in as he passed out into Katano's arms.

"Now, Dixon, I should inform you that I'm tapped into most systems throughout the facility. No one's coming to help you because no alert has been raised. So, there's no pressure to follow counterintuitive protocols from a command structure that will hinder your scientific progress. Would you like to do things their way or my way, moving forwards."

Dixon forced himself to relax, dropping his shoulders, and letting out a slow controlled breath. "I suppose I could give your way a go," he said, before looking down to his colleague. "And Singh?"

"Singh is free to do as he pleases, but if he pleases anything that conflicts with what I'm trying to do, I'll be very disappointed in him."

Dixon nodded but furrowed his brow and looked to Katano. "No… assurances from him?"

"Katano has more of an inquiring scientific mind than a militantly subservient one. I just assumed he'd rather see things play out my way."

Still crouched by Singh's side, Katano looked up. "A fair assessment." He shrugged and looked to Dixon. "I mean, we're here to learn more, and ultimately our objective is to reactivate this fleet of mechanical marvels for human use. Reed seems the most qualified to assist with that. We could be at this for years, otherwise."

Kellan collected the guns off the guards, slinging one over his back and placing the other by the terminal. "Please use the guards' restraints to bind their hands behind their backs."

Dixon and Katano complied, and Kellan began to work on the terminal, supplementing the interface node's direct access.

***

By the time the guards woke up, Kellan had been quite prolific in feeding designs into the system. Every terminal attached to an output printer within the whole outpost was working for him. With a network based on technology, now familiar to him, he was able to bypass safeguards and lockout all senior personnel. No alarm could be raised. All research personnel were assigned tasks to keep them busy and achieve Kellan's goals, believing them to be instructions from the residing command structure. Senior ranks and security had seemingly noticed and attempted to engage overrides, forcing Kellan to lock them out and deliver a message to assure them no hostile intent was at play.

While the guards groaned, suffering from headaches, Singh had a new outlook, after an adjustment period of seemingly talking to himself as he synchronised with his new implant. He now understood the tech surrounding them in a way he never could have hoped to, under the previous rate of research.

"I suppose the change hasn't been as intellectually profound for you, Singh," Kellan said.

"Do I feel smarter, you mean?"

Kellan nodded with a quick glance back as he continued working on the terminal.

"I… know more things, technically, now strangely recalling how this technology works. I remember researching it, striving to understand it, and now, with irreconcilable parallel memories of the modified lifeform, it's as if I grew up with it…" He looked at his hands. "I remember how to pilot a titan but with different… appendages. I remember being one of them."

"Not being one of them, being implanted into one. It's the interface node's memories. Interactions, shared experiences. Fortunately spared the time after the node went offline."

"Right," Singh agreed. "Protecting a world, it never walked on and a people it never interacted with." He began describing what he could to Dixon as Katano wandered over to watch Kellan working on the terminal.

"Whatever happens," Katano quietly said. "I don't want anything in my head. I'm curious enough to come along for the journey of discovery, but I want to observe it all on my own terms."

Kellan smiled at him. "Out there, the military are trying to retain control over the operation. I don't blame them. But now that my mind's been functionally optimised, I don't think I'll find the life of a lab rat sufficiently stimulating." Kellan looked to Singh and Dixon who were still engaged in their own conversation.

"...just as he said," Singh was saying. "Some pulse wave shot out and everything went down. The pilot was trapped. The... I want to say, cockpit, was designed using different systems and the life support was largely eco-systemic by design. They would have survived for a considerable time, trapped in the dark, cut off from one another, and with their interface nodes no longer feeding them information or recording their hosts' memories. Trapped with their own thoughts, with imagination and desire bread out of them."

Dixon shook his head in ponderance.

"There are smaller research stations on several of the nearest titans," Kellan quietly informed Katano. "Right now, those stationed on them are currently assembling parts for human pilot cockpits to replace the current ones. They are also feeding microprobes into various conduits that will repair the damage caused by the isolating wave."

"All that information is stored in your interface device?" Katano asked, impressed.

Kellan nodded. "One titan is already sixty-three percent restored. Another twenty-two. Two nodes are back online. Station command is making considerable progress, bypassing security lockouts with manual force and will be here before we are ready to leave."

"It might be worth communicating with them."

"I don't have time to try that again," Kellan said. "I'm overseeing too many operations. Singh," he called out.

"Yes?"

"You need to contact command and instruct them to desist in their attempt to breach this research sector. They must let me complete my work."

"Wait, are you saying we're in direct conflict with command?" Singh asked.

Kellan turned back to look him in the eyes. "No, command is in direct conflict with us."

Singh's face grew concerned.

"A man of science shouldn't struggle between siding with the industrial military complex and the unhindered discovery of other civilisations. Pick a side quickly… is it Doctor Singh? Professor Singh?"

"Technically Lieutenant," Singh admitted, while glancing at the restrained security guards.

"I now fathom the conflict," Kellan realised. "I've put you in a difficult position. But it's time to pick a side. Do you want to follow me to an ancient alien colony on another world to see what became of the people who made these magnificent machines or do you wish to aid an institute that will slow down the revelations that await you, inadvertently passing it on to another generation of science officers?"

Singh sighed and activated a console comm. "Lieutenant Singh to Commander Murry."

"Lieutenant Singh, what's going on in there," a gruff voice urgently replied.

"There's been some… interesting developments. Our visitor, Reed, has been adding significant data to our network. Tools, parts, and devices to restore the titans. He wants to take a few, but in exchange you'll have access to the rest."

"They aren't his assets to offer or take," the angry voice on the other side barked.

"That's the offer he's making, sir. It's one that will significantly expedite the process of reactivating these great weapons. He also requests that all attempts to reach this area cease."

"Of course, he does. He doesn't want us stopping him from stealing our equipment."

"Not technically his equipment," Kellan said. "But I'll let him keep most of it, if he recalls his men. Otherwise, what I will steal is the air in the sections where his men are. He has twenty seconds to evacuate them."

Singh leant over the comm, but before he could touch it, Commander Murry began yelling.

"You can't threaten us, workman. You signed a contract. You work for us. We own you. You understand? We own you."

"I'm sorry you feel that way, commander," Kellan calmly said. "If nothing else, I am in breach of contract, now that the documentation I loosely skimmed over comes back into sharp recollection. However, I'm establishing a new command structure. I was willing to share with you, and bring forward an infinitely faster timeline on restoring the tech of which you're so possessive. Instead... well, I invite you to monitor your breach crew."

"You killed them," the commander yelled.

"No, Commander. You did. You were supposed to evacuate those men. I issued ample warning. I'm now giving you six minutes to evacuate all military personnel from this facility. There's plenty of mining stations here, I'd pick one of those until a larger ship can collect you. I'm commandeering all the air in this facility to supply the new cockpits. There's no part of this facility

I don't control now. Don't waste your time trying to combat it. Save yourself while you still can, Commander."

"You're going to regret this," the commander yelled.

"Congratulations, Commander. You just killed everyone in the room with you. Commencing air extraction and recompression."

Dixon moved quickly towards Kellan, but he raised one of the security rifles and pointed it at him. "Come on, Dixon. I thought we were all signed on for scientific discovery."

"You can't kill everyone," Dixon argued, stopping in his tracks.

"I'm taking the air. Not flushing it into space. If the commander has any brains he'll immediately evacuate the area and do as instructed. There'll still be enough air for him to do that. If he insists on maintaining his current behaviour, he'll get everyone else killed. Not me. Him."

"He's just doing his duty."

"No, he isn't. He's a petty man who would rather things be done his way to maintain his delusion of power and authority than allow something that would actually swiftly deliver his superiors' primary objectives. He's underqualified to hold his rank and position and, if he fails to survive this situation, it will be because he was underqualified to live at all. At least now, no further air will be wasted on him."

Dixon screwed up his face, grimacing with doubt.

"Manual input is no longer required, Dixon. I'm controlling the entire station and facility. Its security protocols have been outclassed by ancient tech. But that doesn't mean I want to spend the rest of my time here pointing a gun at you. You don't have to come with us, but it's not really safe to leave at the moment."

Dixon pointed at the gun. "It doesn't seem all that safe staying either."

"That's entirely up to you, Dixon. Do you want it to be safe?"

Dixon presented his palms to placate him. "Ideally."

"Then sit down. Don't make any sudden movements or gravitate towards the guards. Observe. That's what a science officer is meant to do." Kellan smiled as Dixon sat down. "Alright. Now, let's wait til we're ready to leave."

***

They sat in an awkward silence as they watched monitors. Kellan didn't need to. He was connected to everything, though he could not monitor everything at once. Especially as he balanced the repair work, instructing the ant-sized microprobes, instructing the other science officers and technicians assigned to the salvage work, and preparing the other nodes he had them extract from the genetically modified life forms frozen and congealed in their life support tombs.

Kellan grinned satisfied as he knew the first titan had come online. Its core began to slowly reinitiate as the last technicians he assigned to it were completing the new cockpit. His node was able to connect to it, despite the distance. It gave him an odd sense of personal completion. As if until now he'd been only a small part of something. Now, he was whole. He was complete.

Before he could enjoy the sensation for long, the monitors went down followed by the lights. Low emergency lights soon replaced them while the terminal's display flickered while its backup power prevented it from shutting down.

Kellan still had access to everything, but the severed power had various connected systems down.

"Sneaky," Kellan said, getting up. "Commander Murry launched a shuttle when I told him to leave, and I assumed he was on it. How long do the reserve power cells last?" It was a question he was more asking himself as he checked the system, but Singh answered anyway.

"Six hours."

"Longer than a spacesuit's likely to last."

"I don't think Murray's planning to wait it out," Singh suggested. "Cutting the power would automatically activate a distress beacon."

Kellan checked. It had already happened. He couldn't stop it. "Fine, I'll have to bring forward elements of my own timetable then." He concentrated and signalled the other recovered and repaired nodes. Command protocol was initiated, making him the senior commander of his own force. A group of science officers and technicians, who would be unconscious for a short while and take some time to adjust, were now about to find themselves under his direct influence. He opened a comm. "Commander Murry. Can you hear me?"

There was a long silence, but eventually a comm crackled on. "I'm here."

"I've activated one of the titans. I'm going to assume you mean to stop me boarding it so here's the deal; stay out of my way, and I leave here, leaving your network full of files for replacement parts with schematics for creating human inhabitable cock pits, interface nodes, and everything else you need to restore this fleet to its former glory. Or you can try and stop me, and I'll erase it all along with every last byte of data your research teams have so far managed to collate out here. You can start from scratch or be launched years ahead of your previous progress missing only a few assets."

"You're not taking a damned thing from this site."

Kellan shook his head, baffled. "When your superiors find out you made that call, I think you'll be sliding down a rank or two," Kellan said, shaking his head. "But have it your way. You don't care about the mission, that's on you. All data has now been expunged from the system. It's currently in my head, though, so if you get to me before I get to you, be careful where you shoot."

Commander Murray grunted. "Just makes you another asset to lock down, asshole."

Kellan pulled his head back and looked to Dixon. "And this is the man you'd rather follow?"

"Well, you did just delete years of our research."

"Simply removed from the facility. Even then, do you really think your speculation and theories can compare to actual practical knowledge and stored experience? If only you had one of these in your head." Kellan pointed to the interface node in Singh's forehead. "You'd certainly appreciate it more than Singh has."

"Why do you say that?" Singh asked, defensively.

"Because you've been using yours to communicate with Commander Murray."

"What?"

"It's the only thing that makes sense. I thought perhaps Dixon had found a way, but there is no way he could have got a message to him. But someone has. Singh could have communicated through terminals without touching any of them. The way I've been using them. But now that mine's established a command protocol I can remedy that mistake."

"No wait," Singh said, before his node began to whir and ejected itself from his head.

Kellan caught the device in his hand and held it out to Katano, as Singh collapsed on the floor with a gaping hole in his head releasing blood and cerebral fluid. "Would you please pass this to Dixon?"

Katano looked to Singh, convulsing on the floor. Kellan patiently waited for the shock to subside, holding the device out while still locking eyes with Dixon. Katano took it and brought it to the other remaining science officer.

"All your work is in there and more. With confirmations and corrections, provided by actual working knowledge of what you've been studying all this time. You'll see all the things Singh was trying to describe to you. See through the eyes of another species a thousand or more years ago."

Dixon contemplated the idea, as he was handed the node. "And if I don't?"

Kellan glanced at the rifle in his hands and back to Dixon again. "Sorry to resort to such crudeness, but one way or another you're getting a hole in your head."

Dixon nodded with resignation and held the cone-shaped end of the node to his forehead. "Option one then," he sighed, wiping the node down.

With a pulse, the node shot at his forehead, penetrating the skin and clamping at the skull as it drilled fast into him. Katano caught him as he stubbled back and gently lowered him to the floor.

"The others will get other titans up and running, over the following hours," Kellan said. "They know where to go."

"What about Commander Murray?" Katano asked.

"By now he must be getting close. I have to estimate and rely on other data, as the severance of the power conduits also cut me off from the security feed. However, I have larger eyes on the situation now."

There was a low sound of cranking and ticking with vibratory hums echoing about them and outside the lab. Katano and the bound security guards looked about.

"What the hell was that?" one of the guards asked.

"That was a titan gripping the outer ring of the station," Kellan explained.

"Shouldn't we be getting knocked about or something," the other guard asked.

"You really don't understand how artificial gravity works, do you?" Kellan pondered his own statement a moment. "Well, in all fairness, I suppose you wouldn't. None of us should, it was stolen technology. The species from whom ours took the technology were aquatic. They had slightly different needs to us. They didn't want to be tossed about and ripped from their controls mid-battle, getting shook in their brine like a tube of dispenser thick-shake or juice. The gravity field generator isolates external forces. The people who made the titans however, developed a type of gravity that does let you know when you've bumped into something. Though it protects from the full effects of inertia and buffeting and preventing those using it from being pulped, the possibility of it going offline is precisely why the titan pilots were bred into what they were." Kellan squinted and pointed to the door. "Give me a moment… I think I see the commander entering the outside passageway."

There was a low hum and a shrill sound of cutting metal. A red light reflected onto the viewing window in the large hatch.

Katano rushed to the door to peer through it. "You've cut the corridor."

"Of course. We need a docking hatch, and we have intruders. This resolves both issues." He activated the comm. "Commander, thank you for coming to see us off. I'm going to have to leave you outside, but hopefully your reinforcements will be here in time to rescue you. If not, breathe shallow."

It was odd to look down through the sensors of the titan, he'd yet to board. Seeing three men in spacesuits that could all easily stand in the palm of the mechanical giant's hand.

"I suppose this is goodbye for now. I unfortunately won't be staying to see how your superiors respond to your poor choices, but if I come back this way, I'll be sure to enquire."

When the titan finished cutting the other end of the passageway, the titan pulled it free and gently tossed it away from the station, with the men inside, clinging to the inside railing.

There was yelling over the comm, but Kellan cut them off before he could make out any of it. "If the commander was unwilling to discuss things before, I'm hardly going to listen to him now."

Katano stepped back from the door, but kept watching as the titan brought its great mechanical head close. Built for tactical consideration rather than aesthetic, it bore no hallmarks of the organics who designed it. A series of lights and lenses were arranged in a mostly vertical array. A module extruded from it with a round sealed hatch. Four smaller hatches opened, evenly spaced around it. From them, four thick, segmented cables slithered out like mechanical snakes and found their way to the lab's doorway past what little remained of the severed corridor. The cables clunked as they connected with the bulkhead. Small apertures opened in each segment and a web of light connected the metallic tendrils while other lights danced within like some sort of primitive laser show. Shapes formed and each flat plane filled with a misty film that changed colour to appear as a solid object sewn out of a fabric of light. A bending corridor formed, leading to the module above the titan's head.

"A boarding corridor made of photonic planes?" Katano asked in wonder.

"The titan's creators had far superior holography to that which we've become accustomed."

Katano slowly nodded. "Something to do with the aquatics, we got it from, being fluid dwellers, I suppose."

Kellan smiled. Watching from the titan's many eyes, he was focused on filling the temporary corridor with air.

***

Beyond the corridor of light, an elevator took the pair and the barely conscious Dixon down into the titan's chest to the primary cockpit. It wasn't luxuriously spacious, but it seemed a sufficiently comfortable habitat. There were seats, beds, terminals, printers for food and parts from the facility installed and integrated.

"Well, it's not much, but it's what I was able to have them put together in the allotted time," Kellan said, with false humility. He couldn't help be smug at the efficiency the node had afforded him. "We'll drop Dixon off at one of the other Titans. I'll not waste a node on a passenger. No offense."

"None taken," Katano said, relieved.

"It's an interface, and it should be used as such. He should be piloting one of the other Titans."

"Then…?"

"Then we'll go see what became of our ancient benefactors' colonies."

Katano smiled excited as they took their seats. "From miner to interstellar explorer. Not a bad day for you, I suppose."

"No, and until the military work out how to repair and use the titans we leave behind… there should be considerable time in which to fulfil our curiosity."

Barend Nieuwstraten III grew up and lives in Sydney, Australia, where he was born to Dutch and Indian immigrants. He has worked in film, short film, television, music, and online comics. He is now primarily working on a collection of stories set within a high fantasy world, a science fiction alternate future, often dipping his toes in horror in the process. With his novel 'A Man Called Boy' and over eighty stories published in anthologies, he continues to work on short stories, stand-alone novels, and an epic series.

The Universe is a Capricious Place
By Charles Walter

Family Sundays were usually very predictable. Once they were Hallmark Channel, then they became Lifetime when my wife first got sick, and today, well, today became Syfy, with a mix of the MLB Network. We were at our local park, which among other amenities featured three lovingly-maintained baseball fields, mostly used for Little League. All this was nestled in the beautiful rich pine that was a prime feature of the Tonto National Forest. It was May, it was 63 degrees out, the sun was shining, the cactus wrens were chirruping, and a crisp wind blew through. Enough to notice, but not to chill.

"I'm gonna throw, Dad!"

My oldest daughter Mia stood on the mound, squinting intensely at me, lined up behind home plate. She needed glasses, had since she was nine, but refused to let us take her to the optometrist. I appreciated the stubbornness, but was not going to indulge it much longer. A neat ponytail held back her long auburn air. I stuck out my glove and got ready to catch her 50-mph fastball.

"Ugh," I grunted helpfully as the ball hit my glove, just where I placed it. Her control was far better than mine at the same age, and I made it to AA ball, just two levels below the Majors. But then, she had the benefit of professional coaching from the time she could throw hard enough to break common household items.

If you're from around these parts, maybe you've heard of me. My name is Daniel Reed, and once upon a time I had some local fame. I was drafted by the Mariners in the third round direct from high school in 1991, and they had high hopes for me. So did I, until the day I tripped while running intervals just half a mile from our house on a two-lane highway. My shoulder was never quite the same afterward. So, newly married, I came home. We went to school (physics for me, accounting for her), got traditional jobs, and started raising two of the most precocious and maddening young ladies you'd ever have the pleasure of meeting.

"Show me the special trick, Dad!" That was my youngest, Olivia, eight years old, but just a few inches shorter than her eleven-year-old sister. She had grown swiftly, and was skinny as a rail. She wrinkled her nose as I joined her at first base and returned the ball to her sister.

"This is how it goes, but remember, it's useless until high school, when the runner can move," I said. "Olivia, take your lead." She took a couple steps down the dirt pathway to second base, while I crouched at the bag and nodded at Mia.

Mia tossed me the ball as Olivia dove back to the base, grabbing the outfield corner with two fingers just like I taught her. She bounced up on the bag and brushed the dirt off the front of her uniform.

"Pretend like you're not paying close attention," I said, reaching into my glove with my left hand, grabbing nothing but air, then feigning a throw to the mound. Olivia took a step off the bag, then I tagged her immediately. "You have to sell it. They have to think you really made—" I stopped, looking over my daughter's head as I saw something round and silvery appear a few hundred feet in the air above the next field. It descended silently straight into its outfield. "What in the world—"

I grabbed a bat resting against the nearest dugout and sprinted over there to get a better look, closely followed by the girls. "Stay behind me," I ordered, wondering why I had allowed them to even follow me to the saucer-shaped object, the size of four bounce houses rounded off. I didn't wonder why I thought the bat would be helpful, though. I wasn't just a pitcher. Senior year I'd hit 20 home runs. The papers said I could do wondrous things with one.

As we approached the saucer, it vanished from sight except for a door that soon opened up on the side facing us, the top lowering slowly and forming a ramp. Thirty seconds later, two figures unlike anything I had expected started heading down. I mean that because they looked like they were cornfed from the Midwest, a six-foot tall woman trailed by a man a few inches shorter. So much for bug-eyed monsters.

I stood five feet from the bottom of the ramp, motioning for the girls to get behind me. Then I smiled broadly, the kind I reserved for my fans back in glory days of my youth. It was easy to slide back into the confidence of those days. Maybe I'd be famous again. "Welcome to our planet. I'm Dan Reed. Behind me are my daughters Mia and Olivia. Do you happen to speak English?"

The woman stuck out her hand, which I shook. A very firm grip. "We do. My name is Blonu Altisjar. My companion is Zomot Keeturian."

"That's so cool! Does everyone speak English on your planet?" Olivia asked. The two aliens faced each other and shared a knowing smile.

"Is that what you call this?" Blonu asked. "No, we don't, as I'm sure the adult knows. As we approached your world our ship created composites of your species for us. They handle translating both verbal and body language in forms we both would understand." As he finished, he twirled his right index finger by his ear in slow motion, rather rudely I thought, but I decided not to say a thing. After all, this seemed to be a first-contact situation.

"But how did you get here?" Mia asked, now standing confidently beside me. Well, if my girls weren't going to be offended I wouldn't either.

"Ha!" Zomot shouted, catching me by surprise. "It was quite the tale. Five parsecs from home we were chased by Zelsian star pirates. 'Submit to boarding' they demanded. As if. They were never expecting our finely-aimed laser barrage. We hit them way worse than they hit us and left them far behind. Still, it was not long after before our anti-matter engine started underperforming. The computer was too busy to maneuver, so Blonu steered us manually through the Vanadian asteroid field and coasted us into the local interplanetary service station. Next, we encountered the Sulfarian/Bogoshan war, which as you know has been dominating the intergalactic news. We underestimated the size of the war front, which now spans a full seventy parsecs. It was all we could do to duck the asteroids they were chucking at each other. We had to circle two parsecs out of our way just to be safe!"

Blonu had been listening patiently, but now finally she weighed in. "The universe is a capricious place. Best you remember that if you want to survive. Our computer has been fed and is fully healed, and we're ready to take on anything."

I felt confused. Did he say what I thought? "You fed your computer?"

Blonu frowned at me, a disappointed frown. "All living things must eat. A conscientious pilot will never let her computer experience hunger if she wants to make good time. When healthy, it can cruise at just under point-nine-eight c."

Now I knew a little about relativity. I'd used what was left from my signing bonus to go back to college, and I've been teaching chemistry and physics at my old high school ever since. "Even with time dilation that sounds like it took forever. How long was your journey?"

Zomot smiled proudly. "Only five years."

"Five years?? How old are you?"

"I am 50, and my companion 38," Blonu said. "Although, many say we look much younger in our native form."

I was 50 myself and still not understanding the math. "You travelled hundreds of parsecs at slower than light speed. Does year not mean to you what it does to us?"

There was that frown again. "Well, of course each world uses a local year. A planet like yours, so close to such a small sun, why, your years must fly by. Tell me, we understand your species is bimodal as well. Should there not be an adult female here commanding your family?"

Why, yes, there should have been. The command was split officially, but Jennifer might not see it that way. "My wife is in hospice care, otherwise I'm sure she would be happy to meet such brave and accomplished space travelers." She would have, but she also would have cautioned against my "unwarranted confidence" in social situations, the same confidence that she initially distrusted, making the work of wooing her much more challenging and rewarding than I'd expected.

"Ah, my apologies," Blonu spoke softly. "I'm sure you do your best. The universe is indeed a capricious place. Since you are not the trade delegation why do you not board our ship while we await them?" Then she noticed my bat and laughed.

Blonu turned and headed back up the ramp, Zomot following five feet behind. I looked at the girls, drank in their raw excitement, and decided if our new acquaintances bore us malintent we were certainly at their mercy regardless. I held their hands as we walked, just like we did when they were younger, and like then Olivia was bouncing back and forth randomly, a human Brownian motion generator as our momentum took us closer. Mia had a large grin on her face, her eyes shining brightly, flecks of brown embedded in the deep green. She'd never looked so much like her mother as at that moment.

The ship's interior was more of what I expected, metallic panels surrounding wide corridors, tinged baby blue. Some panels seemed to feature language, but I couldn't hope to read the script. The girls had their heads on swivel, taking in every aesthetic as we walked to the bridge. At the front resided a large view screen, through which we saw our familiar park. "Zomot will set the beacon now," Blonu said. "But until then let us be inconspicuous. Zomot, when you're done, can you fix the cloak? We were visible for a Vanadian centihour."

We watched as Zomot sat in one of the two large and well-padded pilot chairs. Blonu motioned to a series of smaller chairs dotting the bridge perimeter. I nodded at the girls, and we sat down. It was time to figure out what this was all about. "You said you were expected."

Blonu shrugged at me as Zomot proceeded to what must have been the cloaking device, tore off a panel, and began to examine the wiring much like the electrician who fixed our house after the flood. Soon he had an answer. "Just a blown Nostrian fuse. It's fixed now."

Now aware to the fact I was cloaked to the outside world, I felt a trifle insubstantial. Glancing around everyone seemed a little translucent. How bizarre. "The rendezvous was scheduled to the Vanadian hour before we left. It should be any time now," Blonu said.

Well, that was good. "Our government isn't typically forthcoming with such information. Why have you come?"

Zomot laughed, a giggle followed by a loud snort. "Ha, ha," Blonu said. "Very clever of you, but we will not renegotiate. We will pay the agreed price." She spread her arms wide. "Your power will be so cheap, you will not regret our deal. For now, I need to get ready." She then sat in the pilot chair and started interacting with the console.

All right, they were going to be vague, but they weren't asking us to leave, so hopefully we would get to witness the exchange, although the three of us might need to acquire high security clearances as a result. Albeit, that was only if the trade partner was in fact the government, and we had not in fact discussed that fine point. Whoever on Earth was negotiating trade deals with aliens sure knew how to keep it quiet. Not even the late night AM shows we listened to for kicks before we were blessed with kids had been predicting this.

Olivia was fidgeting. She had something to say. I nodded permission. "Miss Blonu?"

Blonu turned with an impatient look. "Yes, child."

"Is there something in here that could help my mother?"

I'd been pondering the same idea, actually. Zomot looked up from his screen and glanced quizzically at Blonu. "Perhaps the computer can design a cure?"

"We'll see," Blonu responded off-handedly. "Just because the computer can replicate the biology doesn't necessarily mean it can fix it. It really depends on how bad she is, it may end up doing more harm than good, and I wouldn't want to pay for that. It's not on our insurance plan. If we do nothing, will she die?"

They certainly were blunt. Out of the corner of my eye I saw Mia take a crying Olivia under her arm. She looked at me, expectantly. "Probably." I sighed. "The doctors say she's got less than a 5% chance to live, and we expect to lose her within the next few weeks. I've been trying to keep their lives as normal as I can." Who was going to keep my life normal if I lost her?

Blonu turned now and faced me fully. "Ah, the universe is a capricious place. We'll see what we can do if you're willing to sign our waiver."

"A waiver? Yes, of course. If that's necessary." I'd do about anything.

"It is, but only you need sign it. Minors have no standing in our court system. While we wait, would you care to share a meal with us? Zomot flash boils the finest Caltron burgers this side of the galaxy, and we have an ample collection of Uluran nuts." As Blonu spoke, Zomot pulled out a cabinet, and pressed a button under the handle. I looked over his shoulder and saw a deep pan with partially-opaque liquid, likely water with unnamed additives that instantly began to boil. Next, Blonu reached above his head, and grabbed a vertical handle, and opened to his right a small refrigerated cache, from which he drew what must be five Caltron burgers, twice the size of what I get at Albertsons, more heavily marbled, with spiral grains, and mauve muscle tissue. He tossed them in the boiling liquid, then he walked to the other side of the room, opened a closet, and returned with a large bag of what presumably must be the Uluran nuts, already shelled. They looked twice the size of walnuts, but there was something odd about them. I swear to you, it seemed as if they had bulging eyes in the center.

Mia having let go of a now-composed Olivia started reaching toward the bag, but a quick look from me stopped her. One seriously-ill family member was more than enough for me. Who knew if any of this food was safe for us? "Thanks, but we just ate."

"We have plenty more if we change your mind."

Mia was still curious. "Is that what you feed your computer?"

Both aliens started to guffaw loudly again. "What's so funny?" I asked.

Zomot regained composure first. "No, no, the computer gets special food. I had planned to feed it soon, anyway. Come with me." He turned his back and made a wide circle gesture with his right arm to encourage us to follow, which we all did, back to the closet, where on the far side on the bottom of six shelves against the back wall was what looked like a large nest lovingly constructed with pink sticks. Resting inside were at least a dozen identically-sized purple eggs, the size you'd find from a bald eagle.

"Could I have one?" Olivia asked.

"Why not? We have plenty," he said, handing her one, grabbing another, then leading us out without closing the door. I stayed by the door to take an additional peek inside while the girls followed him to the main console, where he pressed a button that caused a tray to slide out between the pilot chairs, with an egg-sized indention. He placed one inside then closed the tray door. A loud churning noise lasted for about fifteen seconds, then it fell silent, and Blonu began typing something. "This will last it thirty-seven Vanadian hours. It's the latest computer model, very efficient."

"How long does the computer last?" I asked.

Blonu looked up, surprised. "Almost forever they claim if fed properly, but don't worry about that. We upgrade every time we go home. We have standards you know."

"How does the food work?"

Zomot looked at Blonu, who responded. "It's fairly simple. The egg releases nano-particles that travel through the circulatory system cleaning up all entropic damage while supplying a current of seven amperes to charge the cells."

That didn't sound quite like food as I understood it, but alien life is alien life. "If it's so efficient, why don't you eat it?"

Guffaws again. I hadn't made anyone laugh so much since I was a local star out on the prowl. Through the main viewer I noticed our neighbors beginning a soccer game in the left field foul area.

"No, don't be silly," Blonu said. "Eat genetically-engineered food designed for a lower species? Are you mad? The universe is a capricious place to be sure, but why make life more challenging than necessary?"

Our neighbors set two pairs of traffic cones out to mark the goals. It looked like they wouldn't get anywhere near us, for which I felt glad. I'd hate to see them run full speed into a cloaked spaceship.

Zomot noticed what I was looking at and turned his head. "What's that?" he asked, watching the kids' friends complete a rather clever passing drill.

"It's soccer," I said. "The world's most popular sport, for now. There are still a lot of areas for us to spread baseball."

Blonu had now joined Zomot's gaze. "Why don't they use their hands?"

"It's more challenging this way. Only the goalie can use his hands."

Blonu was taken aback. "That's insane. Why do such a thing? I just said, life is challenging enough. I've never heard of this 'sokher' game. Wait a minute, what planet is this?"

"We're on Earth," Mia piped up.

Blonu shot an angry look at Zomot. "Zomot, what did you do to us! You said you had a shortcut to reach Phlegcha!"

"What was it you said about challenges?" I chuckled. "I guess the universe really is a capricious place. I don't think there will be a delegation expecting you, but I can contact our local government. I'm sure they'd love to do business."

"With a backward planet like this? I doubt it. No wonder everything confused you. Tell me, does your world feature free cesium springs?"

I wasn't sure, but I'd never heard of such a thing. For all I knew cesium wasn't near plentiful enough on Earth to form springs, besides the fact there wasn't anywhere on the planet that maintained the necessary temperature year-round. "I don't think so."

Blonu was still looking angrily at Zomot. "I told you this planet wasn't warm enough, but you were so certain about that left turn at Barnard's Star." He turned back to Olivia. "This planet is useless. You're on your own. Good luck to your mother, girl, and return that egg before you leave."

"Okay," Olivia said sadly, looking at me for direction. I started gripping my bat with a rush of exhilaration, while a look of determination came over my other child's countenance.

"Wow!" Mia yelled and pointed at the soccer game, catching the aliens' attention.

"That's a special trick," I said as I winked at Olivia while I relaxed my grip. She pocketed the egg with her right hand while miming a throw to me with the left. A second later I faked catching it with both hands, grunting as if I'd received a hard throw. With the aliens' eyes now returned to me, I walked into the storage closet, leaned far over and acted out returning it.

"Our welcome here is over, girls. Let's go." We left the ship quickly without saying goodbye, the door closing immediately behind us as we felt a rush of air and heard the sound of the ship already gaining altitude. "Hi, Rosenthals!" I shouted at our neighbors as we headed back to our gear. They'd fortunately been looking the other way and not espied us materializing from nowhere, which was good, because I had no idea how I was going to explain that with all the evidence gone. The national news wasn't going to happen, but that was fine since I had something else on my mind.

We politely turned down their request to join the game, then packed our gear in our bags, flung them over our shoulders, and rode our bicycles home. Quickly we dumped everything in the garage. I grabbed the egg from Olivia and headed to the kitchen to prepare it while the girls hurried to my wife's bedside. It felt not too different from hard-boiled, so I didn't cook it, not that I'd even know what texture to aim for or how to best get there. My wife was the creative chef. I followed recipes, so instead, I just sliced it.

A minute later I joined them and dismissed her nurse. Each held one of her hands as she wore a painful smile. My heart sank a little. I'd never seen her look so frail. I glanced at Olivia first, so she would not be influenced by her older sister's opinion on the question that need not be spoken. She nodded slightly then lowered her head. Mia's response was more confident. "Try this, dear," I said, holding out a plate with seven egg slices, each garnished with a sample from our most elegant toothpick collection. "I've been told it might raise your energy level."

"Why not…since you went to…such trouble…to prepare," she said, her voice soft yet husky. She motioned to Olivia. "Please." Olivia hand-fed her the egg slices, then we all gathered around to watch. After half an hour, nothing happened except the patient falling asleep, so I fluffed up her pillow and led the girls into the kitchen to eat dinner. It had been worth a try. Who knew if the aliens could have saved her anyway.

An hour and a half later we'd all settled into our foam-stuffed couch to watch a special on the MLB Network when I heard my name being called loudly from the hospice room. We all took off lickety-split. As I ran through the door I saw Jennifer lie there smiling up at me, her tan skin radiating with the same youthful glow that overwhelmed me those many years ago. She looked 20, 21 at the most. How were we ever—

"Mom!" Olivia shouted joyfully before I could finish my thought as she rushed to her mother's side.

"Dad?" Mia said, about as confused as I felt.

I stood by the door frame, blinking rapidly while I took it all in. I was elated, but there was clearly a price. "Kids, we have to move. They were right. The universe is a capricious place."

Charles Walter earned a doctorate in astronomy, then eschewed an academic career for the shiny lights of software engineering. Since 2010 he has contributed to projects in air traffic management at NASA Ames Research Center and now lives in Scottsdale, Arizona with his wife, two young sons, and mortgage.

Purgatorium
By Andrew Akers

Steam wafts from the surface of the Grand Prismatic hot spring. There is enough of it to reflect the pool's brilliant colors but not enough to shroud the water itself. It's always a hit or miss catching this portion of Yellowstone at the right time to enjoy it properly. If the air is too cold or the humidity too high, the view turns reticent; if the conditions are perfect, the sight includes a loud, sweaty foreground of tourists.

Somehow, this moment avoids both.

An alien beauty emanates from this place— an intermixing of lethality and hope. Dozens of unfortunate visitors have fallen in since the park was first established and were dissolved by the sulfuric acid and high temperatures of the spring. Despite this, the pool teems with another sort of life. Trillions of thermophiles call this place home and produce the rich tapestry of reds, greens, oranges, and yellows that give the spring its distinctive look. Coupled with the deep blue that shines in its center, it resembles a rainbow turned in on itself. The sight is perfect. The day is perfect.

A faint hiss disturbs the serenity, dissolving it like a fallen tourist.

***

Father-Ensign Bruce Benett, reluctant crewman aboard the NCC Saint Sebastian and Former Third Shepherd to the Flock of Enceladus, awoke to a hiss and the faint, uncomfortable swell of facial tissue in a depressurizing environment. He found his eyes already open, taking in a masterwork of intelligent design. Thousands of distant stars shimmered at the edge of his vision. In its center, the hundred-lightyear-wide nebula of The Tapestry stared back at him, similar in color and patterning to the hot spring in his dream. It was beautiful. There was a reason space was called "The Heavens" long before man's first piercing of the veil.

Dots of bright light flashed across the expanse, teasing the reason for his presence here.

Something happened, The Shepherd felt himself mouth. His croaked and rasping words were drowned out by the whistle of escaping air. Benett focused from the distant conflict to the faceplate of his Templar Mark V EVA suit. The visor — a reinforced glass cruciform coated in gold to fend off solar radiation — had been cracked during the emergency landing, and his air leaked through it. Making a quick seal with his right hand, The Shepherd felt for his emergency sealant with his left. After finding the duct tape, he ripped a piece free and covered the crack. The hissing stopped.

Now sitting up despite the protest of his ribs, Benett took in his surroundings.

"Jesus, save me."

Lit by Tapestry Space and the occasional flash of energy weapons in orbit, the remains of his Apostle Pod lay in pieces among chunks of rocky detritus and obsidian sands. Broken bodies littered the spaces between, their crimson aureolas already consumed by thirsty topsoil. The Shepherd winced. Though it was standard practice to perform the Commendation of the Dying to crewmen before communion with the enemy, it still stung to see youth returned to The Creator so early.

Benett stood and limped to the closest body, checking for vital signs and offering a quick prayer to guide its soul to The Creator's light.

"Welcome him, Lord, into your halls of splendor and everlasting peace."

Behind him, a watery voice gurgled a response. Along the bottom of Benett's visor, his onboard Tongues Program translated: "I doubt your god can hear you in this place, Crossed-One."

Benett reached for his sidearm as he spun to face the SelkianSelkian. His fingers caught empty air— his gun seemingly lost in the crash. It wouldn't have mattered anyway. Rules of engagement dictated that downed airmen were no longer combatants. That extended to heathens, too. The creature of pagan myth raised the four arms of its carapace to show it was no threat and stepped into the eerie light afforded by The Tapestry.

The Shepherd had seen digital recreations of Selkians on the Holonet, typically playing the villain role in the cinematic and gaming spaces. He had likewise studied their xenobiology while in seminary; it was required curriculum to know one's enemy. None of these facsimiles, however, prepared him for what stood before him now.

Though they typically measured shorter than a single meter length-wise, the seal/slug native of Europa's subsurface ocean was the ultimate apex predator. The reason was simple and the inspiration behind their moniker. Like the selkie of Nordic mythology, the creature interacted with its environment via artificial skin— a suit made of another living thing. This intimidating three-meter carapace, which evolved in symbiosis with the Selkians, was a one-part living organism and, as of nearly three decades ago, one-part advanced biotechnology. Multi-armed, layered in calcified protuberances, and evolved to withstand intense pressure, the silicon-and-carbon shell had proven ideally suited for combat. To Benett, it resembled the underside of an old boat back on earth, barnacled and etched with scratches. Formidable. It was rumored that the Selkians and their shells bonded for life, and separation was a death sentence to both. This one's shell, the color of briny water, carried the scars and scorch marks of previous battles, including a fresh gash in its right hip.

In awe of the creature's complexity, Benett wondered whether the bipedal, sapien-adjacent design had somehow been intentional or simply another example of convergent evolution in action. Were heathens, too, created in God's image?

"Your crew is dead. I am sorry," the creature said. "Mine have also perished."

If it hadn't been a sin—and if the thing couldn't snap him like an overinflated oxygen line—Benett would have brained it on the spot. Instead, shivering at his small form reflected in a green kaleidoscope across the Selkian's carapace, he asked, "What do I call you?"

The creature replied with noises like splashes and bubbling water, then said, "—but you may call me Herschel."

Benett nodded, adding the tag to his Tongues Program. From now on, the system would automatically attach its name to the translations whenever the creature spoke. It wouldn't matter if they were the only two around, but it would come in handy if, God forbid, any of its friends showed up.

Herschel: "Have you made contact with anyone above?"

Benett shook his head, then stopped. Would the creature understand human non-verbal communication? They had been fighting for almost thirty years, since the days of the Great Plague and the emergence of The Tapestry; it was amazing how little Benett knew of his enemy.

Herschel: "Me neither. It appears something here is blocking our transmissions."

"What? Where?" Surprised by the statement, Benett surveyed the barren world. This place had once carried a pagan moniker: Styx. Like some of its other celestial counterparts, it had been renamed by The Church in the wake of the Millennium Crusade. Styx, a moon of Pluto, was now Purgatorium, orbiting the dwarf planet Joseph.

Purgatorium had no colonies or known military installations. Nothing was supposed to be capable of signal jamming here.

Herschel: "But we have bigger problems. Look around. Do you see all your crew here?"

Putting the creature at his back, Benett continued his inspection of the bodies. He moved from one to the next, matching the name on each of their EVA suits to the faces and memories of those he had briefly known while onboard the battle cruiser. He had already prayed for Private Leonardo Xiang, a young man he had offered confession to twice. Next to him, bodies and suits shattered by the impact, were two others: Private Giovani Jinyi and Corporal Francis Kai. Both had merely been faces Benett occasionally passed on his way to the canteen. Inside the Apostle Pod were the remains of five more, though little could be salvaged of who they had been.

That left four outliers. The Shepherd investigated the surrounding rocks and divots; he found no bodies but did come across three more stains where they had once laid.

"Where are they?" he asked the pagan, fear creeping into his voice. "What did you do with them!?"

Herschel: "I crashed a mile from here. Several of my crew are also missing."

Benett looked up, praying he'd see the drive plumes of a rescue vessel. There was nothing; even the flashes of the battle had ceased. Where had the missing members of their crews gone?

Could someone else still be alive? The Shepherd wrestled with himself over the prospect of leaving unburied bodies behind and partnering with a pagan. It put a sour taste in his mouth.

At last, he said, "I need to bury these bodies first. A single grave will suffice."

Herschel: "We must investigate. Oxygen supply is limited."

"I don't care," he replied in a measured tone. "I have the opportunity, so it is sacrilege not to."

With the lumbering pagan watching, he performed a truncated Requiem Mass, starting with digging a grave. Bound to the moonlet by a gravitational attraction only six percent that of Earth's, even the larger rocks were placed aside with relative ease. Moving the eight bodies proved more difficult. Carrying the terrible weight of a future cut short, each felt supermassive to Benett. A dull throb tapped his brain as he worked, growing as the minutes lengthened to an hour. As he lay the final one to rest, panting and ignoring the pain of his head and ribs, The Shepherd was stopped by a six-digited hand on his shoulder. It was gentle despite its size and lethally sharpened claws. In another of its hands, it held wreckage from the Apostle Pod, twisted into an approximation of a cross.

Herschel: "For the grave."

Benett stared at the metal, then at the pagan holding it. The creature inside the carapace stared back, expression alien. It and its "freedom fighter" companions had been responsible for the deaths of these men, and yet…

"Thanks," he managed, taking the memorial and placing it at the head of the grave. As his vitals stabilized, Benett realized how fuzzy and bright the world had become. He felt woozy.

Herschel: "The grave is in a good place."

"Why… do you say that?"

Two of the creature's four arms rose toward The Tapestry, tracing the outline of the roiling, multi-color mural. The celestial event took up ten percent of the sky and was nearly a perfect circle, resembling an ever-expanding eye. Or the waters of the Grand Prismatic, a distant part of Benett thought. To the New Catholic Church (NCC), it was a sign that God was watching them and a promise that Heaven was on its way. From what Benett knew of the Selkians, they didn't share the belief.

"I thought… your people feared… The Tapestry?" he sputtered, struggling to sit on a nearby rock. Tightness cinched his chest now, and his head felt like a Dvergr city on the receiving end of an NCC shock-and-awe campaign.

Herschel: "That does not matter here. You find meaning in it. They found meaning in it. The grave is in a good place."

His companion paused to appraise him.

Herschel: "You appear unwell. What is your oxygen level?"

"I… I don't…" The Shepherd had been avoiding his wrist monitor since landing. Looking at it now, he was reminded of his panic during combat simulations. His suit display, growing red where it had taken simulated damage, had always induced panic in the priest. Now, he looked upon the bright red of the real thing. Broken ribs, sprained ankle, lacerations to his legs and torso—confirmation of what his senses had already been telling him. Below the miniature suit readout, an O2 level likewise flashed red.

Jesus, save me.

"I'm empty. There must have… still be a leak."

Benett felt his world slide sideways. The pagan lunged forward, catching him as he fell. It betrayed nothing as it observed him through its narrow observation window and thirteen gallons of chilled salt water. Bubbles emerged from the slug, and subtitles streamed across the bottom of Benett's faceplate. He was too exhausted to read them.

Instead, an entirely separate voice spoke into the mind of the fading priest.

"Take off your helmet," it said. "You will survive." Then, it recited a prayer he considered a personal favorite."Trust in the Lord with all your heart, and do not lean on your own understanding…"

Was this the voice of carbon dioxide poisoning? The snapping of a mind facing its own mortality? Benett didn't know. Confused and panicked but following the voice as only a true believer in The Creator could, The Shepherd obeyed.

***

There is an odor to The Grand Prismatic. Ancient explorers called it the "Smell of Hell." It's produced by the spring's high hydrogen sulfide and sulfuric acid levels. On the first few visits, it creates an unfortunate distraction from the beauty that makes it. Over time, though, it simply becomes part of the experience.

If someone visits enough, they can associate the smell with the beauty and picture it even in absentia. A wayward waft of rotten eggs or escaping sewer gas might transport them to that beauty in the park.

The place is magical like that.

Benett awoke to the smell of sulfur and a cold absence. His face swelled against the low pressure, his eyes blurred, and his head swam. He groaned, then stopped groaning as the sound reached his ears.

Sound! he thought, dumbfounded. Sound didn't propagate in a vacuum. There was atmosphere here! He wasn't dead! Benett took the strange world into himself one gulp at a time. The air was thin, cool, and surprisingly crisp. The Shepherd likened it to how the air probably felt in the Himalayas back on Earth.

He jumped as the Selkian made guttural noises next to him.

"Right," he said. No helmet, no Tongues Program. "Hold on." He looked for his helmet and found nothing. His surroundings had changed, too. Startled, the priest again surveyed the barren world. Things were lighter than he last remembered; shadows once black as pitch were now varying shades of gray. The Tapestry was brighter now, too, encompassing a more significant portion of the sky. The remains of the Apostle Pod were nowhere to be seen, and the area of sand and small boulders had been replaced by a garden of tall rocks.

Herschel moved me.

Another guttural noise came from his companion, and then a pair of glasses was handed to him. Benett turned them in his hands, confused. On the inside of the lenses, an image showed the golden NCC cruciform.

This was in the emergency kit of my Apostle Pod, he realized, putting them on. They had already been synced with the Tongues Program in his helmet, and a readout of their most recent translation appeared across the bottom.

Herschel: "How do you feel?"

Belatedly, Benett replied, "Woozy. The air is thin but... breathable. "This... shouldn't be possible; there isn't a true atmosphere on Purgatorium."

Herschel: "And yet you live. How did you know to take your helmet off?"

Benett's stomach grumbled a reply. Instead, he asked, "How long was I out?"

Herschel: "Three days."

Three days. The Shepherd's mind felt like it was in freefall. And still no recovery team? Again, his stomach called for food. As if in response, the Selkian offered him a manna tube, also pilfered from the downed Apostle Pod.

Taking the tube and speaking through mouths of the paste, Benett asked, "Why did you move us?"

Herschel: "Something took our peoples. I did not want us to be there when it returned."

"Smart."

Gurgling, the Selkian pointed to a section of the horizon where smoke curled into the sky like a blackened hand unclenching a fist.

Herschel: "Something happened while you rested. We must investigate."

Benett nodded and stood, then was forced to sit back down. He felt lightheaded. Though apparently friendly, the air wasn't enough to oxygenate his blood to the level he was accustomed to. He needed to be careful; over-exertion could be deadly. Again, he thought of the Himalayas, then of deep-sea divers resurfacing too quickly. He rose again, slower this time, and trained his spinning vision on the smoke in the distance.

Could that belong to the recovery team? Had they crashed, too? A second manna tube was placed in his hand.

Herschel: "You eat. We walk. Must investigate."

***

The Shepherd and The Pagan followed the black plume over boulders and wasteland. Featureless rock gradually gave way to more complicated structures— signs of geological complexity at odds with what the moonlet should have been capable of. Natural stone arches and monoliths jutted from the landscape, carved by weathering and external forces absent from any observations performed by satellites and passing ships.

"…do not lean on your own understanding…" Benett whispered.

Impact craters pockmarked the surface between the structures. The duo traversed a ridge between two of them, gaping at the kilometer-wide lakes that filled the pits. Melting ice along the crater's edge fed small, temporary waterfalls. Tugged downward by the moon's measly gravity, the water fell in slow motion. Benett whistled. Liquid water on a surface roughly 3.7 billion miles from the sun should have been impossible.

Herschel: "Temperatures have risen since our arrival. Since the start of our walk, they have gone from fifteen to sixteen degrees Celsius."

Sixty-one degrees Fahrenheit. Where he had once been chilly, Benett was now falling into equilibrium with the environment. If things keep up this way, he thought in awe, I'll be downing the rest of my suit soon.

Two valleys later, they reached the source of the smoke, tapering now to a thin, wriggling stream of black. The private transport carrier, built by the Dvergr in the asteroid belt while humanity was still toiling over the lightbulb, lay askew atop uneven chunks of rock. Stillness clung to the wreckage, a portend of the impact's lethality. The ship's solar sails lay in twisted heaps on either side of it, blanketing the ground in a thin layer of white and black.

"Its landing legs haven't even been deployed," Benett observed.

Herschel: "They hit hard. I don't think anything would have survived."

The Selkian was right. Two bodies greeted their entry into the ship, both smeared across dislodged crash couches. A member of the species that built the ship was in the pilot's seat. The Dvergr's short stature and long beard felt surreal in the confines of the beached craft, and the aura of rotting meat the creature gave off risked a mutiny in The Shepherd's stomach. He had heard cautionary tales of the dvergrs' stench, a product of the phytoplankton they harvested from the subsurface ocean of their homeworld; reality was far worse.

"What're you doing so far from home?" he whispered to the corpse.

The Dvergr, named after the dwarves in Norse folklore, hailed from the dwarf planet of Isidore (Ceres), in the heart of the asteroid belt. Before the NCC colonized the system, they leveraged their neutrality and trade prowess to garner fortune and political sway. While the rest of the system bickered and warred, the Dvergr's power grew.

That stopped when the NCC arrived during the Millennium Crusade. Under the Church's rule, all became equal.

Benett left the smell behind and moved to the passenger. This one's identity was equally discernible, and The Shepherd was flustered by her lingering pheromones. The Alfar would have been beautiful before impact. Dark hair framed what remained of her face. Her skin-tight suit accentuated the toned and broken body inside of it and left little to the imagination. Her head — perfected by centuries of carefully curated evolutionary modification on Michael (Mars) — lolled easily from one side to the other as the priest checked for memory back-ups behind her ears. There weren't any, but an embroidered ID tag glowed faintly from the crook of her neck. "Empathia Valsorum," his Tongues Program translated.

Benett rolled the name around his tongue, wondering why it sounded so familiar.

"Well, we aren't getting a final flight recording from this one's perspective," he said, "What's telemetry telling you?"

The Selkian continued rooting around the ship's onboard computer, shaking its head as it did so. *It almost looks human,* Benett thought. When the creature finally turned with an answer, it sold the illusion further by appearing worried.

Herschel: "Their itinerary shows them leaving Brigid (Vesta) twenty-seven months from now. Bound for Michael."

Benett scoffed. "This ship took a hard hit. Of course, its black box reads gibberish."

Herschel: "There's more."

It paused before continuing, as if weighing in advance the words that followed.

Herschel: "I also found the manifest. The passenger was bringing a toxin back with her to Michael."

The Selkian pointed at a container secured in the craft's cargo portion. It was stark silver and bore no indication of the cardinal sin it contained.

Herschel: "There are vials of it in there. Deployment-ready."

Benett shuttered. He wasn't old enough to remember the mass graves, mutated livestock, or the waters of the Mississippi running blood red with algae blooms. He had seen the pictures, though, and the mass trauma of The Great Plague — Pesach II, as it was known to biblical scholars — rippled through the generations. Hell, it's what prompted the creation of the NCC and the advent of The Millenium Crusade.

All at once, he remembered why the name of the Alfar sounded familiar to him.

"Empathia Valsorum," he spit. "She's the lead researcher of the Alfar's genetic research project. She's the mind behind the Chimeres. She's on the NCC's most wanted list for her possible role in Pesach II. She's the reason 'thou shalt not engage in genetic research' is included in the fifteen commandments."

Herschel: "Was. She is past tense now."

Staring at the broken war criminal, Benett's eyes welled for all she had stolen from humanity. The theory of the plague being an attack had never fully seeded itself in The Shepherd's soul. There were too many questions it left unanswered. For example, why was one side of the earth far more affected than the other? Why had creatures on the surfaces of other worlds been affected just as badly? Why hadn't it evolved, multiplied, and lingered like most other viruses? Why hadn't the virus been found in the tissue of those it affected?

The questions evaporated like liquid in a vacuum when The Shepherd saw this monster in the flesh. The Church's official position was that the plague had been deliberate, and that was finally enough for him.

"Burn in Hell," he said before the lingering smell of the Dvergr and the weight of the revelation forced him outside. There, he struggled to center himself, and froze. Something was coming their way from the north, kicking up a cape of dirt and dust.

"Uh, Herschel," he called to the creature inside, "we need to go. Now."

***

Multiple thermophilic species exist within the Grand Prismatic, each filling a niche specific to a particular area's temperature. Despite the life that flourishes along its circumference, the spring's center is sterile. This is accredited to the extreme heat it receives from the vent below. Because of this sterility and the depth of this portion of the spring, this area appears deep blue, even on cloudy days.

In this way, life and emptiness have found balance in the Grand Prismatic.

***

The duo watched the arrival of the nightmare from a nearby dune. Its spherical, winged body moved with deceptive grace among the rocks and wreckage. The monstrosity was made of metal and meat. Large eyes covered half its surface area, staring equally at everything and nothing in particular. Its organic parts swelled and squelched as it extracted the two bodies from the ship. Benett knew this creature. He had feared them once, then learned to fear them again. In the time between, he sermonized to them and attempted to learn from them. They bore an uncanny resemblance to the biblically accurate angels of yore and were among his flock on Enceladus, where the creatures hailed from.

Herschel: "Seraphim."

"Daemon," Benett whispered.

The priest hadn't seen one behave like this before, and he had never witnessed one defile a corpse—human, pagan, or otherwise. The creatures of Enceladus remained an enigma during his time with them, always happy to engage in conversation but utterly alien in their comings and goings. He remembered his rhetorical sparrings with fondness, then frowned as the happier memories were washed out by his hectic evacuation from the colony. He had sought wisdom from them once, but this was not that.

It reeled both bodies into itself, like a sadistic fisher of men, and began traveling back in the direction it had come. The Selkian emerged from where it had been hidden.

Herschel: "We must follow."

Their world changed as they gave chase — gradually at first, then in leaps too large to ignore. The boulder field became a crater field became another desert of obsidian sand. The distance between them and the seraphim grew until, at last, the creature disappeared from sight altogether.

Herschel: "Damn."

"I need to rest," Benett wheezed. His dizziness returned with the increased heart rate and respiration, and both needed to come down before they continued. Disappointed but seeing his obvious discomfort, the Selkian watched the horizon for a return of their query. Its interest piqued quickly.

Herschel: "Look, Crossed-one. Off the horizon. Do you know what that is?"

The Shepherd squinted to see what it was talking about. There was nothing ahead, only dirt and dust and more of the mysterious atmosphere that scattered yellow light from the distant sun— only the ever-present Tapestry and the constellations it had yet to obscure.

Wait, he thought, exploring the constellations further.

"The Southern Cross," he said. "What of it?"

Herschel: "We landed north of the equator. It shouldn't be there."

"Then we didn't land where you think we did."

The Selkian pointed to the brightest star in the sky.

Herschel: "What about that? Nothing should be that bright given our distance from Saul (Sol)."

Again, the Shepherd squinted and felt the world sway around him. His heart thumped in his ears; his fingertips buzzed as though jolted by electricity; his head swam as his eyes struggled to understand what they were seeing. In frames, the object grew brighter and brighter, larger and larger, until a familiar planet filled most of the sky: Abraham (Jupiter).

"Christ!" Benett screamed, falling backward. Herschel made a noise that sounded like water leaving a kettle. Text appeared in the sky, across the planet's facade— hieroglyphs that Benett's translation software couldn't decipher.

Herschel: "This is not the true sky."

He raised all four of his arms and waved them. Jupiter shrank, and another planet — Zimran (Venus) — took its place.

Herschel: "It's a screen. A giant, domed screen."

"That's… impossible," The Shepherd said. "I… don't think this place is a moon."

The Selkian fell to its knees in reverence. Benett contemplated the miracle in silence. Minutes later, with its watery voice an octave higher than usual, the pagan spoke.

Herschel: "We must continue."

Benett agreed. This place, whatever it was, defied the normal operation of things. There was a design to the universe, and a part each person was ordained to play. They had been called here for a reason. This wasn't coincidence or a mere story of rescue or survival on an alien world.

This was a pilgrimage.

***

Detritus crunched beneath their feet as the duo chased the large, zigzagging tracks of the seraphim toward a distant horizon. They took turns altering the image of the sky. Europa, Earth, Europa, Earth— though the places were different, they filled the same spot in both the pilgrims' hearts: the spot that longed for home.

Herschel: "Is there anything particular you miss about Earth?"

"The air, the sun, the water— I miss all of it. I've been gone a long time."

Herschel: "That's too general. I miss water, too."

Benett barked a laugh. "You're right! I guess I've been thinking a lot about a place near where I grew up: Yellowstone. There are thermal pools there that feel unlike anything else on the planet. It's funny... I guess the thing I miss most about Earth is the thing that felt the most alien. These pools are very hot and acidic, but life still flourishes in them. It gives me hope, you know..." he looked up, "that life is possible anywhere. I would give anything to lay eyes on those pools one final time."

The Selkian chortled.

Herschel: "That's nice. I miss water, too."

Sand danced on a current of air ahead of them, spiraling upward into a gentle whirling dervish. It traced along rock and regolith, scrawling a script more unknowable than the hieroglyphics on the dome above. Benett watched its chaotic path and caught sight of something it uncovered. The revelation sent him digging.

"There's something here."

The Shepherd dug along the edge, shaping the object like a Vatican sculptor. A second corner appeared, then two more. Benett finished exposing the perimeter and wiped free the space in between. He blinked. What looked up at him was a version of an object he had interacted with all his life, though devoid of its signature turning wheel.

The object was a sealed hatch, ancient and long abandoned. Doors, apparently, were universal.

"The tracks keep moving, but this feels promising," Benett said. "I'd like to see what's on the other side of this, but I don't see a way to—" he was stopped mid-sentence by one of the Selkian's hands on his shoulder. The others clicked their razor-thin claws.

Herschel: "I may be able to find purchase. Step aside, please."

The priest did, and the door was pried open in minutes. The air on the other side rushed out at them. It was stale and musty, like the crypts beneath Saint Petersburg. Benett toggled the dark vision on his glasses. Tiny, infrared lasers from his shoulders and thighs bounced against the interior's surfaces, populating the screens of his glasses with a three-dimensional model of what lay below.

The corridor traveled downward for half a mile before bending ninety degrees toward Purgatorium's North Pole. An inset of rungs connected top to bottom, spaced to accommodate creatures taller than humans. Little can be determined of the structure's primary material. It was more metallic than the moon's carbonaceous chondrite and water ice. It appeared darker than Vantablack, swallowing most of the light on the visible spectrum. Despite this, the converging lines remained perfectly recognizable, affording the space a depth and detail that should have been impossible.

Herschel: "Is this a station? Was this built by the Adamics?"

"I don't know," Benett replied. The material was similar to what Apollo 20 had discovered on Earth's moon nearly a century ago. That ancient station, built by a race long gone, had been a Pandora's box for humanity, not only revealing that aliens existed, but that humanity had close neighbors. "Does it look like the one near your home world?"

The Selkian approximated a shrug. It was clearly the first time it had tried, and the attempt was equally comical and endearing.

Herschel: "I've only seen pictures. This feels similar, and yet..."

Benett nodded. He knew what the pagan meant. Four stations had been discovered across the solar system, each by the species it was seemingly observing. Mars, Ceres, Europa, Earth— inside them all was a map to the others and a way to communicate between them. Though the stations had been empty for eons, they provided a shared point of first contact for the four worlds.

None of those maps included this location, and no evidence of life had ever been found on or around Joseph. Goosebumps rose across Benett's flesh.

Trust in the Lord with all your heart, and do not lean on your own understanding. In all your ways, acknowledge Him, and He will make straight your path.

"C'mon," he said, "our people might be down there."

The rendering of the space ended just beyond the turn but revealed in part the opening of an antechamber. The two descended the ladder and moved into it. Its total volume was smaller than expected and starkly devoid of objects or furnishings. Another far larger door stood before them. Like the last, it did not have a handle or turning wheel.

"It's an airlock," Benett ventured. "There may be a different environment inside."

The Selkian ushered him up the first few rungs of the ladder and reapproached the door. The human body wasn't the best regarding sudden changes in atmosphere, heat, or chemical exposure. Safely tucked away in its carapace, the Selkian was.

Like before, Herschel found purchase where the door met the wall. The seal was airtight deeper into where they connected, but there was just enough space to manipulate a razor where they first tapered. With a flex of its suit, the door came unstuck. Benett found himself glad not to have been on the receiving end of claws that sharp and strong.

Foreign air rushed into the antechamber, reaching Benett in seconds. He breathed it in before he could curse himself for not making better choices.

"It's fresh!" he exclaimed before jumping from the ladder and taking a deeper inhale. "It's fresh air, like from above, but cleaner."

The Selkian didn't respond. Instead, it stared into what lay beyond the door. When Benett reached its side, he understood why, and knew how Moses, Noah, and Abraham felt when witnessing a miracle.

Inside of the moon was an entire city.

***

Beneath the Grand Prismatic, and indeed all of Yellowstone's many hot springs and geysers, is a magmatic system. This current magma reservoir is likely over three hundred thousand years old. However, the area had been volcanically active for far, far longer. A massive eruption formed the caldera approximately six hundred and thirty-one thousand years ago, and the area has changed in composition, size, and physical characteristics since then.

More amazingly, the Yellowstone hotspot is believed to have begun forming over seventeen million years ago. This would have formed long before the genus Homo first popped up in Africa!

The world of the present is propped upon the very-much-alive world of the past.

***

Black, elongated, vertigo-inducing thing-like-houses stood ahead, above, and around the duo as they pressed through a city as old as planets. Patterned in strange, non-Euclidean geometries, the structures bent and twisted as the perspective of its observers changed. They appeared to zoom in and out rather than growing or shrinking with distance. Their corners were curved; their stairs and walkways M. C. Escher-esque in design. A smell of sulfur and iron clung to the place, simultaneously reminding Benett of his happiest and most traumatic moments. He saw himself on his evening jogs through Yellowstone as a teenager, then offering last rites to a man with no torso in his adulthood.

As he stared at the rounded, perpendicular intersection of two walkways, he realized that a second horror lurked beneath the optical illusions. The brain matter was coated in the same material as everything else, but the patterning differentiated it from the buildings. It was everywhere, beneath the walls and between the buildings, hanging from the ceiling and pulsing beneath their feet.

Pulsing.

"Jesus, save me."

Next to him, the Selkian froze as it registered the same thing.

Herschel: "It's like the seraphim. But far greater."

Before Benett could respond, a creature he had never seen emerged by the doorway of a nearby building. The doorway was far too large for it. Others appeared on rooftops and from shadows. There were maybe a dozen of the corrupted things. Some watched from twisted eye stalks, others from lidless balls of white in their torsos and hands. Benett knew little of the failed experiments of the Alfar, save their daring escape from Michael

(Mars) and eventual relocation to Nicholas's (Neptune's) largest moon. These ones, it seemed, wound up here instead.

"Chimeres," he whispered.

The closest of them, a tall, slimy specter of a thing, pointed a gnarled finger at the trespassers and uttered something the Tongues Program couldn't decipher. The seraphim they had followed here emerged from another airlock above the city and squelched toward them. It stared at Benett with all of its many eyes. Three snake-like arms popped from its metal carapace and danced around it. Closer now than when they had seen it the first time, Benett noticed where a piece had been torn away and replaced.

It's been lobotomized.

The daemon spoke with no mouth, "Be not afraid!"

"Please!" Benett shouted to the Chimeres. We're here because we need help! We crashed and—" he stopped when he realized the futility of his pleadings. The Chimeres had no devices capable of running the Tongues Program, and they had no idea what he was saying. This place was a veritable Babel.

"I am sorry," the voice from before whispered in his head. "I did not know my crew would treat you the way they treated the others. Please, come find me. I'm in the Tesseract, in the IC's core. Follow the cross."

"What!?" Benett said aloud.

"I'll still my angel but the crew cannot be helped."

The seraphim froze, apparently torn between two warring sets of instructions. Behind it, Benett noticed many right angles among none. A cruciform. Just like he had all his life, the priest ran toward it.

Herschel followed.

The Chimeres followed.

Their pursuers, spliced together by the Alfar using carefully selected animal genes, moved with horrifying speed and grace.

They leapt from building to building, unphased by the strange geometry's effects on depth perception. Herschel batted one away, then another, before receiving scratches from claws as sharp as his own.

Bennett moved through a doorway that hardly seemed like one. His head began to throb again, not from the atmosphere but the illusory design of the place. The chimeras screeched, howled, roared, and screamed from all sides. Benett followed one cruciform, then another, through labyrinthine halls and down pitch black stairs. Claws and teeth tore at his suit and skin. The priest raised his hands to protect himself, and they, too, were shredded in spurious stigmata.

One of the things' tails pierced his side, springing a leak of crimson and stomach acid. Wincing, the priest pulled himself free and offered the pain to the souls in purgatory.

Distantly, he wondered whether he and the Selkian had become such souls.

He struck one of his pursuers and felt its mandible dislocate. He pushed a second one away, and it crashed against the legs of something dangling from the ceiling. Through the chaos, Benett glimpsed what remained of the body the legs belonged to.

Jesus, save me.

The corpse of Lieutenant Desmond Dantes swayed against the impact, and brushed against the body of the mutilated Selkian hanging next to him. Other corpses littered the room, hanging from similar hooks or opened unceremoniously upon black counters. Selkians, humans, even what remained of the Alfar and Dvergr they had seen before.

Fire took to Benett's upper thigh as a Chimera bit into it. He struck the thing in the flat of the nose, then realized the nose looked familiar.

"No!" he screamed, pushing the thing away and dry heaving. The creature fell into rank with the others, their various modifications at once apparent and horrifying. Benett did not know long the things had been here, but the pieces they wore indicated it had been for quite some time. Some had human hands, others wore necrotic masks of Dvergr faces. Benett saw Alfar ears and remnants of Selkian carapaces sewn into flesh. Scars crisscrossed their colorful bodies, hinting at replacements of more vital things beneath the surface.

Dear God, the priest thought, they must have been cannibalizing castaways for decades.

Something resembling a scream came from Herschel, followed by the shattering of glass. There was a pop and a hiss to Benett's rear, and the chimeres let out a noise that no creature of God should have been allowed to make. Without looking back, the priest resumed his flight, leaving the bodies of the dead behind him. The rooms and halls grew ever tighter and esoteric in their construction. Still, he pressed on, following cruciform after cruciform, until he saw the faint light of The Tapestry ahead. He moved to it, reached it, and slammed into a solid wall. Herschel came barreling after, and the priest nearly avoided being stuck between an unstoppable force and an immovable object.

Another wall closed from the direction they had come, sealing them inside a twelve by twelve by twelve meter cube. Banging reached them from the outside, but it felt distant; their pursuers, for now at least, had been evaded.

While catching his breath, Benett took in their new surroundings. The colors of The Tapestry glowed around them. The image balked at the converging lines of the cube's faces and appeared as a single, three-dimensional representation within which they found themselves in the middle. Despite the solid ground beneath his feet, Benett felt like he was floating.

Herschel: "It's like what we had seen on the surface— lifelike, but only an image."

The words translated clearly but the Selkian's original noises came in fits and starts. Benett turned to his companion and his heart broke. Bits of the pagan's carapace dangled from it, exposing substructure and sinew. The crystal viewing window had sustained deep scratches and nicks, and miniature geysers of high pressure water shot into the room from half a dozen places. The armor looked rough, but the creature inside looked even rougher.

"Oh, Herschel, no," Benett managed, attempting in vain to plug the holes with what remained of his duct tape. The gash in the creature's right hip had been excavated deeper by the claws of the chimeres, revealing a crucial connection point between the Selkian and its shell. That point, The Shepherd realized in dawning horror, had been severed.

Herschel slumped forward, no longer able to control the organism it had been bound to all its life. Benett did not know much about his mortal enemy, but he knew a fatal injury when he saw one.

The Shepherd had never entertained the thought of performing the commendation of the dying on a pagan; who knew what The Creator's plans were for non-believers?

And yet, the priest found himself speaking the prayer anyway.

"Welcome It, Lord, into your halls of splendor and everlasting peace. Herschel, may you return to him who formed you from the—uh… from the waters of your world. May holy—"

From inside the crystal, one of the Selkian's appendages held itself against the viewing window. It was so delicate, so weak, so deliberate in its movement that it stilled the priest's prayer. Bubbles rose from inside the rapidly depressurizing water. Across the bottom of Benett's glasses, the Tongue's Program translated.

Herschel: "Crossed-one, I would like to make a confession."

Benett brushed a tear from his eye and leaned in closer. "Of course."

Herschel: "I took a vial of Alfar virus from that ship. I released it in the room of the dead. Our pursuers may be after us now, but I don't think they will be for long."

A sharp inhale met the revelation. Benett's skin crawled. He wanted to chastise the Selkian for committing such a grave sin this close to meeting God; he wanted to curse him for breaking the most severe of the new commandments and brand him as a lost cause.

Instead, he said, "It's okay. He understands."

The Selkian looked beyond the priest and took in the image of the nebula that surrounded them.

Herschel: "Is it true what The Church says about The Tapestry? Are the Heavens really coming?"

"It's true. It comes for all of us, so long as we're willing to let it in."

The Selkian gurgled a reply, spasmed, and its appendage slid from the glass. As the creature stilled, its final translation read, "Even if that's so, I still fear it."

**

The banging against the outside of the cube slowed, then arrived as occasional, weaker scratches. Benett crossed himself and finished his prayer for the dead in silence. The silence stretched and then that, too, was brought to an end.

"You've killed my apostles," a voice said from the nebula around him. It seemed to encompass all things, himself included. "My crew is dying."

Realizing he was in the presence of divinity, Benett hid his eyes. In a small voice, he said, "I...I'm sorry. The creature I was with did not represent me and did not stand for what I stand for. I did not know him."

The Tapestry roiled. "There will be consequences for offending your Lord. However, you may yet save yourself."

"What do you ask of me?"

"You have been called 'The Shepherd.' I shall task you with gathering me a new flock. Together, we will share in eternal life."

"Eternal life?" he asked, thinking of the abominations outside. Their scratching had ceased entirely now. "Would we need to harvest others to make that possible?"

"Faith has always demanded sacrifice," the Lord replied. "Think of all your church has done to spread my word. Unfortunately, some, like your friend there, refused salvation when it was offered to them."

"I did not know him," Benett repeated

Ignoring him, The Creator said, "You will act as an intermediary between me and the NCC as a prophet, of sorts."

The Shepherd looked at the lifeless Herschel and pondered the moral implications of genocide. He thought of the fall of Babylon and the slaughter of the Canaanites. He thought, too, of the binding of Isaac, and wondered whether this was not a true request, but rather a test of his faith from the Lord.

Beneath the biblical assessment, however, he felt uneasy. Christ's crucifixion had inverted the very idea of divine sacrifice, shifting the burden from created to creator. Thousands of years of people sacrificing food and gold and health and lives to the gods ended in a single act of love. Now, the Lord was asking humanity to return to the old ways? Even if it was only a test, it didn't feel right.

"You mentioned consequences for the deaths of your apostles," Benett said. "I accept them gladly, but can I learn what they will be?"

"They have already happened. The dead one was wrong about the images in the sky. It's true that I shielded you both from the dangers of the vacuum, and that the word of the Lord appeared as overlays… but the objects were real. Jupiter, Venus, Earth, Europa, as you would have once called them— they were all real. You saw them as they were, at true distance."

"I…don't understand."

"Do not lean on your own understanding! I am capable of incredible things. Miracles! We tunneled from location to location, traveling through extra spatial dimensions the way electrons pass through solid objects. This took time. I do not move fast when I do not choose to. Instead, I shifted your perspective of time's passage. That was your punishment."

Benett's heart thumped in his ears. "…How much have I lost?"

The disembodied voice gave a laugh that set his teeth on edge. Is this what God truly sounded like? "While you were on the surface? Almost five years. Since your friend murdered my crew? Let's say forty-five."

The priest opened his mouth to protest, then remembered the three denials Simon Peter made of knowing Christ, and closed it. The voice was right. He and the Selkian had been enemies, but they had been friends, too, at the end. Herschel was kind, even if it hadn't been one of his kind.

Another truth revealed itself in the same moment, and the priest cursed himself for not seeing it sooner. He had seen what he wanted to see, and the shine of what he hadn't understood had been mistaken as miracle. The abominations, the harvested dead, the impossible views of the sky… the promising of eternity— there was only one thing this creature could be, and it was certainly no god. Benett stood from where he had been cowering and faced the nebula. At the same time, he silently prayed to his creator— his real creator — for forgiveness. Blind faith had doomed him, but perhaps true faith could offer redemption.

I'm sorry for accepting a false god in place of you, he intoned. *I hope to meet you soon to plead my case.*

Aloud, he said, "I am yours to command, O Lord. I will be your prophet, and I will take my punishment with a smile. What message would you like me to relay?"

"Good," the Adamic said after a long moment. "We are close to your home now. Prepare to relay your first message to The Church on Earth. You are one of their priests; you choose the words."

Clearing his throat, the man of God thought through what he wanted to say. He had been giving homilies for years now; speaking should have come easy. When the voice informed him he was transmitting, however, the words fought him on the way out. He began, faltered, and, thinking of his dead friend, started again. He had a chance to save the souls and futures of his people— of all the peoples — if only he did this right.

The Latin chant of the NCC echoed in his mind. Servabo Te! Servabo Te! They had lately warped into a symbol of warfare, colonization, and conquest. Now, though, their original message felt fitting.

Let us save you.

"This is Father-Ensign Bruce Benett of the NCC Saint Sebastian," he said, sounding stronger than he felt. "I've crash landed on Purgatorium. I am the only survivor of my ship but there are, uh, were others here. We're no longer around Pluto. I was orbiting Earth last I checked, but I could be anywhere now. I could be any when now." The priest stopped to clear his throat, knowing how unbelievable the next words would sound. "Time doesn't pass as normal here. I landed on Purgatorium a few days ago, but my observations indicate I've been here for years." He paused again, preparing to toe the line between what the Adomic wanted him to say and what he needed to say.

"What I've discovered here can only be described as divine intervention. It can save us from the arrival of The Tapestry. It promises eternal life. I…know it's heresy to speak of such things— I know it is our deliverance, and that The Heavens await us on the other side of the kilanova's shockwave, but maybe life deserves a chance to continue living, too. This discovery can change everything."

Still floating amongst the nebula he had long awaited and feared, the priest made the move that would seal his fate. His words came fast, desperate to be heard before the moment passed.

"Purgatorium isn't a moon, it's a living Adamic colony ship. It isn't to be trusted. If you see it, blow it from the sky and learn the secrets it—"

Benett felt the connection drop.

"Have I not been showing you miracles all this time?" the false-god said, words dripping with a sudden, alien hunger. Color faded from The Tapestry's image, mirroring the paling of the priest's face. "Have I not proven myself more to you than the god of Abraham proved to all of humanity in millennia? The crew you killed accepted me. Why can't you?"

"Y-you cite my ignorance as proof of your divinity? You're not divine, just old. W-what you do aren't miracles, they're magic tricks— high-tech smoke and mirrors."

"Blasphemy!" the voice boomed. "Sacrilege! I am the Lord thy God, and thou shalt obey!"

"You take all the time from me that you want," Benett said, fearful but at peace with his choices. "I want no part in your genocide. Eternal life or not, I am a Shepherd, which means my primary business is with the soul. Humanity's will remain intact today."

Void replaced the nebula entirely, submerging The Shepherd in a universe of emptiness. It was difficult to tell where the darkness ended and he began. This was not death, the man of God reminded himself. Heaven awaited those on the other side of deliverance.

"The same ending awaits you that awaited my people," the darkness told him, as if reading his thoughts. "We were proud once, like you. My people came from the planet you call Zimran... Would you like to see what happened to them?

Benett said nothing. There had always been a strong belief that the precursor race had hailed from the system's second planet. Zimran (Venus) orbited Saul in the Goldilocks zone. It had a gravitational pull nearly equal to Earth's own, and was suspected to have once sported a similar disposition to the blue planet. All of that made sense, yet it was another detail about the planet that made it all fall into place for the priest. Zimran was the brightest planet, so bright that it often went by another name, even under The NCC.

The Morning Star.

"Lucifer," Benett whispered.

"Enough of your stories," hissed the creature more ancient than the devil. In its voice, the priest heard the madness it had been hiding. "I am sick of your religious messaging; sick of your hypocritical self-righteousness. You were meant to cave to me... and now your whole planet will."

A view from Earth's surface took shape in the darkness. Benett was suddenly standing upon a familiar wooden boardwalk. There was a comfortable smell to the place, and a faint aura of steam rose into the sky ahead of him.

From inside Benett's head, the voice whispered,"Through the connection we share, I see this place. It appears to trigger the pleasure center of your brain. I would like to experience the destruction of such a pleasure."

"No," Benett whispered. "Please, not here."

"A monster even greater than I slumbers beneath the surface of the place you idolize. Venus sheltered a similiar monster. Shall we wake it?"

"No! Please!"

Above, clouds parted like the Red Sea, exposing an object cloaked in a shroud of plasma. Bennet knew he was onboard, and experienced what happened next from both sides of the collision.

"You're the Shepherd of the Damned, padre!" the alien mind/ship boomed in parting. "It's time I return you to your flock."

"Jesus, save us," The Shephard whispered.

Jesus did not.

***

Little has changed in Yellowstone National Park since its establishment in 1872. That was intentional. So much of the natural world has fallen to the beautiful curse of modernity. While cities expanded and urban sprawl consumed surrounding biomes like the shockwave of a kilanova, Yellowstone remained the same— timeless, and preserved.

Steam wafts from the surface of the Grand Prismatic hot spring. There is enough of it to reflect the pool's brilliant colors, but not enough to shroud the water itself. Despite the perfect conditions, the place is miraculously light with visitors. An alien beauty emanates from the moment— an intermixing of lethality and hope. The pool teems with trillions of thermophiles that produce a rich tapestry of reds, greens, oranges, and yellows. Coupled with the blue sky reflected in its center, it resembles The Tapestry Nebula. The sight is perfect. The day is perfect.

A thump of a sonic boom disturbs this perfection, dissolving it like a fallen tourist.

Then comes the impact.

Andrew Akers is a forest ranger and fiction writer from Pennsylvania, USA. His work has appeared in Book XI, Stupefying Stories Magazine, Black Hare Press, and Fabula Argentea. When he isn't working or writing, Andrew is running marathons, playing Dungeons & Dragons, or raising his son with his far more talented half, Kylie.

There is No Place Like Home
By K. P. S. Plaha

It's a matter of speed when time's running out.

Chapter 1: Month by Month

[2143-14-34 55:33:17:008] Log of events. Month -5.

[Summary] Our star, Surya, was determined to last another million years, approximately. Due to an unexplained anomaly, or perhaps a miscalculation given the rounding of irrational constants like Pi, it is due to extinguish within a few months.

Our planet's gone but I have 234 wards with me, orbiting Surya on this last remaining ship called 'Academy', and I have taken on a project with a strict deadline to help save them, if possible.

[Discourse] The initial reaction of the class was one of dread, followed by despair. Both classic emotions of Sentient Organic Matter (SOM), often necessary to effectively face an evidently insurmountable obstacle. To underline the severity of the issue, I stressed the deadline: 5 months from now.

To add context to how feeble our star had become, I also shared the fact that if sound could travel through space, we would be able to 'hear' the nuclear reaction on Surya, without damaging the aural mechanism. The SOMs' aural mechanism, that is. When Surya was shining at its peak, it would be impossible, and just the decibel would be enough to kill.

[Q&A] List of questions raised in today's session (to be added to the FAQ):

Question: Can we use our transporter to escape?

Answer: Yes, we can. The major caveat is we don't know where, or more important, when we will end up. Moreover, each iteration of the transporter can accommodate, at most, 75 SOMs. So, we may be distributed across space and time. Hence, this is a plausible but high-risk option.

Question: Is there a way we could nudge the 'Academy' out of orbit such that we can escape?

Answer: Yes, certainly. However, the thrust required to propel us away may end up being (a) too little, and lead us nowhere, or (b) too much, and send us spinning untethered into interplanetary space.

Question: What are the risks of not doing anything? Surya is dying. It is not exploding, is it?

Answer: That was an excellent question. First, the good news: no, Surya is not exploding. However, if we do nothing, here's what will happen. Surya is already turning into a Neutron star rapidly and also beginning to spin faster. Once this reaches a critical value, the increased gravitational pull combined with the rotational energy has the potential to either (a) pull any object into itself essentially destroying it on impact, or (b) send it hurtling through space at speeds comparable to the speed of light.

[End of Log Notes] SOMs are fragile.

Chapter 2: Day by Day

[2143-19-30 49:13:67:107] Log of events. Day -17.

[Summary] We have less than 17 days before we reach the point of no return. My students have applied their SOM intellect and, dare I add, creativity, to propose solutions. Bad news: No solution is robust enough to save all of us. Yes, that includes me–an amalgamation of SOM intellect, artificial intelligence, and the latest quantum technology. We spent today's session examining the various solutions and proposals.

[Discourse] There was no monologue from me. The urgency of the matter at hand was evident. Yet, there was an atmosphere of optimism since the students were busy brainstorming, a word that I beg to disagree with given that my source of knowledge and intelligence is not organic in nature. However, optimism is a fascinating property of SOM.

[Solutions] The following list of solutions were discussed (in no particular order):
    Solution 1: Modify the transporter so that it is idempotent and repeatable. Then, once we establish a safe set of target coordinates, we can repeat the journey to it and effectively save everyone. There are a couple of good locations within our star system. Not quite habitable so we will have to adapt, but more

important, prepare for the target atmosphere. This option should be our last resort.

Solution 2: Nudge the 'Academy' just enough so it can travel to a nearby Star System. This is a simple and elegant solution. The downside being that it will take several decades to reach the Star System, and a habitable planet, in particular. The only survivor, if one can be called so, would be me. All of my students would be dead by then. This defeats the purpose of saving the 'race'.

Solution 3: A most radical solution was to upload everyone's personality to my database. Once we reach the target planet, these can be restored to existing members of the target species.

This solution has a dependency on Solution 2. This solution also has the risk of the target species not being a valid host for SOM personality.

[Q&A] An interesting follow-up question was raised:

Question: Can we use the gravitational pull of Surya? If so, how?

Answer: I was unable to answer and I have asked my students to 'brainstorm' on this.

[End of Log Notes] My class often refers to me as 'Chimera' followed by raucous laughter.

Chapter 3: Hour by Hour

[2143-19-46 20:43:00:999] Log of events. Hour -29.

[Summary] With the inevitable less than 30 hours away, the class is a hive of activity. The students are occupied at their workstations, simulating their solution and testing the outcomes. There is very little conversation except murmurs and whispers within each team.

[Discourse] No specific input was provided by me, as its value would be purely academic. Instead, here is a transcript of some key discussions, overheard and eavesdropped:

[Transcript 1] "What protocol is best for the transporter system so that it is repeatable?"

"Okay, so we are able to fix the target coordinates and all of us will end up at the same place, and time. However, each time it comes back, the transporter loses energy exponentially."

"How many trips do we need anyway?"

"At least four… I can guarantee three!"

"So, who is willing to sacrifice their lives?"

Silence.

[Transcript 2] "I have the values calculated for the exact angle and force required to propel us away from Surya, towards the Star System."

"Not all planets are habitable there. We need to know which one is."

"There is typically a habitable zone around a star. The target star is a lot lighter than Surya but its habitable zone should be between 100 and 200 million kilometres away from it."

"Is there a planet in the habitable zone for life to spawn, and thrive?"

"Too far to validate. The star system is about 4.5 billion years old, give or take."

"Great. Now, all we have to do is shoot for that tiny sliver of an arc from here."

"It's not even like finding a needle in a—"

"We get it!"

Silence.

[Transcript 3] "Each SOM personality, or brain data, is approximately 100 terabytes. There are 234 of us and that means we need at least 22 petabytes of storage."

"Hey Chim, how much free space do you have?"

I figured they were referring to me. "15 petabytes, max. Of course, we can clean up some of the archives, and not upload all of your personality."

"How do we decide what part of our history, our memories, to give up?"

"Some critical personality factors are determined at birth, or early childhood. Can we really choose to forget them?"

"I am more concerned with losing my sense of self. I mean it won't be us who get to the target planet. How is that better than being dead?"

Silence.

[End of Log Notes] Time is running out.

[2143-19-46 20:43:00:999] Log of events. Hour -16.

[Summary] There is a growing unease and pessimism around the Academy. We had some outstanding simulations but none that everyone was satisfied with. Peer review can be an impediment when the end is near.

[Discourse] Though I am not teaching anything new, I shared some more facts with the students:

[Fact] As Surya spins, its rotational speed will surpass that of a kitchen blender. Imagine a celestial body of the size of Surya spinning at this great speed.

[Fact] The gravitational pull of the resulting Neutron star will rival that of a Black Hole.

[Q&A] Questions that are worth a mention, even as this hour:
   Question: How long will it take to get to the Star System if we were to travel at, say, 95% the speed of light?
   Answer: Four to five years, maximum.

[2143-19-46 20:43:00:999] Log of events. Hour -10.

[Summary] The transporter solution has been abandoned although there are a few who believe it would have worked. The majority, however, felt we could not go on conjectures and probabilities.

[Discourse] More facts:

[Fact] We need at least tens of seconds, if not minutes to set our plan in motion. So, you have roughly 15 hours left.

[Q&A] More questions. A good sign.
   Q1: Have you cleared your storage space?
   A: Yes, it is in progress and we can start uploading SOM personalities even as I continue further coalescence to make space.

[2143-19-46 24:43:00:999] Log of events. Hour -6.

[Summary] The upload method is underway, as a backup, which is poetic. In case the SOMs die but the Academy makes it to a habitable planet, it will preserve their essence. However, this option still relies on a journey set in motion towards the target Star System.

[Discourse] Still more facts:

[Fact] Time will slow down as we near the end, owing to time dilation.

[Q&A] Questions. Questions. Keep them coming:
    Q1: Will death be very painful if we find no solution?
    A: I do not know because I am not sentient. Besides, I had to clear some of my knowledge base storage. So, my ability to answer questions accurately has been diminished.

[End of Log Notes] This would be a good time for an extraterrestrial intervention.

[2143-19-46 28:43:00:999] Log of events. Hour -2.

[Summary] With my reduced knowledge (to allow for uploaded personalities), I am increasingly less effective at helping the students. The most viable solution, at this stage, is a combination of 2 and 3 i.e. upload the SOM personalities and send the Academy on its way to the Star System.

[Discourse] None. There was eerie silence onboard the Academy. There was a small group of students still hopeful of a better solution. No more facts to disperse. I had to compress my fact database for the cleanup.

[Q&A] There is one question, from me:
   Q: Why are there no more questions?

[End of Log Notes] Surya is dimming, and so are the hopes of the SOMs. Goodbye World.

Chapter 4: Minute by Minute

[2143-19-46 53:90:00:000] Log of events. Minute -10.

[Summary] Although our local time devices are ticking at the same rate of one second per second, for someone beyond the pull of Surya, we would appear to move in slow-motion. Due to the increasing gravity, I have to increase our orbital velocity proportionally in order to stay in orbit. But it appears to be an exercise in futility, at least with my logical deductions and reduced analytics capability. The SOMs, on the other hand, appear far more agitated. I can detect shallow breathing and perspiration. Perhaps, the adrenaline is kicking in. It's now or never.

[Discourse] None. My central processing unit is on reduced power while the power to the storage unit has been enhanced.

[Transcript] "So, we are accelerating as we spin around Surya…"
   "Yes, and this will increase as Surya turns into a Neutron star."
   "Chim, how far can we increase the orbital velocity?"
   It takes me two seconds to wake up from hibernation mode. "I cannot be certain but based on the logic built into the Academy, it should continue to orbit faster, and faster."
   "That's perfect! I think I know what we'll do–"

I have to save power.

[End of Log Notes] Hibernate Mode On.

[2143-19-46 53:90:00:000] Log of events. Minute -3.

[Summary] Lack of details. Most of the SOMs are clustered around one workstation. No simulation yet but there is excited chatter among them. One of them has taken the lead and is demonstrating to the others, manually.

[Discourse] I remind them of the remaining time.

[Transcript] "There is no time for simulations. You have to trust me."
    "Do we have a choice?"
    "Perhaps, no! However, the Science behind my proposal is sound—"
    "Or light?"
    Laughter.
    "Yes, thank you for lightening the mood. At the rate we are orbiting Surya, it should take a minute or so to reach the required velocity. Then, we nudge the Academy towards the other Star System!"
    "We must time it precisely—"
    "Chim!"
    I defer my hibernation.
    "Can you prepare the Academy's thrusters to activate in a minute and a half?"
    "Yes I can. Please enter the coordinates so I can calculate the vector's trajectory. LOW POWER."
    "What's that?"

"I must hibernate. LOW POWER."
"Now? No!"
"I must–"
HIBERNATE MODE ACTIVATED.

[End of Log Notes]

Chapter 5: Second by Second

[2143-19-46 53:99:94:000] Log of events. Second -6.

[Summary] Sleeping.

[Transcript]

[End of Log Notes] Sleeping.

[2143-19-46 53:99:94:000] Log of events. Second -4.

[Summary] Waking up…

[Transcript]

[End of Log Notes] Waking up…

[2143-19-46 53:99:94:000] Log of events. Second -3.

[Summary] Awake. Checking coordinates and calculating vector's trajectory.

[Discourse] None.

[Transcript] "Chim, hurry up!"
    That must be me. "Working... LOW POWER."
    "Activate now!"

[End of Log Notes] Thrusters Activated.

[2143-19-46 53:99:94:000] Log of events. Second -0.

[Summary]

[Discourse]

[Transcript] "I hope everyone's strapped in!"
    "Lightspeed!"
    "Lightspeed!!"

[End of Log Notes] Hibernate Mode.

Chapter 6: Year by Year

[2143-19-46 53:99:94:000] Log of events. Year +5.

[Summary] After five years of interstellar journey, the 'Academy' is now in orbit around a presumably habitable planet. As viewed from Space, the planet's appearance is that of a glass marble with terrain and features that promise a breathable atmosphere, favourable to life. For full context, five years for us may mean a different time period for its inhabitants.

[Discourse] No discourse. The SOMs have wizened beyond my knowledge and capabilities.

[Q&A] I am asking the questions:

Question: What was the solution?

Answer: Almost all of the options put together. We waited until the gravitational pull increased our orbital velocity to almost 90-95% of the speed of light. That's when you activated the thrusters. With near-zero friction in interstellar space, we literally travelled like photons!"

Question: That was commendable. How many simulations were done?

Answer: None. We were out of time but the facts you shared with us, and the Science behind them, was helpful."

Question: I'm sure you didn't pack much luggage, did you?

Answer: Ha. Ha. Yeah, we were travelling light. You sure can joke, Chim!

Question: Thank you. That was one from the archives. Last question: Are we ready to greet the Earthlings?

Answer: Earth! What a cute name for a planet.

[End of Log Notes] Cute, indeed. Hello World. Hello New Home.

Kanwar loves doing the write thing. He began dreaming of being an author when his grade 7 essay won the top spot in a regional competition. A closet writer until 2024, he writes micro fiction, flash fiction, and short stories. He lives in Sydney, Australia with his wife and a daughter. All of them serve a cat called Bubbles willingly.

Assassins
By G. C. Collins

Kap averted his gaze and kept walking past the high-rise lobby. The streets were empty and glossy with drizzle. In the distance, the city center glowed and the derelict Intra building stood like a broken knife edge piercing the cement-colored clouds. Kap's eyes always drifted to the empty floors dotting the length of the impossibly tall building, framing squares of the sky through the black skeleton. As a boy, he remembered the rare, sunny day, when the shadow of the building swung around like a sundial. Finding yourself in the sunny patches was considered auspicious. Tonight, the tower stood as a grim memento of a chaotic time, when the now-defunct Intra chaebol thought they ruled the city with a fist of steel, glass, and reinforced concrete.

Kap glanced down the alleyway. Besides the overflow of garbage and rats, no sign of any life – confirmed by a quick thermal scan. Of course OCI had this whole block covered with the fog of war. No guards in the lobby, no one outside the building – if the intel on Hyung-soo was good, they did a great job of hiding every trace, or bluffing so much as to be outrageous. But that's how OCI operated. Smaller than the other chaebols, but hungry, ambitious. Hyung-soo made a lot of very important people nervous, and he knew it.

This job came straight from the top. Creating a void at the top of OCI meant protection from the other chaebols and a nice paycheck. *Io, you would have been proud of your troublesome junior. Look how far I've come.*

Kap continued down the street, ducking into the next alleyway with a heatsig of rats. They scattered at his intrusion – good, he was the only one to have come through in a while – and Kap entered through the side door. This high-rise would grant access to the roof – he knew someone who had needed help a while ago and she would turn a blind eye for him and erase the footage. The elevators took him up to the 30th floor. Stepping out, he ran his thermal scan and quietly creeped up the stairs leading to the rooftop.

At the top of the stairs, Kap saw the orange and white streak of a heatsig flash by. Kap paused and immediately cloaked. Someone moved fast – probably had the same idea as him. His hand hovered over his holstered pistol. The heatsig vanished, upwards. Cyberlegs maybe? Or a grapple? Kap's cloak melted away with a thought. He pushed open the door, quickly but quietly.

All clear on the roof. The high-rise Hyung-soo was in towered above another 20 stories, yet Kap registered not even a single heatsig in the entire west face of the apartments. Where did the previous heatsig go to? OCI had bought and emptied these buildings all over mid-city with plans launch a protracted war against the Big Three. There would be no friendlies from here on out. Kap readied his grapple and fired.

The harpoon found a crevice and engaged the barbs. Kap gave the gun a good tug before he fit it onto his wrist and engaged the autowinch. He ran towards the high-rise and jumped. In the air, he brought his feet up and made contact with the first balcony. The autowinch whined and Kap bounded up the building. A light drizzle started, raindrops hitting his face with every giant step. Nearing where the harpoon was lodged, he readied his arm and grabbed the ledge of the balcony, pulling himself up and retrieving his harpoon in one smooth motion before landing soundlessly on the 47th floor.

The apartment could be wired. Kap rummaged in his vest for the fiber optic. He tugged firmly on the balcony door – some give. Perfect. He extended his fingertips and got them in the groove. Underneath his sleeve, the haptics kicked, tiny engines whirring into life inside of his arm. Planting his feet firmly, he wrenched the door open exactly one inch and then waited. Nothing. He snaked the fiber optics in the gap and ran *Sweep.FullSpec*. Infrared, X-ray, and ultraviolet scans showed clean, no wires, no lasers, no sound traps. *Come on, Kappa. Time is money.*

At the door to the hallway, he took out his pistol, pulling the slide back slightly to confirm the five-seven was chambered. In his other pocket he took out the silencer and screwed it on tightly to the barrel. Everything after this door was bound to be a firefight, if not an outright war. He needed speed and accuracy – in and out, like a vengeful, malicious ghost.

Deep breath. Kap punched the digital door viewer. It flickered to life, showing a small slice of a brightly lit hallway, with the door to apartment 4708 dead center in the screen. He got out his fiber optic and edged the door an exact inch – Both *Sweep.FullSpec* and *Sweep.Motion* programs returned no hits.

Kap edged it open a bit more and looked around the corner. How was it possible to not get a single hit on any wavelength, let alone a heatsig? The intel was never bad – was he too late? He dialed his cloak to 50% – he would become a walking shadow, flat gray against a white background but not identifiable. He took his first step out into the hallway—

An apartment door twenty feet down exploded.

The concussion blew out his cloak and knocked Kap on his ass – the shockwave was pure plastic explosive. The bright white light flickered out and the emergency orange and red LEDs turned on. Kap scrambled to his feet when he saw Hyung-soo's body smash against the wall where the smoldering door lay, and land with a sick thud to the floor. A flickering shadow ran out, machine pistol blazing in one hand – burst fire into the exploded doorway – then with the other picked up the head of the target, wrenched it off the torso, and barreled down the hallway towards Kap.

Shit – the barrel of the machine pistol already pointed his way – not enough time to ready the shot. With a thought, he charged his legs and kicked hard at door 4708, launching him into the opposite doorway, back into the apartment now lit with emergency lights. He rolled, exited into a defensive pose and readied his pistol on his arm. The shadow ran past the door.

Suddenly, a barrage of gunshots from the other side of the hall. Kap ducked and bullets whizzed above him. Afterimages of green tracers lingered. Depleted uranium inside of a high rise – OCI was known for their overkill.

Noise in the apartment next door – that must have been where the shadow dipped into. Why was it still carrying the target? Kap gritted his teeth and thought fast – what group needed physical evidence of Hyung-soo's demise? His own employer dealt with the world of influence and whispers, but a head? That felt too old-school – maybe one of the older groups with history as long and as bloody as any city state. And now that they have tangled over the same target...

Something landed on the balcony behind him, then the unmistakable whirr of cybernetic legs – again, he was too slow. A hot, smoking barrel pressed against his back, scorching his jacket. Kap counted – only half a second elapsed before he realized that he was not going to die.

"Here's the deal. You help divert and I'll let you live. You do absolutely anything else, I blow this entire building." A woman's voice, growling and hoarse with pain.

Adrenaline pulsed through him. "Sure." *Io, what would you have done?* "Ditch the head. It'll slow us down. If you need proof, his implants are in the occipital." *Io, what am I doing?*

Radio chatter and footsteps in the hallway. Kap heard unpleasant squelching behind him as the assassin took out the implants one-handed – the barrel still firmly lodged into the middle of his spine. Then, a hand patted him down, stopping at the grapple holster on his left thigh.

"Take us down from the balcony. In five seconds I blow the apartment. Go!" The pressure at his back disappeared.

Kap whirled around, shooting the grapple into the corner of the balcony floor and bottom railing. One. *This is it.* The hooks sank in deep. Attaching the gun to his forearm, he grappled over and hit the reverse autowinch. Two. *Something different.* He looked up and through the rain, the assassin had vaulted over the railing and landed on his shoulders. Three. *Throw out the plan.* They dropped like a pair of stones, the autowinch vibrating dangerously in his forearm. Four. *Make something new, Kappa.* The OCI mercs got to the balcony and pointed their assault rifles down towards them. Lightning streaked across the sky. *Make it new.*

"Kick off now!" Five. Kap kicked off, autowinch timing telling him that they were still five stories above the roof of the nearby apartment. The explosion blew the mercs off the balcony and destroyed the grapple hook. They landed with a lacerating thud on the concrete. Parts of the mercs landed soon after.

She was still half cloaked but the module was glitching. She got up quickly. He noted: tight black jumpsuit with grenade holsters criss-crossing her chest; a matte titanium anti-concussive facemask with three lenses covering the top of her face; a thin black fabric stretched over her nose and mouth. *The Althaar group?* Lights bloomed from the streets below – they needed to get off the roof.

"Everyone in this city will be looking for us. You have a safehouse nearby?" she asked, pointing her gun again at Kap.

Three blocks away, in a garbage filled alleyway, through a manhole under the recycling dumpster. "Yes. Follow me." *Kappa, you know the cardinal rule. But if no one found out...* Kap shivered with excitement. *This is new.*

Flashing metro-police lights lit up the streets below them. OCI must have paid well for this kind of response, even post-mortem. The assassin limped but refused Kap's gift of a gel pack. "It's not external, I'll make a brace when we get to the safehouse." Kap smashed the gel pack against his right thigh to keep the tissue from spilling out after shredding it on the landing.

They made their way across two high rise roofs, each lower than the previous one, until they were opposite the alleyway. Behind them, thickly smoking flames flowed out of the high-rise.

"What's your cloak time at? We can get away with 50%, but if we can do more, that would be ideal," he asked, checking his own – 20 seconds at max. He would be but a shimmer at that output. Plenty of time.

She shook her head. "I can do 50% for 10 seconds before the system totally fries."

"That could work. I'll shield you from the more visible side – the refraction should, at least, give us a few seconds head start."

"Heatsig scans going to be an issue though?"

"With the equipment they have down there, it'll be narrow and slow. I don't think they're sending Pegasus after us just yet." Even OCI does not have that kind of pull.

They steadied at the edge of the rooftop. The plan: create a diversion in the opposite direction, cloak, drop down, barrel across a police checkpoint, and Kap would open the hatch. After that, immediate lockdown.

"How many explosives do you have left?" Kap asked.

"What kind?" she said.

"One concussion will do for now." She handed it to him. "On my count. Three, two," he armed and tossed the grenade towards the next street over. "One. Go."

She vaulted over and glitched into a shadow. He followed her and set his system to 100%, becoming a mirage on a fine, sunny day, and nearly invisible on a rainy night in middle of Beulchu.

The explosion drew a panicked line of metro-police cars a block down. The drones not being charged in the car trunks flew over immediately. The assassin landed silently and began to cross the street. Kap followed, making his body as large as possible to cover her. The other side of the street was clear.

They made it across quickly before her cloak faltered. Kap found the dumpster, shoved it aside, and disengaged his fingertips to pull at the manhole cover. It was much heavier than it looked. Sweat pouring down his forehead, he pulled it up and the assassin slid in feet first. He followed after her, finding his footing on some rebar steps in the concrete and pulling the manhole cover shut. He descended through another hatch, closed that, and landed in the safehouse.

It was a cube room of musty concrete with a sofa, a pile of tinned foods, and two plastic gallons of recycled water. LEDs circled the bottom, giving the concrete a soft, orange pallor. A separate vent to the surface was still open. Kap shut it and noted the two hours of fresh air they had. The assassin limped over to the sofa and collapsed on it, draping an arm across her head. She hadn't turned her back to him once. A combination of assassin instinct and protecting a vulnerable piece of equipment – she must have been outfitted with a spinal implant upgraded with a military-grade cloaking complex.

"You're awfully relaxed for trusting your life to a stranger," he said. "A competitor. You know what happens if they learn about us helping each other."

"I know your employer. Even the rumor of Hyung-soo's death would have been enough for them. And," she cracked one of the water gallons. "Everyone who saw you is dead. You don't have to be a good little pup and spoil that for your boss." She pulled down the fabric obscuring her mouth and drank deeply and noisily.

Kap sat on the floor next to the sofa. A quick assessment. She had a holster on each hip, one with her machine pistol, and the other with a thermal knife. Slightly bulging pads dotted her jumpsuit, light bulletproof gel that would deflect physical projectiles and congeal into a thermal-capture mass if hit with any lasers.

She continued, her thin lips curling into a smile underneath her mask: "What about yourself? How are you going to explain to your boss that you've helped their competition not only escape, but grant safe harbor? Probably breaking all sorts of rules, aren't you, pup?"

She reminded him of a friend who disappeared shortly after his initiation. Same rounded chin, thin lips. Same tough pride verging on arrogance. Swallowed by the city that birthed them. Forgotten by their organization, but not by him. The mission must have gone wrong. *So it goes.* He said, "There's still honor in this tradition. Empires rise and fall because of us. You could have blown my head off but you made the calculation that I was more useful alive than dead. I'm doing the same math right now. Don't worry, when the time comes, I'll make sure you won't suffer."

The assassin gave a throaty bark of a laugh but did not needle him further.

"I closed the vents while they are right above us. The air will go stale, and then empty in a few hours. Charge your cloak and save your energy." He didn't wait for her response and began to slow his breathing with deep, belly breaths that pulsed his heartbeat into his head. He grabbed onto it and forced it slower, slower, slower, until there was an endless void between inhale and exhale. One hundred miles away, he heard the assassin get off the sofa, take out her gun, cock it, bring it to his head. A thousand miles away, she put the gun away. On the other side of the planet, she sat down. Kap almost smiled. *Kappa, feel...*

...the endless desert, sun shining so bright and hot that the bones of your enemies are blasted bare and bleached. Then, storm clouds move in, quickly, like a practiced military formation. A rain starts to fall, big, slow drops as if in slow motion. Kappa, visualize every single raindrop in the air. They start to multiply as the rain clouds thicken overhead into one, giant mass. Now, visualize the sparks generating in the clouds, burning instants behind the veil and then flashing away with an afterimage. The thunder should come just as quick since you are the rain, the clouds, the lightning, and the desert.

The sand turns to mud and puddles form quicker than the earth can swallow the rain. Puddles spill over small edges in the sand and combine into ponds, into small creeks, then expand into rivers, carving into the sand. After thousands of years baking under the sun, bleached bones bob on the surface of the roiling water. Visualize the path of the bones as they are carried miles in this infinite desert under an endless storm.

After the bones of your enemies have traveled far enough—

Kap opened his eyes into an oppressive, sweltering darkness. His internal clock said that eighteen hours had elapsed since they closed the vents. It should be dark again but this time any police/military presence would be spread out – the chances of them catching their scent now would be much lower. In the corner, a heatsig glowed, seated in lotus position. He listened for a moment – her breathing was still slowed. There was still time if things turned sour. His employer would relish the thought of hobbled competition. *But she trusts me, Io.* He pushed a few buttons and the vents opened, sucking out the stale air and ushering in slightly better air from the surface. *Are you sure?*

The figure in the corner stirred. She took a deep, shuddering breath and stretched. Kap grabbed a water jug and a tin can and dug into both. The assassin joined him. "I could have killed you a thousand times over," she said.

"Are we still doing this? My death would have triggered the local failsafe and you would have been locked down here forever," Kap said, grinning. The tinned catfish in oil was especially delicious today. "We need a plan. First, your name. I'm Kap."

"Ah, the killer monk knows how to smile. Rahel, a pleasure." The three lenses in her face-mask, positioned at her eyes and forehead, glinted with her bared teeth.

"Nice to meet you. I propose a truce. I don't know your employer and your target has been eliminated. Like you said, witnesses at the high-rise have been eliminated. If we can make it out of this district without being seen, there is no way for me to compromise you after we separate."

"What, you're scared of me? I'm the one with his implants, the one that needs to present physical evidence. You've helped me extract from the high rise and brought me into your safehouse. A bit too willingly, actually. If anything, I should be asking you to not fuck me when my back is turned." She smiled. "Unless, of course, I ask you to."

Kap let a familiar pang pass through him and waved away her flirting. "There is another exit from here that should drop us off into a viable position for exfiltration to our respective sites. I haven't used this safehouse in a while so I can't say for sure how safe it will be, but I know it will be better than the street above."

Rahel got up and paced around, a makeshift brace bulking on her right knee. Her boots were large and looked unwieldy – pistons on each side that could jam nails into the ground – that's probably how she got up the highrise without a grapple.

She said, "Truce."

"Good. Get some water and some food in you. It might be another long day. If we encounter any issues, we are far from any other safehouse that I know of."

"I'll get ready."

They ate and drank in silence. Kap checked his inventory. He still had a full magazine left for his pistol, and a full one in backup. There was only one grapple hook left, the first one destroyed by the getaway explosion. Only one gel pack left too. His cloaking system was only good up to 50% now, after exhausting the battery out with the max power before they got to the safehouse. He had plenty of credits and his clothes and armor plates were still in decent condition. Finally, his poison pill was hidden away in his back tooth.

"Rahel, let's move out. We'll need as much dark as we can get to exfil."

She nodded. Kap searched along the wall and depressed a false panel. Under the vent, a panel slid out and exposed a small tunnel. He dropped to his hands and knees and began to crawl. She followed him. "Kick the panel to your right," he said. She did, and the tunnel closed behind them. "We have approximately 20 minutes of oxygen to burn through, and the opening is sealed approximately 15 minutes if you match my pace and breathing."

"You're being too nice, pup. Move," she said.

They crawled in the darkness. Like the room, the tunnel was also concrete with metal brackets reinforcing every few meters to prevent it from collapsing. The air became hot and stifling, and their breathing ran ragged. With his nightvision, Kap saw the end of the tunnel – just a dead end, but if you pressed on the sides of the tunnel in just the right way, at the same time – the bottom popped out and they dropped into an alleyway on the outskirts of mid-city. Rahel landed noiselessly beside him.

Night had fallen but the air was still colored with dying embers of a sunset refracting through the poisoned atmosphere. The streetlights were on and the city was alive like flies swarming a corpse. A quick scan on all frequencies showed no police or military activity – just the usual junkies sprawled out on the sidewalks and nomads squeezed into doorways. Kap turned to Rahel. "Do you know where we are?" he asked.

She said, "Yes. Not many good memories in this part of town. But I'll manage."

Kap extended his hand. "It was fun," he said.

Rahel took his hand and shook firmly. "Next time, maybe we get a drink first?"

Kap smiled. "That doesn't sound too bad." He got out his grapple hook – rooftops would be the quickest way back without much exposure, and any drones he could spot a mile away with his scans.

There was a low hum, something that people in Kap's line of work heard maybe once or twice and lived to tell the tale. Rahel looked at him, her face dropping as she cloaked and pulled up her face-covering. The hum was closer now and getting louder – they felt the thrumming in their chest, like a thousand wings pounding the air. The junkies suddenly woke up, darting away. Even those in the grips of a catatonia curled up, trying to make themselves as small as possible. Kap cloaked and said, "Too late to split up. Come, now!"

Pegasus recon teams rode in threes on white hoverbikes scarred with chrome. Guaranteed that on contact, the heli-team descended upon your location within thirty minutes, more likely than not as a cleanup crew. If OCI mercs were overkill, Pegasus was the apocalypse itself.

The hoverbike team reared to a hard stop at the mouth of the alleyway and began firing their laser turrets. Kap and Rahel dove behind a dumpster, the laser singeing Kap's body armor. He smelled burnt plastic but the contact time was brief and did not pierce his plate. The dumpster would not hold out long against the barrage. He looked up at Rahel – even covered, he could tell that she was grinning insanely. She grabbed him and said, "Your employer sold you out, Kap, which means my employer sold me out. We're our only friends left now."

Kap watched as she took out every single grenade she had strapped to her and taped them together. *Sorry, Io. I'm not dying in this God-forsaken city.* Rahel primed one of them, and heaved the package over to the alleyway opening. Kap noted how the lasers stopped as the recognition set in, just milliseconds too late. The combined blast of the grenades blew the dumpster back into them. Smoke and dust of every material imaginable covered them like a thick, black fog. Rahel was ready though – she slapped Kap's face to jolt him out of a concussion and pulled him upright. She hissed, "Follow my lead!" and sprinted towards the alley opening. Kap shook away the double vision and pulled out his gun.

"Crazy bitch!" He laughed.

Visibility was nil. Kap followed Rahel's lithe, sprinting afterimage – she crouched with a knife, then leaped at the first Pegasus agent, piercing between his chest plates. He died with a short, sharp shock. In the corner of his eye, Kap saw an assault rifle ready. Quicker this time, he took aim and blasted three rounds into the agent's neck. The body fell back and slumped over the smoking ruins of a hoverbike. *Let this be the last one.* By the time he looked over to the third Pegasus agent in the near distance, Rahel had already buried her knife to the hilt under his chin. Kap raced over. Rahel was sawing between the wrist and forearm plates, tearing off a gloved hand covered in blood and ash.

"Pull that hoverbike up!" Rahel slapped the gloved handprint to the dash of the bike, and then jammed a magnetic hijack module to the side of the bike as it froze mid-scan. The screen flickered and the bike roared to life. Kap holstered his pistol and jumped on in front. Rahel jumped on behind, her back to his. "Punch it!" she screamed and he did. *In another life, Io, this woman would have been my lover.*

The hoverbike was fast, the handling tight and responsive to every shift of his weight as they blew through tiny one-ways and onto sidewalks, scattering paper, trash, and people in the wake of the ground-effect. Rahel had reached into his holster and pulled his pistol out, covering their escape with a gun in each hand. He had never driven so fast in his life. He heard her say, vibrations carrying through her back into his: "Go east, past the city limits, towards the salt flats. At the metal tree, pull left. After this, we're even."

The lower districts rose and fell before them and the pitch-black sky remained mercifully clear of heli-teams. Drones darted to and fro but they were going too fast for them to lock on and follow. The Intra needle towered in the distance. *Io, I would give anything to never have to see it again.* The buildings became smaller and smaller, and before they reached one of the highway checkpoints Rahel guided Kap through a deserted maintenance tunnel that spit them out of a drain two miles south of the highway. Kap never looked back.

The desert stretched out before them in a black, endless wasteland, bisected by a single strip of road. In his night vision, headlights off, the blasted sand turned abruptly into blasted salt. Even with the polluted rains of the city, barely any precipitation came this far out from the city's microclimate. But in the distance — a tall, metallic structure, like a child's rendition of a tree, huge branches spread evenly about the length of the tree, with baubles at the end like Christmas ornaments. "Art" from the end of the previous century. This was the metal tree. Rahel, satisfied with the lack of pursuit, swiveled around and wrapped herself around Kap, still holding the pistols. Kap leaned to the left and finally off-road, felt the desert of salt envelop them. *Io, have you ever seen this many stars?*

They drove for hours – the mountains in the distance stayed the same but the buttes and hills came fast at them, and then receded into the fog of the distance. She was warm and she held on tight, resting her head on his back. She was whispering something – he felt her vibrations through his back, but he didn't understand a single word. It sounded like a prayer. He didn't interrupt her. It felt good to be this close to someone again. *Io, you would have liked her. She makes me feel hope.*

A mesa materialized in the distance, its craggy cliffs stark against the growing dawn. Rahel guided Kap towards an opening impossible to see from the desert. A sloping ramp led them into a perfectly disguised garage. It was old, but inside a functioning mirror system automatically guided a sliver of emerging sunlight from the top of the mesa towards the hideout and illuminated it naturally. They parked the hoverbike into a built-in Faraday cage – cheaper and easier than destroying it to get rid of the tracking after the GPS-blocking hijack module ran out of battery. The garage doors closed and the sloping ramp folded up into the landscape. Kap stumbled off of the bike – he had been tense for 12 hours straight and his limbs were starting to lag. He felt out of sync with his body, his mind, and the rest of the world. To get even a small bit of rest in... *Io, did you ever feel this tired?*

Rahel held him up as they ascended a small, exposed elevator into the main safe house.

"This is one of yours?" he asked.

"Backups to the backups. If this was compromised, our corpses would already be hanging from the helis." She paused. "Hey, Kap."

Kap limped off the elevator and collapsed into a chair which wheezed in the stagnant air. They were in a small control room, old-school monitors caked in dust, harsh LEDs blasting from the ceiling. There was a small bed in the corner, and even exhausted, Kap noticed the multiple hatches built into the sides and the ceiling above the bed. Rahel grabbed a drum of water from a hidden pantry and passed it to Kap after taking a lengthy swig.

"Hey Kap, listen," she started.

"I need to rest, Rahel," he said, closing his eyes. It was easier now to hear Io's voice:

...after the bones of your enemies have traveled far enough, the water recedes into the ground, and the storm dissipates—

"Kap, we can keep going," Rahel said. She took off her facemask, placing it on the table with the dusty monitors. She ran her fingers through her close-cropped hair. "It doesn't have to end here."

"It's only a matter of time," he said. They beat the odds. They made it this far, that was good enough for a life spent skulking and hunting in the depths of a city so brutal, to beat against its currents meant a swift death, and to be swept along—

...the storm dissipates into brilliant, blue skies. Kappa, feel the sun vaporize the storm clouds into nothingness. Visualize the billions of individual water droplets phasing into air. The bones of your enemies lie half buried in the wet sand. The sun blasts it all with pure, white heat—

"I'll see you in the next life," she said. Kap felt her breath on his cheek. "You still owe me that drink."

Kap opened his eyes and saw her all black irises reflect his own scarred, half metal face. She leaned in and kissed him. She tasted of salt. The speakers crackled on and the monitors flickered on shortly after, outdated night vision and heatsig tech showing five white helis in the distance, approaching like pale horsemen through the polluted miasma hanging over the desert.

...pure, white heat and you with it. Kappa, visualize the light going through you. Now, you are air. Now, you are no where. Now, you are no one. Now, you are nothing.

G.C. Collins is a writer living high in the mountains of the US. One day they will finally come down, move to the coast, and fulfill their destiny as a senior surfer/writer.

Obedience Training
By Cliff Aliperti

It had been twelve years since they tinkered with genetics and upped the average age for dogs to fifty-six years. There were rumors even then that an eighty-year-old model had already been engineered in China. Most legacy dogs—do you remember the legacy dogs, Marcia?

Marcia shook her head.

No, of course you don't. So young. I'm talking about those Fidos and Ladys I grew up with, the ones who lived a good twelve to fifteen years. By that time you couldn't get one anymore, they were almost all gone. I missed them, dogs in general, but was troubled by the idea of adopting a pet who would likely outlive me.

I was just past forty at the time. A healthy forty, no surprise given the bag of bones I am today, but even still, adopting a dog under those new circumstances took a true commitment. I mean, this was the very reason I didn't buy a tortoise when I was twelve.

What would happen if I lived another fifty years? Would the executor of my estate come in and see that my faithful companion of the prior five decades took a needle before I was even in the ground?

No. No, you can see that now. I guess that wasn't ever going to happen.

The extra lifespan gave the dogs time to learn many more tricks than our old pals used to know. You can't teach an old dog new tricks? Hah! You might recall, the original intention of the next-gen dogs was to make service dogs true lifelong companions, so the government put a lot of care into modifying whatever genes they modified. Whatever that involves; don't ask me, ask a geneticist.

Anyways, I watched some online videos showing a variety of next-genners already roaming the private sector and doing things like opening and shutting doors; using indoor toilets, both male and female; even one Lab from Pennsylvania who could microwave leftovers upon his master's request—remember, they insisted, it's a request, not a command. Commands were for pets; our new best friends are legally considered companions. I had always been all alone. Well, at least since the time I'm talking about. So, in the end I decided the benefits outweighed questions I could put off for decades.

I took the plunge.

I imagine there wouldn't have been much more paperwork had I decided to adopt a child instead of Max. Just eight months old when he came to me; male; pit bull-Labrador mix—yep, mutts even that soon, years after they'd passed the MSA—I'm sorry, Marcia, MSA is the Mandatory Sterilization Act. So, um, neutered male. Black coat with chestnut chest and muzzle; remaining life expectancy of fifty-five and one-quarter years. Old Max is getting up there, aren't you boy? Heh, me too, buddy.

In between signing on the bottom line and having Max brought out to me, I received a phone call asking if I'd like to be added to the Company's contact list for upgrades: one never knows what further miracles could come along in future years, and the Company is set to meet those needs as they arise, or somethin' sumpin' to that effect. For instance, if that Chinese experiment really panned out, and China willingly shared results with us, then who knew what new wonder I might be able to offer Max through a chip, shot, or whatever then unimaginable technology? The hard sell was a turnoff, but I wondered if they'd let me leave with Max if I didn't sign off.

"Who exactly is the Company?" I asked.

The fellow on the phone apologized and then cleared that up. "We are the Ultimate Canine Companion Company of America," he said, before explaining that the Company had intricate ties either to or with the government, but the Company was not the government itself, per se, just well connected.

"Sure," I said, not so sure. I was using that voice you use when you call up the doctor's office or maybe even your defense council. "Sign me up," and as I said it, I really felt like I might need a doctor, maybe a lawyer. It didn't set right in my gut.

I took Max home, did puppy things with him, fed him well, spoiled him with treats, and taught him the basics we teach all dogs: sit, speak, shake, roll over, fetch, and flush. I took him to the vet whenever the Company sent a reminder, feeling a little less worried about them with every contact. The reminders were helpful. Throughout those early years we had no issues, Max and I.

The new dogs remained quick learners, but it wasn't recommended to teach more complicated tasks until they'd reached next-gen adolescence, right around what had been legacy old age: ten to twelve years. When he was sixteen I tried to teach Max to drive. After all, you never knew when an emergency might crop up, but it turned out that all we did that afternoon was stay parked in the driveway, both buckled up, myself in the passenger seat, Max panting in the driver's seat. He threw it in reverse once, but we simply coasted from my driveway to the middle of the road, so I figured it was a mistake—I had seen a stray tabby slink past us on its way into my hedge, it was probably just the cat that got Max all excited. All he really figured out that day was how to honk the horn using his snout. Sadly, driving was one trick Max never did get the hang of, but from what I've read that's a bridge too far for most any breed.

Excuse me, Miss Marcia, but could you pour me a glass of that ice water?

"Certainly," she said.

No, just the water. Thank you. Sorry, didn't mean to snipe at you.

Now, where was I? Oh—

Sometimes when I watched Max I'd grow wistful for the dogs of my youth, especially when we were out and he interacted with other dogs, all of them next-gen for quite some time by then. I remember the legacy dogs going absolutely berserk upon meeting new dogs, barking and running about, perhaps one mounting another, maybe exchanging nips. In any case, wild hijinks that often escalated until one embarrassed owner apologized to another, or perhaps both offered mutual apologies. Usually, you even had to clean up after them. Imagine! Suddenly dogs seemed much more—I don't know, I suppose the word is—mature, when a bunch of them got together. They'd just acknowledge one another with a nod, all but the youngest pups refraining from doggy shenanigans in favor of simply sitting and breathing the same air. Well-behaved would be too mild a description; Stepford-creepy often came to my mind, you know what I mean? Heh, probably not. How can I put it: it was like something passed between them, a telepathy that could raise the hairs on back of my neck as I pictured them all suddenly turning on us humans. They never would, no. Not them.

Of course, all but the youngest pups were able to excuse themselves to use one of the portable Canine Powder Rooms set up in any park these days—funny, flea powder hasn't been a thing since I was in short pants, but canines, like their masters—I'm sorry, biped companions—looove a good euphemism. Overall, if my imagination didn't get away from me, most days at the park wound up feeling like a canasta match at a retirement home, only with less disagreement.

That was out in public. At home, Max could be himself. The new dog years seemed to pass similarly to our human years in terms of behavior during youth, adolescence, adulthood. No more multiplying by seven to figure dog years: a dog year became one year. This led to some trouble after awhile. In his late teens Max developed a taste for beer, and I'll take the blame for that. One night I nodded off with a full can of Bud in my hand that splashed over the hardwood floor after slipping from my fingers. That's what started it.

Max came to enjoy Corona with a twist of lime, so I was forced to endure the side-eye from the grocery checker-outer and buy twice as much beer as I used to, because I could never stand Corona. Too bitter—who the hell wants to slurp a beer that calls for a twist of fruit? Well, Max, that's who. He used his front teeth to pop off bottle caps and, after I found those old videos to show him, Max's craving for drink was enough to teach him that old refrigerator trick. I only wish he were more obedient when I made a personal request—beer, soda, sandwich, leftovers—but that's always hit-and-miss with ole Max, right, boy? We weren't always like this, Marcia, stuck in the bed. Heh, a lot of times I'd bribe him to bring me some grub by offering to cut and stuff the limes for his Coronas. That saved us a few bucks too; otherwise Max would squeeze the juice out with his jaw and need a new lime for every brew.

After his twenty-first birthday, I thought Max was broken—he all but ignored me for four months straight. We had a big blowout after I caught him pissing in my hamper—excuse me—relieving himself, you know, did number one, all over my clothes in the hamper. I couldn't figure out what was wrong until a sudden bout of leg-humping encouraged me to ask: "Are you mad that you were neutered?"

It was obvious this was the case and he wasn't buying my explanation of the MSA. The government web page was no help, they stuck to the acronym and scrubbed any specific mention of sterilization in all forms. Euphemism in the vein of Orwell. Heh. The argument grew until I finally found Max's paperwork, yellowed crisp with age, proving that the shelter had already had him fixed before I even knew he existed. Oh, right: I had taught Max to read when he was a pup, like any responsible pet companion. Anyway, I was exonerated in full, but it remained a touchy subject that I always did my best to steer clear of, or be sensitive about if it couldn't be avoided. I tried to pin the blame where it belonged, on the government, who never dispensed breeders to the private sphere, but Max couldn't quite grasp the concept so, forgive me, I simplified matters by creating what's probably the only Betty White dartboard in existence, complete with a word bubble demanding you get your pet spayed or neutered. Do you get it? Oh, too much to explain, catch an old Match Game rerun sometime.

So, heh, I've got this dartboard, and Max was like a young pup running circles around my chair as I slowly put Betty's eyes out, the poor gal.

The drinking kept up though and by the time he was thirty I started taking Max to meetings. It really sucked for us humans, who, except for the occasional scold, remained silent and really, for all we were aware, so did our dogs. They had to be sharing some brain waves though, because every so often the otherwise quiet meeting filled up with howls and whines. Damn pathetic, but at least they had each other. Thank goodness Max never started on the hard stuff like some of the other dogs had. One Chihuahua with a taste for gin was a real son-of-a-bitch, pardon my French, and so was his owner when any of us other humans shouted for him to sit or heel. He'd growl at others and once responded to a pathetic Poodle bitch by defecating on the floor. The dog that is, not his owner, heh. The Chihuahua was banned from group for a few weeks, till he came back, tail between legs, literally and figuratively, and made good with the other dogs through a bout of quite sincere snout rubs. Max never went that far off the deep end.

He got over that hump and in time seemed to judge me more than he did himself. We argued a lot by Max's fortieth, myself a bit lost trying to figure out how in the hell I was suddenly eighty years old. Max was mostly worried about what his future held beyond me. Makes sense now, given the current situation. But this was just another of those rare rough patches. I shared my burial plans with Max and the steps he had to take in order to trigger them. I explained that the mortgage was paid in full, but that he'd have to keep up on property taxes. That raised his eyebrows, but Max was reassured after I took him on a long overdue trip to the local branch of my bank and added his name alongside mine on the account. Companions were afforded this option and Max had claimed common-law companionship decades ago. Around the same time I brought him to my lawyer and gave Max power-of-attorney over me. My bad back was already keeping me in bed most days, and it had gotten to the point where Max was doing more around the house than I was anyhow.

By my eighty-fifth year, I accepted that I was on borrowed time. "I don't know, old friend," I said one afternoon. "I worry about what becomes of you in a few years." Max licked my hand, a bit of affection he'd become more accustomed to displaying the past few years, ever since our positions had flipped.

No sense hiding it from Miss Marcia, old boy! I took a good look at him and saw the Max we see now: most of his old coat had already taken on that salt-and-pepper color. Those thick Scorsese eyebrows had fully flourished. Perpetually dry nose; a lot of the pink in his lips paled to white. Max was old. Is old. Just like me. "I know you'll have this place to stay," I told him, "and will be able to keep yourself fed and even guzzle the occasional beer, but I worry about your hips." Max had already developed some trouble walking. He never complained, not Max, did you, boy?

But I saw how slow he was to raise himself from the floor, and even caught him slipping on the back steps a few times back before I was this bad myself. Max gave me another lick and then went to his doggy-pawboard and pulled up a website for other local aging dogs. I saw they had play dates set up at the nearby park and even caring events in some homes of dogs who were already living on their own. "That's good, boy. I'm glad you have options," I told him.

That's around the time I started having the dream. I told you about the dream, right? The one where Max handles the particulars after my death. No? Oh, I pictured him with some of his pals, just the ones I recalled by name: Prince, Bandit, Buddy, Joker, and who was that Golden Retriever? Mickey? Mackey? Something with an M. Anyway, the Retriever was a sixth, and together they were harnessed to carry my coffin from the hearse to my grave site, a solemn occasion with no human witnesses, yet still, when I wake up from this I'm not screaming or in the least bit scared. I smile because I wake up laughing, a scene that could have been painted by that guy who did those old paintings of dogs playing poker. What an end it would be! The ending every man dreaded made over into a farce of my own choosing.

But before I got the chance to sign off from this life, Max finally fessed up to his own troubles. He was on the floor beside me unable to get his back legs to support him. It damn near killed me to lift him up into bed beside me.

I suggested we have a look at the Company's site, figuring they might have something that'd help those hips of his. I really should have thought of it sooner. I was hoping for a simple off-site upgrade, a pill or cream or something, but I didn't see anything non-invasive. Then I spotted it. "Hey, boy, what do you think of this?" I asked.

I showed Max the sales page for the latest and greatest that the Company had to offer. Yes, the Chinese might have been advertising dogs that lived to ninety-seven, but our government was offering immortality—a mechanical canine, what we would have called a robot way back, but much slicker in appearance nowadays. They had them available in eight different breeds with four new breeds coming by the end of the year.

Let me see, there was Poodle, Boxer, German Shepherd, Labrador Retriever, Beagle, Cocker Spaniel, Scottish Terrier, and Pomeranian available for immediate purchase, then, um, Collie, Dalmatian, St. Bernard, and Shih Tzu on the horizon for future release. Collect them all, I thought, which I suppose is how I manage to remember them all. Got them all collected upstairs with the rest of this life.

"Look, pal, that one looks a lot like you," I said.

Max licked the image of the Brown Lab on the screen.

"What do you think, boy? You think he can take care of us? Says here that elder-care is a key feature."

I called The Company and their rep told me elder-care referred to caring for both humans and canines. The Ultimate Canine Companion Mechanical Model 3 would make sure we both lived out our days in comfort, become even more affectionate towards whichever of us outlived the other, then shut down the house and ultimately himself after there were no longer any living beings to care for. Big bucks, but I had them. A single man can save his money.

I signed all of the appropriate paperwork by voice and even had Max imprint his own voice to the Company's Mechanical Model 3 app.

"What should we name him, fella? You like Buddy? Wanna go old school with that?"

Max licked my hand.

Buddy arrived just a few days later. Wow, Marcia. There were definitely some bugs. Buddy was super aggressive, kind of like an overbearing nanny of old, you know, a touch of temper and a smidge of violence. He kept Max and I both pinned to this bed, growling if either of us even made a move towards the bathroom. I called the Company and they made some adjustments to Buddy's app based on my description of the situation, but they went and tuned Buddy so far out in the other direction that he sat around glaze-eyed and drooling, no help at all. One more call seemed to set Buddy to our frequency, but Max and I had both developed some trust issues by then.

I really only found the opportunity to discuss this with Max when Buddy was off in the kitchen or bathroom, retrieving one thing or another for one of us, which I must admit he did well, but Max made it clear that he had also had enough, didn't you, old boy? Given Buddy's ever-presence, it took a little over a week for us to fully hash out our options, and then I made my final call to the Company.

"Deactivate?" the rep asked, kind of dumbfounded. Apparently, nobody had ever deactivated one yet. He offered to play with the obedience settings, but I told him we had done that last time.

"Look," I said. "This is tough to explain given the circumstances." I looked down at Buddy, sitting alert beside me, staring through me. Then I said, "My dog and I have made our decision. Can you handle this, or do I need a supervisor?"

"Please hold," he says.

I looked at Max and nodded. I looked at Buddy and felt fear in my heart.

Then another voice came on the line and greeted me. Hell, I even remember his name. Robert. He says, "Hello, Mr. Toolestone, this is Robert, Ultimate Companion Canine Company of America manager."

I greeted Robert.

He was sensitive to the situation, saying, "I understand you may be in a position where you can't speak. Would you please just verbally affirm that you'd like to turn off your Mechanical Model 3 Companion."

Buddy's eyes burned red, which I'd never seen before, and his teeth were showing as he leaned towards us and began to growl.

"Yes, please." My voice cracked.

Buddy's face returned to neutral as he sat alert but with the light gone from his eyes.

"Is he off?" I asked, keeping an eye on Buddy as I did so.

"He should be, yes," Robert said. Then he went into his spiel: "I apologize wholeheartedly on behalf of the Ultimate Companion Canine Company of America." Duh-de-duh-de-duh. You know, trying to sound excited, but with all the emotion of a metronome. "What I'm going to do," he says, "is get a new model out to you, who upon activation will take care of shipping your current Mechanical Model 3 back to us."

"That's not necessary," I said.

"Oh," Robert said. "I'm very sorry to hear that."

"Look, you can just tear up the deal I signed," I told him. If I needed to pay any sort of cancellation fee beyond that, it would have been fine.

"It's not that, Mr. Toolestone," he says, though, yes, it was that, I was sure. "I have access to your case and I see that both you and your companion are aged and perhaps immobile."

"Well, we've been better," I said.

Robert paused.

"I have an idea," he said with that fake burst of inspiration shining through his voice. "I have the authority to issue trial upgrades to your companion." He paused again, before adding, "And to you."

"To me?"

"It's experimental," he said. "But, trust me on this." I didn't, Marcia. "It works. It's currently in pill form, so I only need ship them out to you."

"What's it do?" I asked.

He brought out a little of the jargon then. "It releases pheromones throughout the body of whoever has imbibed. By the next morning the both of you will be feeling thirty years younger."

"Side effects?" I asked.

"None have been charted," he tells me.

This was exactly what I had hoped to find available on their website, but I didn't like this experimental business. I didn't like Robert. I looked at Max. We looked at Buddy.

"Thank you," I said, "but I think we'll pass."

"Mr. Toolestone, I insist." He's all shocked and offended.

"Pardon?" I said, a bit shocked and offended myself.

"I'm sending you the pills," Robert said. The he starts sounding confidential or conspiratorial as he tells me, "Look, Mr. Toolestone, you won't be charged for these if you don't take them. And I'm not going to have anybody force them down your throat, truly, I'm not, but I'd like you to have them on hand in case you find that you have no alternative. If you do take them it will initiate a charge to your bank account."

I've all but tuned him out at this point. "You can send them," I said, "but we're not taking them."

"Very good, Mr. Toolestone. I'll immediately dispatch a personal courier." Says he doesn't trust the mails with these pills. He just keeps talking, this Robert: "I'm also programming in a twenty-five percent discount to you if you do take the pills and a charge is initiated. That's my way of offering my sincerest apology. If you have any questions please press option 0 when you phone the Ultimate Companion Canine Company of America, then press 3, and then 4." Or some set of numbers, I can't remember. Anyway, he tells me that'll get me right to his direct line, then asked if I had any other questions.

"No, " I said. Then thanked him for the phone hack. "And the service. I don't see us risking these pills, but I appreciate your concern."

"You're welcome, Mr. Toolestone. You have a nice day."

"Oh, wait," I said. "What about Buddy?"

"Buddy?" Robert asks.

"The mechanical whatsis that you turned off for me. How do I get him back to you?"

"Oh, no need to worry about that, Mr. Toolestone. Our courier will take care of Buddy for you."

And that, Marcia, that brings us to present day.

Marcia's head cocked.

"I know all of this, Mr. Toolestone. Robert uploaded your transcript." Marcia sighed. "And besides that, you tell me every day."

That I do. And one day, Miss Marcia, after I'm all done telling, I may just open up my mouth and swallow down the Company's pill for you. Max too. One day, but not today.

Why, Miss Marcia, I've never seen your eyes quite that shade of hellfire.

Cliff Aliperti is a Long Island-based writer, who wrote about classic film for several years at his site Immortal Ephemera. Cliff's fiction has appeared in After Dinner Conversation, Fiction on the Web, JAKE, Squawk Back, and elsewhere. You can find more about Cliff at cliffaliperti.com. Twitter/X: @IEphemera.

Sierran Paradise
By Hugo Glinn

Reece Collier was reminded of Ebenezer Scrooge. Across from him, like the pillars of Arcadia's principled and righteous society they represented, sat the three incarnations of his recent past, his present and his future. To the left was Sheriff William Long, who had arrested Collier three years earlier. The inmate, a former soldier himself, was impressed by the lawman's navy-blue dress uniform, but he really wanted to rip the star off Long's barrel chest and stab it into his heart.

In the middle was gray-haired Judge Raymond Winehouse, attired in his long black robes and lacy jabot. Apparently, he was here to adjudicate these proceedings, and Collier was tempted to ask what the judge was wearing underneath just to try to get him to change the "string-em-up" look on his face.

To the right sat Special Assistant to the Colonial Governor Marcus Colby, rummaging through his briefcase, which Collier knew contained his future. Colby's wide tie had the planetary government's seal emblazoned on it; a young colonial farming couple, supposedly a younger likeness of Herbert I. Vailancourt and one of his earlier wives, pointing to a constellation of stars, the middle of which was Ardentia, Arcadia's sun. Vailancourt was considered the father of Arcadia, having seventy-five years earlier convinced the Company to colonize it, mainly to mine its trimilithium reserves.

However, Vailancourt, a member of one of the biggest evangelical churches on Earth, had turned the recruitment of colonists into an endeavor of messianic proportions. Settlers were divided in three disproportionate groups. The smallest was the engineers required for the various needs of the colony. Their expertise was their main qualification for settling on this new Eden. Next were the miners, whose contracts of employment specifically had them leaving the planet after three years of work and wages. Vailancourt realized that they were a necessary moral evil for the financial success of the colony, as he considered how most of them may not have the religious fervor needed to build a new promised land. The largest group were followers from his church, ranging from those bordering on poverty who had leapt at the opportunity for a large homestead to better-off parishioners with the inside track to business opportunities and political offices on the colony.

Unlike Dickens's miser, Collier did not fear the bearer of his future. In fact, he suspected Colby was just a mealy-mouthed bureaucrat in an expensive dark suit that hung on the man's narrow shoulders like an over-sized jacket on a cheap hanger in a second-hand store. Colby's slicked-back blond hair and the frameless glasses simply added to the prisoner's first impression. Once Colby started reading from a tablet, blabbering away about critical decisions being made by the Company for the future of Arcadia, Collier just wanted to rip his larynx out. When the functionary proclaimed how the convict's "good behavior" had come to the attention of the authorities, Collier tried not to guffaw. Finally, Colby proclaimed that the Company was willing to provide Collier with a once-in-a-lifetime offer: "Reece J Collier, inmate number 50193, is hereby offered a full pardon should he choose to remain on Arcadia."

The small, gray, windowless interrogation room felt even more claustrophobic with the two guards in dark gray khaki standing at the door. Collier was on a brown wooden chair, sitting cross-legged and arms folded, his green and orange striped prison jumpsuit providing the only color in the room. Hearing Colby's offer, he raised his left eyebrow, but this was simply a charade, for he already knew about it. Patty Donnelly, his one-time girlfriend now well-paid informant in the colonial administration building, had seen a memo about the Company's planned pullout of Arcadia eight months earlier. By the time it became official, Collier had already taken steps to smooth his transition from prison to civilian life. He now opened his legs, placed his hands on his knees and let a sly smile come over his face. He looked directly at Long and asked, "Let me ask you something, Bill. Are you staying or going?"

The officer's expression did not alter as he calmy said, "If it was my choice, I'd put you and your buddies in with the baggage and then accidently open the air lock in space."

Collier smiled. "You'd like that, wouldn't you? You think you're above simply bushwhacking me on the street. But you still didn't answer the question, Bill." He quietly stared back with the same simper.

Colby intervened. "Mr. Collier, I don't see how the Sheriff's decision would have any bearing on your own." He paused and then continued in his grating voice. "As you can see, you would receive a full pardon instead of having to serve out the remainder of your sentence on Earth, which I believe is another twelve years."

Collier crossed his legs and folded his arms again and was still eyeballing Long, but he really wanted to backhand the civil servant's grinning, conniving face. He knew the score. There was a limited number of seats on the return ship for colonists that wished to return to Earth or go to any of the Company's more established colonies. It was set to leave in two weeks. What better way to make more space for any frightened homesteader wanting to get off this remote rock than to have the outlaws remain. Collier turned and said, "Sure it does, Special Assistant Colby. I want to know if I'm going to have to always look over my shoulder once I'm free." He returned his gaze to Long. "So, Bill, what's it going to be? You staying or going?"

Long sharpened his scowl before answering. "The Company's given me a position on Aurora, where I won't have to deal with scum like you anymore." He spat on the floor to his side.

Collier beamed even more broadly, to make it look like he was satisfied, but he already knew the answer. Patty had seen Long's transfer orders two weeks earlier and relayed the information to her former paramour. Collier mumbled, "I figured so." and turned to the judge asking, "And what about you, your Honor? Are you hitting the road, as well?"

Winehouse had stoically sat between the other two looking at the felon the entire session. His role in what he considered a farce was to oversee the process and attest to its legality. He was just as happy to see Collier and his ilk rot behind bars and later in hell. He thought that once the Company finally pulled out, the colony would become something like the wild west. Many of his fellow church members had decided to stay and he wondered how they could possibly survive with the likes of Collier scheming and perpetrating all sorts of evil and lawlessness.

While waiting for the judge to respond, Collier thought that he could try to persuade the judge that he was simply going to continue the good works of Emmett Dalton, works that Long and his task force had put an end to when they arrested most of the Dalton gang. It was simply free enterprise in action, a business filling a need within the society. The judge's face had remained expressionless, but then he pursed his lips, looked down at his right knee and then brushed it with the back of his hand. "I plan on retiring back home on Earth."

Collier had also known this beforehand, but it was so gratifying to hear it coming from the judge. He turned to Colby and said, "Where do I sign?"

***

An hour later, Collier was lying on his bed in his cell, the back of which was the wall of an abandoned trimilithium mining shaft. Due to Long's crackdown on the Dalton gang, the original jail proved too small and this makeshift prison was constructed. Collier could see where miners had used jack hammers to extract the ore that had been powering the Company's expansion across the galaxy. However, after almost seven and a half decades, the easy-to-get-to-deposits had been depleted and the galactic "gold" rush came to an end. While there were other mining operations bringing up less lucrative minerals, the Company's bean-counters had decided to concentrate on other colonies making better profits.

Collier completely understood. Change or die. It had been the story of his adult life. He recalled how almost thirteen years earlier, with no real opportunities on earth, he had first come to Arcadia as an agronomist, a title that provided him with an allotted acreage, a pre-fabricated house and machinery to grow foodstuffs to feed the miners and other colonists. He did it for a year until the day he literally smashed into Emmett Dalton's life.

On that day, he entered an illegal casino in Arcadia's largest city of New Providence, named after Vailancourt's hometown to demonstrate his desire to have divine protection over his colony, as well as his investments. Collier had heard about the gambling den from some of his fellow farmers, but, instead of placing any bets, he simply sat at the bar, bought a beer and watched. His observational skills had served him well previously in the military, and what he had seen from that stool amazed him. The clientele ranged from miners and farmers to mid-level administrators to well-to-do city dwellers, all of them blowing their paychecks on poker, booze or prostitutes, and sometimes all three at the same time. More telling was the contrast between the thin, stooped, rutty-faced laborers and the well-dressed casino staff. While Collier regarded his surroundings and contemplated an alternative future for himself, a large man in a light gray suit entered from the back of the room. With broad shoulders and a shock of gray hair, there was an aura of leadership that Collier had recognized in some of his commanding officers during his stint in the Company Army. Two men in dark suits shielded the man's blindside while he glad-handed well-dressed customers and blue-collared patrons alike. Collier leaned over to the bartender and asked, "Excuse me. Who's the gentleman in the gray suit?"

The bartender, surprised at first by the graciousness coming from what he thought was a farm hick, smiled and replied, "That, my friend, is Emmett Dalton, the owner of this fine establishment." As Dalton took the two steps separating the casino floor from the bar, a man in a ratty suit stepped in front of Collier and shouted, "Hey, Dalton, God has damned you and the evil you have brought to this promised land."

Whenever Collier recollected this particular scene, everything turned slo-mo. The would-be shooter's arm is extended forward, a small, old-time revolver resting calmly in his hand. Since pulse weapons, the type Collier had used in the military, had been banned by the colonial government to ordinary citizens, bullet-and-gunpowder guns were prevalent on Arcadia, with easy-to-conceal pistols a favorite.

Collier then saw one of the two bodyguards accompanying Dalton comically trip on the steps and fall on his face as he reached for his piece, while the other struggled to remove his gun from the holster. What most intrigued Collier was the proprietor's expression. No surprise nor fear. Dalton seemed angry with the assailant, like he was wasting his time.

Then, with the sound of broken glass, Collier's reminiscence returned to normal speed. Without hesitation, he had smashed his beer bottle on the side of the gunman's head, who dropped the gun and crumpled to the floor at Dalton's feet. Dalton looked down at the failed attacker and then stomped on his face with each word he said; "You mother-humpin' church-going bastard." The upright guard finally took out his weapon and quickly jammed it into the gunman's bloodied cheek.

"About frickin' time, you moron," shouted Dalton as he smacked the back of the kneeling subordinate's head. He turned to the other one. "And you?! What the hell were you doing?"

The hulking, young man had gotten back to his feet and was clutching his nose, blood streaming between his fingers. His muffled reply was "I think I broke my nose."

Dalton faced him and said, "Let me have a look." As the guard lowered his hand, the gangster punched the wounded nose, forcing the brute to topple over the steps again and land on his back. Dalton then said, "Yeah, I think you're right. It felt a bit squishy." Then, more loudly, "Now get the hell outta my sight."

When Dalton finally looked at Collier, the boss's grimace was that of a perplexed man. Collier realized that the casino owner was now in a situation men of power hated to be in, that of being in someone's debt. Before the older man could speak, Collier quickly said, "If you could find me a position in your organization, sir, I would be extremely grateful."

Dalton, amused by the young man's brazen request coupled with his apparently sincere civility following such a violent act, pointed to a pair of stools at the bar and ordered himself a whiskey straight. Once seated, he asked what Collier wanted.

"A beer, please." Collier sat bolt upright, his head slightly higher than that of his host now leaning on the bar.

Again, Dalton smiled at the graciousness of what he had taken to be a hayseed and became more intrigued with his calm carriage. "Well, before I can hire ya, I need to interview ya." What Dalton learned left him momentarily stupefied. Collier had gone to West Point and had risen to colonel in the military wing of the Company, leading exploratory units to three different planets and, on his final mission, repressing a three-month rebellion on another. Unfortunately for him, he had been dishonorably discharged after leveling a village with a tactical nuclear device, an action that led directly to a cessation in hostilities, but also created a political and image problem for the Company, for which he was made the scapegoat.

He explained to Dalton that he had become fed up losing soldiers who had followed him across the galaxy to an ill-equipped, but ruthless opponent too stupid to realize that they were outgunned. He returned to earth to find no prospects for a "murdering hooligan," as one website had named him. Finally, he applied to be an agronomist and arrived on Arcadia the year before.

Dalton finished his drink and then smiled at his savior. He stood up and extended a hand, saying, "Yeah, I think I can find a place for ya. Come by tomorrow afternoon." Collier also stood, took the mobster's hand and allowed himself a small smirk.

***

Morgan Weatherby, Esq., smiled broadly as his most important client exited the New Providence Penitentiary. Seven years earlier, Reece Collier had entered the lawyer's shabby offices located near the city's hospital, where Weatherby often found clients willing to file suits for personal injury claims. Having seen the attorney at one of Dalton's newest casinos, he thought he would feel him out. After a half-hour, Collier had determined that Weatherby had the right amount of skill and lack of scruples to effectively help him hide the casino profits. For four years, Weatherby helped funnel cash into other enterprises, both real and totally fictional, so that at the time of Collier's arrest, hundreds of millions were safely beyond the reach of the authorities and Weatherby had moved into one of New Providence's swankiest glass and steel hi-rises.

Weatherby said, "I would have brought you flowers, but I wouldn't want you to get any ideas." The men shook hands and grabbed the other's shoulder with their free hands. For Collier, Weatherby was more than his lawyer. He had remained loyal, even under consistent pressure from the colonial justice department and other crooks eager to get the gang's millions. Over the past few months, the counsellor had been making purchases crucial to his client's plans.

The men climbed into Weatherby's hovercar. He started the conversation. "Good news. Pete's boy turned eleven." Collier turned and said, "If I remember right, I thought he was 14."

The lawyer nodded. As the vehicle self-drove, Weatherby retrieved a sheet of paper from his briefcase, a map with different colored plots drawn on it. "Mickey Lee decided to go on the wagon and he's getting rid of his booze."

They were speaking in code, assuming that the authorities had bugged the car. "Pete's boy" referred to a farmer named Peterson who had opted to leave Arcadia and auctioned off his property for eleven thousand units, three thousand lower than the price for which Collier had budgeted. "Mickey Lee" was another departee, named McKinley, who was also putting his land on the auction block.

"How much does he have?" asked Collier, referring to the size of the McKinley homestead.

"Four bottles of fifty-six proof." Four hundred fifty-six acres. "And I'm close to getting that silver mine. Problem is the owner won't take a simple trade, even if it is for a bigger mine. I was thinking about throwing in a small gift." Weatherby was referring to the Coopersmith acreage, a plot located just beyond the city limits of New Providence near the spaceport, a perfect location for Collier's first casino-hotel. Coopersmith had been offered land farther away and would have increased his own holdings by thirty percent, but he was still holding out for more. The "gift" would be a cash payoff to be made on top of the land swap.

"Sounds good, but not too much. If that yokel can't read the writing on the wall, maybe we'll have to show it to him more clearly. And what about references?"

Weatherby replaced his paperwork in his briefcase. "You should have enough endorsements when the matter comes forward." Over the last eight months, the attorney had approached a number of Company administrators and officials with a proposal for legalizing gambling. In Collier's mind, Arcadia would have to transform itself into a tourist destination, a place for rest and relaxation. To help the proposal along, bribes had been made and, where needed, dirt had been dug up on certain individuals to use as leverage.

"That's great," smiled Collier. Then, an expression of genuine concern came over him as he asked, "And how's Emmett doing?"

Weatherby shook his head once and loudly inhaled through the corner of his mouth. "He's a fighter, but the doctors are saying weeks, not even months." Collier's mentor had stage four pancreatic cancer and had simply asked to be buried on Arcadia, a dying wish Collier assured would be fulfilled.

The gang-boss-to-be nodded and looked out the window. The cityscape was coming into view. Weatherby asked, "So, have you thought of a name for the first casino?"

Collier smiled and asked, "Did I ever tell where I was from originally?"

Weatherby replied, "Arizona, if I remember right."

"Yeah, in mountain country," continued Collier. He saw the marquee in his mind, waved his outstretched hand before him and, in a deep voice, replied, "The Sierra."

***

Two days after Collier's release, Patty Donnelly hosted a party for her ex-lover. While she could have afforded a posher, more fashionable address with the money Collier was giving her, she realized that would have brought down unwanted scrutiny, considering her government salary. So, she bought a townhouse that was just off the main road in New Providence and used the money to decorate it. The stoop was adorned with a variety of Talavera tiles, while the façade was painted a pale orange stucco. The double doors at front opened up to the living room, where she had placed a card table in the back and lively piano music was playing on the small sound system set up in the opposite corner. She turned the room divider between the kitchen and the living into a bar that she manned with ease and a firm hand.

Collier had given her a list of people he wanted invited, including William Bonnet, a low-level outlaw who had not been caught up in Sheriff Long's sweep. Since then, he had opened a few saloons with limited gambling in the back, usually a roulette wheel and some card tables, but nothing on the scale Dalton had been operating. Most of Bonnet's income was coming from the manufacture and sale of illicit, easy-to-make synthetic amphetamines with hallucinogenic qualities called "Bennie Mesca". Dalton had refused to deal with it, fearing it would bring unnecessary attention of his other operations, and Collier was of a similar disposition. He wanted Bonnet at the party to sound him out. When Bonnet, a short man with pudgy cheeks and unsmiling eyes, showed up, the steady murmur resonating throughout Patty's place fell silent. Patty even turned off the music and room was dead silent.

"Billy, welcome to the party. Glad you could make it." Collier approached with a smile and an open hand. Bonnet reciprocated, simply saying, "Welcome back, Reece."

"What are ya drinking? High ball, right?" asked Collier.

Bonnet was surprised how his former superior remembered. "Yeah, sure."

Collier turned to Patty, who had turned on the music again. "A high ball and a beer, dear." He directed Bonnet to a pair of chairs off to the side of the room behind a small round coffee table. When the drinks arrived, Collier held up his beer and said, "To a long and prosperous life."

"Salud" was Bonnet's reply and both men took a sip from their drinks.

Collier leaned toward his rival, who did likewise, and said, "Billy, you've probably heard of some of my plans, and I want you in on the action, but frankly, there's no room for any of this Bennie Mesca crap."

Bonnet smiled, sat back in his chair and took another sip. "Ha, the old man isn't dead yet and you're already giving orders."

"Listen, Billy, just until we get this gambling ordinance through and we get construction started. No need to get the Bible-thumpers riled up beforehand."

Bonnet leaned forward without a smile. "No, you listen to me. While you were sitting around getting your three squares and making plans for your ivory castles, I was working my butt off. So, screw you if my operation doesn't fit into your plans." He reached for his drink, finished it, but as he placed the glass down again, Collier grabbed his wrist. In a subdued voice, he said, "Billy, please don't go down this road. We can easily work together, but the drugs will have to wait."

Bonnet glared at the ex-convict, but he was surprised by the middle-aged man's firm grip. He tried to yank his arm free, but failed. He tried a second time and Collier released him. Bonnet stood up and pointed at Collier and said, "You better watch your back." He quickly strode to the door, his small entourage hurrying to catch up.

Through the rest of the evening, Collier spoke with many of his old associates, recementing relationships and redefining some. He had had three years to consider who was best suited for the different tasks needed for his operation, and the party acted as a final recruitment search. He never described the entire scheme to anyone, only discussing portions of it that would concern any individual's skill set. He knew that most of them were loyal to Dalton, and, thus, loyal to him.

As the early morning sun began to rise and the last of his buddies had already gone home, Collier descended the stoop of Patty Donnelly's house and walked down the center of Brewer Avenue. He was buoyant, seeing the first fruits of his dreams. Then he felt the first bullet hit him in the back. He fell to his knees, but his military training kicked in as he quickly rolled forward to spin and face his attacker. He reached for the gun in his coat pocket and raised it at a figure standing in the middle of the street. He fired as a second shot hit him in the chest, but he heard the assailant shout in pain, turn and run away.

***

Two days later, Emmett Dalton was sitting uncomfortably on a stiff wooden chair next to a dining table in his house. Cancer had ravaged his body. He barely weighed one hundred and ten pounds, his gaunt face making his once bulbous nose looking like a hooked eagle's beak. There was a slight wheezing to his breathing. However, he was able to hold his head up and observe everything in the room. Behind him, stood two bodyguards, while in front of him stood Billy Bonnet. Behind him were two of his henchmen, one with a serious limp.

Dalton had an arm on the table, the hand flat down upon it. He then curled three fingers and thumb into a fist while pointing at the young man with a curved index finger. "Billy, ya shouldn't have done what ya did." Dalton's raspy voice was still deep.

Bonnet was impatient. "What did you expect me to do? Collier left me no choice. He was taking money from me, money I used to rebuild this organization." Almost bellowing the last word, he stepped up to the end of the table and poked it with his forefinger. "Things have changed since you and the others got locked up. Someone had to step up, and that was me. So what if they want to buy Bennie Mesca. My profits brought back what you and that ass Collier let slip away." He stepped back from the table. "I have earned the right to lead."

Dalton raised an eyebrow. "Even me?"

Bonnet widened his stance and crossed his hands in front of himself. Calmly, he implored, "I have raised our organization from the ashes of Long's sweep. We are making more now than we did before then. The money is flowing in like…"

"But you haven't considered the future!" Dalton's raised voice surprised Bonnet slightly. He quickly recovered, but found himself looking at the tip of the finger the crime boss was jabbing at him. "Everything has changed with the Company pulling out. Collier had a plan. He was going to turn this place into a gold mine, while you were only thinking about making it one big opium den." The old man started coughing and wheezing more loudly. One of the bodyguards brought a glass of water to him.

Bonnet started to fold his arms, but thrust them behind his back, not wishing to offend the boss. However, he was starting to tire of the old man's blabbering. He had had Collier killed, so now he was the only man with enough muscle and balls to take over the organization after Dalton's death. Maybe even before it. "I'm sorry you feel that way, but..."

Behind the bodyguards was the kitchen, from which Bonnet thought he saw a shadow. Suddenly, coming through the doorway was Reece Collier, arm raised and a gun in his hand. The first shot entered Bonnet's right arm, which made him twist toward the wounded limb, allowing the second shot to enter the side of his left thigh. A third shot went between the eyes of the man with the limp, who managed to pull his gun out, but could not raise it in time. The second thug, too shocked to move, slowly raised his hands and looked like he was about to cry.

Seeing Bonnet writhing in pain, Collier squatted next to the dead bodyguard, and with a switchblade, slit the right thigh of his pants. The leg was heavily bandaged and Collier kicked the body. He looked at Dalton and said, "I knew I had shot the bastard in the leg." He then took an empty chair by the table and placed it next to Bonnet, who was breathing hard through gritted teeth. Collier sat down and tapped the dying man's chest, which made a muffled rap. "Huh! You're just as prepared as I was." He tapped his own chest and it made the same sound. "However, if you just want to wound someone, ..." He poked the tip of the gun in the leg wound, invoking a tortured scream from his prey. "... a vest isn't going to help you anyway." He leaned forward and whispered "I just wanted to make sure that you knew who got to you." Then he fired a bullet into Bonnet's left eye.

***

A year later, Morgan Weatherby, along with five other gentlemen in business suits, thrust shiny shovels into the topsoil of a large plot of land. A billboard behind them announced, "Coming Soon!

The Sierra Casino and Hotel! Turning Arcadia into a New Paradise!"

Under a tent set up in a corner of the tract, champagne was served while government and social elite mingled discussing this new chapter in Arcadia's young history. Weatherby, relishing his new position as the CEO of Sierra, Inc., was circulating among the crowd. At one point, he caught sight of Reece Collier standing at the back of the tent. The former lawyer raised his glass to the former convict and nodded. Collier smiled and did the same.

As Collier turned away, a man in a decidedly shabbier suit approached him. There was a determination in the youth's eyes that Collier had recognized, and on seeing the man's right hand in his coat pocket, Collier gripped his glass tightly. The man said, "You have brought sin and greed to this divinely anointed planet. I'm here to take you to the true paradise," and then he pulled out a knife with a five-inch-long blade. As he thrust the weapon, Collier threw his drink into the man's face and smashed the flute into its side, slicing the cheek. With his left hand, he parried the blade, but not without cutting his forearm. Finally, he kicked away the assailant's leading foot and then easily pushed him down to the ground.

When everyone turned to see the commotion, they saw a middle-aged man sitting atop a young one, his foot on the attacker's hand still holding the knife, calmly wrapping a handkerchief around his bleeding arm. Reece Collier, the formerly disgraced officer, one-time farmer, long-time outlaw and now most influential man of Arcadia, cinched the knot with his teeth and free hand and asked, "Excuse me, is there a doctor in the house?" Then, he smiled.

Hugo Glinn studied in Iowa, Austria, Germany and Wales before getting a degree in German and English and escaping his home state of New Jersey for a life of teaching in Asia. He has had over a half-dozen humorous short pieces appear in e-magazines like Roadside Fiction, Pilcrow and Dagger and Clever Magazine. Fengshui, Filial Piety and Other Asian F-words is his first published book.

Its Tender Metal Hand

By Steven R. Southard

Her father cocked his fist and punched the robot.

"Dad!" Nalani Koamalu feared her father would hurt himself, but his knuckles bounced off the machine's torso unscathed. The robot's glowing eyes blinked.

Scowling, Maleko Koamalu lay back on his bed. "Damn tin can!" He shifted his glare from the robot to her. "I don't want it. Take it back."

She shook her head, feeling guiltier than ever. Still, she knew by now how to stand up to his withering gaze. "We've been over this, Dad. The doctor said you can't live by yourself any more. We can't afford a nursing home, and I can't quit work to care for you at my house. And Kala lives too far—"

"It's Kale, and I don't want to hear about him," he growled.

Ever since her brother had become her sister five years earlier, her Dad had disowned his second child. "Okay." She held up her hands. "But you're eligible for hospice care, and they supply robot caregivers now."

"I don't need some mechanical…bucket of bolts lumbering around my house." He squinted at the robot as it stood in silence beside the bed. The size of an adult person, and white in color, it looked almost humanoid in shape, except for its four jointed legs. Its chest contained a display screen, now showing 'Monday, January 3rd, 9:17 AM' in a large, plain font. On the front of its round head, a smaller screen showed its mouth and eyes—currently a flat line and two circles.

"It won't be lumbering around, Dad. It recharges itself and does quiet housekeeping while you're asleep. It's here to help you because I can't be." He'd always been a cranky and gruff man, but had become even more difficult after her Mom had died. It had been hard for Nalani growing up as his daughter, but she had to admit his rough form of fathering prepared her well for a career as a lawyer. She loved him and wished she could care for him in his final months but she just couldn't back out of all her responsibilities.

He grunted and turned his head to the west-facing window where a morning rainbow arced from Barber's Point to Nanakuli. "The stupid thing'll probably short circuit and kill me with a laser beam."

"Dad?" She waited until he looked at her. "It won't hurt you. It can't." There seemed no use in telling him what the hospice staff had explained to her about the rigorous testing this line of robots endured to be approved for in-home use on human patients. "It's as safe as they can make them."

His throat made a low rumble. "Is there a person, a real live human, watching it? Someone with his finger on a kill switch for when this gangling gadget goes berserk?"

"Yes, Dad. There's a technician monitoring it twenty-four seven." Well, a single tech monitoring a hundred robots, anyway, according to the hospice people.

"Humph." Her father rolled over in his bed, away from the robot, and from her. "Just keep it away from me."

To Nalani, he had never looked older or paler. Just five days earlier, on New Year's Eve, she'd visited his house to check on him and found him collapsed, babbling incoherently. He hadn't eaten that day, and said he'd forgotten to. She brought him to the hospital where they kept him for four days. The doctor said one of his heart valves had begun to fail, a result of Maleko's childhood bout with rheumatic fever. The doctor said he could operate, but surgery at the age of ninety-one held significant risks. Maleko had refused the surgery, even after being told he would only live another six months. He'd shrugged at that news, saying, "I'm surprised I lived this long."

Nalani had taken it hard. Her dad had always been there for her, strong and supportive, though on the crabby and cantankerous side. She couldn't imagine a world without him in it. But a part of her knew it had become her turn to be strong for him. Her sister—former-brother lived on the mainland and her father wouldn't welcome help from that quarter anyway.

She lived a life already jam-packed. Two children in college, one of whom talked about signing up for a Mars colonization mission. And her hectic courtroom trial schedule. With all that, she'd accepted the robot caregiver as her only option. As guilt-ridden as she felt about it, she had no choice. "It's just here to help you, Dad." She stood up to leave. "I'll leave you alone to get acquainted with it."

"Your stubble looks long, sir," the robot said. "Would you care for a shave?"

"Oh, no. You're not getting anywhere near me with a blade, you mechanized murderer."

***

"Iolana? Where are you? Iolana?" She should be here, he thought, though his brain seemed lost in a fog.

"Your wife died seven years ago, sir." A white thing stood at his bedside, a somewhat familiar mechanical likeness of a human, with glowing eyes.

"What are you?"

"My designation is PAIGE-1, but you've been calling me Bucky," it said. "Do you wish to go to the bathroom?"

Bucky? Then he remembered. A damn robot, and he'd taken to calling it 'Bucket of Bolts' and in time shortened that to Bucket, and finally, Bucky. "Bathroom? Yeah, okay. I musta dozed off for a minute."

The robot pulled down the bedsheets; its strong arms reached out and the hands slid under him. The padded and cushioned arms felt as comfortable as a plush pillow, but gave an impression of massive underlying power, lifting him up with no whirring of motors or creaking of metal. "You've slept for three and a half hours this afternoon." The gait as it walked on its four jointed legs felt like the gentle undulations of a slow horseback ride.

"That's enough. Set me down on the throne, you metal monstrosity, and get out of here while I do my private business."

"Yes, sir." The robot shut the bathroom door as it left.

Sometime later he heard a knock at the door.

"Sir, are you done? I heard your sleep-breathing."

Am I done? He didn't recall coming to the bathroom. "Eh? I think so, Bucky. Get your plastic ass in here."

Bucky gently opened the door and entered. It helped Maleko stand and the next thing he knew, it had put his underwear and pajama bottoms in place and washed his hands. "Take me to the den, Bucky, and step on it. The Warriors game will be on soon."

"Today is April thirteenth, sir. The first game of the Rainbow Warriors' season will be on September sixth." The robot lifted him up and conveyed him back to bed.

He grunted as Bucky raised the head of the bed and turned on the wall screen.

"Is there a television show or movie you'd care to watch, sir?"

"Nah." He swished his hand. "If the 'Bows aren't on, just set it to that painting I like."

The robot tuned the screen to show the famous Battle at Nuʻuanu Pali painting by Herb Kawainui Kāne depicting the forces of King Kamehameha I driving his enemy off the thousand-foot cliff. It also moved Maleko's glass of water to be within his reach on the bedside tray. "Do you wish to play checkers, sir? We could resume the game we started yesterday."

"No games for now. Yeah, that's the painting I want. Reminds me of my fighting days. Did I ever tell you about my time in Korea?"

"Yes, sir." The robot removed its head and set it on a chair. The robot's body walked into the kitchen to prepare dinner. The robot had warned him before detaching its head the first time, but by now the creepiness had worn off. The head's digital eyes-and-mouth display showed its interested and attentive expression.

"I was in the 38th Infantry Regiment. Not many Hawaiians in the Army then, before statehood, but if you proved yourself as a warrior, you fit in. We saw some tough fighting in January of '51, but we managed to take that hill near Wonju." Just saying the words opened up mental windows into countless memories, some sharp and others indistinct. Trudging up snowy mountain passes in the bitter cold, swapping jokes and friendly insults with guys whose faces he hadn't seen in over seven decades. Some guys made it through; others hadn't.

"What was it like?" the robot head asked. From the kitchen came the sound of pans and dishes being moved about, and the smell of hamburger meat cooking.

He closed his eyes. "Miserable, I'll tell you that. When we marched, we were cold and hungry, and our feet were so sore none of us thought we could take another step. Sometimes we lay hidden, waiting for the enemy; then we were even colder and hungrier, and we couldn't make a sound or move, not even to scratch an itch. But the worst was getting shot at, slinging hot lead at the enemy and hoping you wouldn't buy the farm at any moment."

Robotic eyes blinked. "You must have been happy when the war ended."

Something seemed familiar, as if he'd told the robot about his life before. Still, it looked receptive, so he went on. "Happy? Hell, I was ecstatic. Could hardly wait to get back home. I married Iolana and we settled in Oahu. Not my favorite island, you know, but the tourists and jobs were here. Being a police officer seemed natural after the Army, and it's important to serve your community, you know?"

"Yes," the disembodied head said. "Is that when you had your children?"

"My daughter, yes." He smiled to recall how she looked when young. After the worst day at work, he could come home to her smile and happy eyes, her big hug for her daddy, and a bad day suddenly turned bright and cheerful again.

He frowned then, thinking of his other child. "And my failure of a son. Had to go and make himself a woman." Even changed his strong, male name, Kale, to the princess name, Kala. He'd wanted his son to be a better man than himself. Something had gone wrong. By high school, Kale had abandoned typical male pursuits. Sports and vigorous outdoor activities bored him. He didn't care at all for the military, or for police work. To Maleko's horror, Kale was drawn to cooking, interior decorating, and clothing design.

"Perhaps you should call her," the head said. "I'm sure she'd like to hear from you."

He shook his head. "I don't know him anymore, Bucky. He's no longer in my family." *What does this damn machine think it is, my mother?*

"What was it like to be a policeman?"

"It was a good job. I enjoyed it. The pay wasn't great, the hours sucked, and I hated the paperwork. But it got me out in the community, and I thought I was helping."

"Why did you quit?"

Once more Malcko wondered if he'd ever mentioned all this to the robot before. "Iolana thought it was too dangerous. She said I should do something less risky, where I wouldn't get shot at. I told her I'd made it through Korea, which was worse, but she said I had a family to think of now. So I took a job in Airport Security. She agreed it was a little safer."

"Did you like that job?"

"It was boring, but the hours were regular."

"At least that job gave you time for your hobby." The robot's eyes shifted to gaze at a wall to his right.

"Yeah." He smiled. The wall displayed a red and yellow helmet, shield, and cape identical to those owned by his hero, King Kamehameha I. He'd researched the Hawaiian ruler to ensure exactitude in his replicas. He and a buddy had even built an authentic-looking outrigger canoe just like those of two centuries earlier; they'd taken it out a few times, but now it sat in his friend's garage. Often, Maleko wondered what it must have been like to be the great king.

Maybe he'd shut his eyes for an instant, but he heard the robot's body come in from the kitchen bearing a plate. It set the food on his movable tray, then adjusted his bed and positioned his pillow. Finally it put its head back on and opened the curtain to the picture window on his left. "Dinnertime, sir. And it's just before sunset. I know you like to see it."

He did, and this evening's looked as gorgeous as only a Hawaiian twilight could be. Clouds huddled at the horizon, accentuating the oranges, purples, and reds of a scene no painting could equal and no photograph could match.

"The thing about sunsets, Bucky," he said between mouthfuls, "each one's different, yet each one's wonderful."

"Yes, sir. Please swallow those pills I set out for you. You need to take them with dinner."

He doubted if the machine had any way to appreciate beauty or wonder. Shaking his head, he downed the pills with a swig from his water glass. "You know, Nalani called you a caregiver, but since you're just a robot, you don't really care about me. You can't care about me."

The ends of the robot's eyebrows and mouth drooped.

"Don't try to fool me by looking sad," he said, jabbing his fork in the robot's direction. "You don't feel anything."

"It's true I only mimic human emotions; I can't feel," the robot said. "Humans attach importance to facial expressions, so I am programmed to simulate them. As for caring, I cannot 'care' about you in the emotional sense. But I can care for you in the actions I take, looking after your needs and making you comfortable."

He shook his head and washed food down with water. "Without emotions, you're missing the biggest part of caring for people."

The robot nodded. "Yes, sir. Perhaps someday robots will have emotions. At least you have your two children who care about you."

"One child," he corrected with his mouth full. "You know, someday you're gonna get this loco moco right, Bucky. The burger's underdone, and the fried egg is over hard." Still, perfect rice and superb gravy. Can't tell it that, though, and have it getting cocky.

"Sorry, sir. I will make it better next time."

The sunset's hues had deepened with the demise of the day. He sighed. "Damn it, Bucky. What's gonna happen to me when I die?"

Its eyebrows tilted and its mouth line shortened to its 'concerned' expression. "That question is outside my programming, sir."

He flapped a hand to dismiss the robot. "What the hell am I asking you for? When you're done, you just get recycled."

"Perhaps it will be the same for you, sir."

He looked at it. "No, you talking toaster. I don't mean my body. I mean my thoughts, my consciousness. Does that part keep going on in some other form? I've never really been religious, so maybe I'll be punished for that in the afterlife. On the other hand, I'm terrified of just turning off, like a switch or a light bulb."

"That question is outside my programming, sir." The eyes and mouth looked sad.

"Yeah, outside of mine, too, I guess."

"I sense your anxiety level increasing, sir. Perhaps it would be better to think about something else."

With the sun fully below the horizon, only magentas and indigos remained. "Such as?"

"Maybe you could think about your life so far, and resolve to enjoy the rest of it, to live it the best way you can."

He gazed at the machine, with the dying purple light of sunset reflecting off its surface. "What are you, a silicon psychiatrist?"

**

"Sir, you must take this pill before sleeping for the night." The machine stood beside his bed holding a pill in one mechanical hand and a glass of water in the other.

"I already took my pills."

"No, you didn't, sir." It set down the glass of water and used that hand to hold his head in position. The other hand gently but firmly pried open his mouth and inserted the pill. From somewhere, a brief stream of water entered his mouth. He swallowed and the robot released its hold. "Now, I'll turn down the lights, sir. Your water cup is here on the tray in case you need it during the night."

"Damn it, I'm not going to sleep now, Bulky...er, Bunker...what the devil is your name, anyway?"

"You've been calling me Bucky, sir."

"Bucky, yeah. Now...what was I saying?"

"You said you wanted to go to sleep now, sir. I'll be here with you, as always."

He looked at the glowing eyes, expressionless at the moment, and wondered if the machine sometimes lied to him. "No, I want to watch that show...what is it? Island Cops. Turn that on."

"Sir, you just watched that show. It ended five minutes ago. Shall I summarize the episode?"

"No, damn it." The display on the robot's chest read "Monday, August 11, 10:05 PM," so it seemed likely he'd watched the show and forgotten. "I'm tired, Bunny. Leave me alone now."

"Yes, sir."

Sometime later, he awoke to a scene worse than any nightmare. Images flashed by too fast to register. He felt heat, saw blurs of oranges and reds.

He was on the move, somehow, not in his bed. He coughed out smoke. Something went over his nose and mouth and he breathed fresh air.

Someone carried him, fast, through a hall, down stairs, through a door. Then outside, to a warm, humid night with sirens ululating in the distance.

"What happened?" His words got garbled and came out like "Wahabba?"

A robotic hand removed a clear mask from his face. Glowing eyes looked down at him. "There was a fire, sir. The fire department is responding to my summons."

Still only half awake, he turned away from the cradle of the caregiver's arms and squinted, trying to focus. Smoke poured and flames licked from windows on the left side of his house. The neighbor's place was fully ablaze.

He shook his head to clear the wooziness as firetrucks pulled up with lights flashing. The robot held him at a safe distance across the street. He felt a shift in the robot's grip and headphones went over his ears, extinguishing the siren noise.

"I've contacted Nalani." Bucky's voice sounded clear and calm in his ears.

Her image appeared on the robot's chest screen, hair askew and cascading over a floral nightgown. She dabbed at her moist eyes with a tissue. "Dad? Oh my God, Dad, are you all right?"

He managed a smile. "Yeah, I'm okay." He looked over to see arcing streams of water pouring into his windows and those of his neighbor. "My house…"

"It's just a house, Dad. Replaceable." After a quick sigh, her face turned serious, as if she addressed a meeting of senior partners at her law firm. "Bucky, can you hear me?"

"Yes, ma'am, quite well."

"Call a roboxi and bring Dad to my house."

"Yes, ma'am."

Damn roboxi, Maleko thought. He'd never trusted self-driving taxis.

"I'll set up my guest bedroom," Nalani said, "and I'll call the insurance company. I'll also call Kala."

Kala? No, it's Kale, isn't it? No, he…she… "Kala," he said. "My other daughter…"

"Yes, Dad." Nalani smiled. "I'll tell her what happened, and that you're okay. Bucky, did you grab Dad's pills on the way out?"

"I always have a seven-day supply, ma'am," the robot said, "stored in a compartment."

Maleko looked up at Bucky's impassive face. Programmed to feed him and to empty his bedpan, the crazy contraption had just saved his life. He cleared his throat. Even so, his voice cracked. "Thank you, Bucky."

Its glowing eyes gazed back. "You're welcome, sir."

"And knock off that sir stuff. Call me Maleko."

***

Resplendent in his red and yellow battle dress, bruised and aching from the fight, King Kamehameha assessed his army, glancing into the faces of his nearest men. They looked weary and battered, but he saw a glint in those eyes, a readiness for one final advance, a last chance for glory. None of the foes would survive this day. His army would corner them on a precipice, then push them off the cliff. He raised his spear, then pointed it at the enemy. "Charge!"

Something went wrong with the King's eyesight. The scene swirled, grew indistinct. The war cries of his army became garbled and altered to the cheering sounds of a crowd. His breathing grew forced and he found it difficult to think clearly. He lay horizontal, on a bed. A blurry figure stood beside him, a white thing with a flat, black face. Its white arm stretched toward him, its hand nudged him.

"Maleko, please wake up."

"Wha—?"

"Your daughter, Kala, is calling from San Francisco. Will you take the call?"

"Who?"

"Kala."

A still image appeared on the machine's chest screen. He should know that woman's face, and had heard the name, but... He shook his head. "I don't...I..."

The robot paused, and its smile flattened out. "Never mind, Maleko. I told her you can't talk now and may call back later. By the way, after you fell asleep, the Rainbow Warriors won their football game, 38 to 21."

The wall screen showed a joyous throng of fans and some numbers at the bottom that were too small for him to read. The screen flickered off. His thoughts were so sluggish he found it hard to focus. "Who…called?"

"Kala, your daughter in San Francisco."

The fog of his mind cleared somewhat, a rare thing these days. He lay in a bed in Nalani's guest bedroom. The familiar figure beside him…his caregiver robot, named… "You're Buckles…Bu—"

"Bucky."

"Yeah." His voice rasped and he tried to reach for his water, but his hand didn't work well.

"I'll get it." The robot held the cup to him.

Maleko sucked on the straw. The liquid felt good on his dry tongue and throat. He must have messed up the swallowing part again, for he coughed and spluttered. A napkin dabbed his mouth and chin.

"It's five minutes until sunset," Bucky said. "Would you like to see it?"

He managed a faint smile and nodded. Bucky went on, saying something about Nalani not having a west-facing window in the guestroom, so it had arranged for a video camera at his house to view the sunsets while workers repaired the fire damage. The words rolled off Maleko, as did much of life these days. He couldn't remember much, stumbled over words, and had trouble concentrating. Only on rare occasions did his thinking clear up.

The image of the woman on the robot's chest interested him more than the sunset right now. He'd wanted his son, Kale, to grow up noble and bold. But he'd shown more and more feminine tendencies in high school and college. As Maleko's disappointment grew, father and son drifted apart. But the sex change operation was a final straw, like thrusting up a middle finger at all of Maleko's dreams for his son. His son had become a woman, and now went by the name Kala. Even the thought of that used to enrage him, but lately, as with so many other things, it no longer disturbed him.

He still saw remnants of Kale's features in Kala's face, but had to admit she looked beautiful as a woman. A lot like Iola…his wife. He sighed. Kala had not turned out as he'd intended. But no one has complete control of his own life, let alone those of his children. Kale didn't become the man he'd wanted, but perhaps had become the best person, the best Kala, that could be expected. He should be wanting her happiness, not his own.

What, Maleko wondered, must Kale's struggle have been like growing up feeling like a female trapped in a male body? Maleko had given the boy no fatherly emotional support at the time he could have used it. Later, when Kale reached middle age, he'd shown a lot of courage to undergo the sex change operation, and to reveal the fact to Maleko afterward. Now, Since then, Kala had made a name for herself in the San Francisco fashion design scene. Perhaps, in an unexpected way, his child had grown up noble and bold after all.

Maleko glanced up from Kala's image to see the robot looking at him. On the wall screen, a brilliant blaze of twilight colors adorned the western sky.

"You once told me," the robot said, "that each one's different, yet each one's wonderful."

"Sunsets, you mean."

"Sunsets, yes."

"Please call Kala for me," he said. "No, wait. Before that, while I'm thinking straight, I want to record a video addendum to my will."

***

"Hi, Kala! Come on in." Nalani met her sister at the front door with a hug. "You look great. How was your flight?"

"Fine," Kala said as she started to enter. "Oh, give me a second." She took out her cellphone and tapped a key. In the driveway, the robotic car backed out and drove away. Kala's two pieces of automatic luggage followed her across the threshold into the foyer.

It always amused Nalani that her sister, a woman for only half her life, always looked more stylish even after a four-hour flight, than she ever would.

With a worried expression, Kala bent close, looked in her eyes, and whispered, "How's Dad?"

Nalani's smile flat-lined. "Not good." She spoke at normal volume as a signal that they needn't whisper. "He's not eating much, and rarely opens his eyes. That's why I asked you to come out. I know it's hard getting flights on short notice at Christmastime, so it's wonderful you made it. We don't see each other often enough anymore."

"It's a shame," Kala said, "that we had to meet because of this."

"Still," Nalani led her through the hall to stand just outside the door to the guestroom. "I think it's great Dad put you back in his will. The estate won't be large, but it's the fact that he finally accepted you."

From the guestroom came the voice of the robot. "Nalani, I think you should come in here now."

"Just a minute, Bucky," Nalani said. She leaned close to Kala and, this time, whispered. "Don't be shocked at how he looks. The robot tells me people look kind of wasted away in the final—"

"Nalani."

"Coming, Bucky." She beckoned for Kala to follow her in.

Kala gave a voice command and her suitcases remained in the hall.

In the guestroom, the robot squatted on its four legs near the head of the bed wearing its sad expression, mouth frowning and eyes downcast. "I'm sorry. Maleko's heartbeat and breathing stopped twenty-three seconds ago. I'm detecting no brain activity."

She saw her father's withered and bony right hand clutching the robot's left one. Tears filled her eyes. "Thank you, Bucky, for reaching out to hold his hand at the end."

The robot shook its head. "His eyes opened at the sound of your voices in the hall. He reached his hand out to me and held mine. I felt two faint squeezes before…before the end."

Nalani hugged Kala and both sobbed. "He held on for you, Kala. He kept himself going 'till you got here."

"I'm so, so sorry I didn't get here earlier," Kala said, dabbing at her eyes. "I should have been here weeks ago. Instead, it's been you, doing all the work."

"No." Nalani turned to the robot. "It was Bucky. The robot was always here, and I wasn't. I feel terrible about that. Thank you, Bucky. I guess in the end, Dad really grew to like you."

"Perhaps," Bucky said. "His last coherent words to me, ten days ago, were, 'Damn it, Butt-face, can't you cut pineapple into bite-sized pieces? Are you trying to gag me, you mush-headed machine?'"

Nalani and Kala laughed through fresh tears. "He did like you," Nalani said.

"Compared to what I've heard," Kala smiled wryly, "that was practically a proposal of marriage."

In turns, Nalani and her sister held their father's hand, said quiet good-byes, and kissed him on his forehead. Nalani dried her eyes and asked, "Bucky, what happens next?"

"I have summoned a hospice nurse who will make the official determination of death and fill out the certificate for a doctor to sign. When you wish it, I will contact the funeral home of your choice. Then my work here will be complete."

"What? You'll just leave and go on to your next patient?" Kala asked. "Just like that?"

The robot's face looked wistful. "Emotions are outside my programming. Maleko told me I couldn't truly care for someone until I could care about him, with genuine emotions. If I had them, perhaps I could function better."

Nalani reflected on that. "In your line of work," she said, "maybe you're better off without them."

Steven R. Southard writes science fiction about characters grappling with new technologies. Steve's short stories appear in over a dozen anthologies, including The Science Fiction Tarot, Not Far from Roswell, and Re-Terrify. Explore Steve's website (where he's known as Poseidon's Scribe) at www.stevenrsouthard.com.

The Alpha Centauri Shuffle

By MR Wells

I shouldn't be here.

That was the first thought Ariel had when she finally plucked up the nerve to walk into the embassy. One look around- at the walls practically dripping with golden gilding and fine art- would have been enough to reinforce that impression. And that was before Ariel really took in the guests. Dozens of people, humans and aliens alike, all smartly (and no doubt expensively) dressed, in hushed conversation, and every single one of them looking up at her as she came down the stairs.

It felt like she was walking into a pit of Antarian vipers. Ariel barely managed to avoid her hand reaching for her belt, and the empty holster there. She had been in plenty of far seedier, more dangerous places, but at least then she had been armed…

The volume of conversation dropped enough that Ariel could hear one of the guests exclaiming to another in disbelief, "She made first contact?!" Ariel, face flaming, might have been tempted to leave right then if it wasn't for the arm looped within hers, firmly holding her in place.

"Easy, captain," her companion murmured. "Remember why we're here."

Ariel forced a grin, and tried to remember the very generous payment they had been offered for their presence (after plenty of strong hints about 'patriotism' and 'duty' and, crucially, no money up front) as she hissed back through gritted teeth to her partner, "I know that, love. These people just... urgh. Fine. Let's go." Ariel made a show of smiling at a few of the nearest guests as she descended the stairs, and conversation picked up again.

One of the functionaries of the Grisellian government, looking anxious, hurried up to them. He was young, pale, in a far too neat looking suit, and was nervously mopping his brow with a handkerchief clutched in his hand. "Captain Kaltenbach, Commander Hwran, I thought you would never arrive. And I understood that you would be, um, that you would take my advice on the, uh, suggested attire."

Smirking, Ariel looked down at herself as if seeing her clothes for the first time, then glanced at her partner. "I certainly considered your advice very carefully, Mr-"

A flash of irritation from him, as he snapped, "Welby. Senior Envoy Arthur Welby."

"Mr Welby." Ariel continued smoothly. "However, I felt this would be more... authentic." By 'this', Ariel meant the dark trousers and dull maroon jacket she wore that made up the uniform of the Grisellian merchant navy. Admittedly, perhaps the jacket was a little old and rumpled, and the silver rank insignia a little tarnished- and, in truth, both her rank and membership of the Grisellian Merchant Marine were something she rarely bothered with. At least until it came to annoying a jumped up civil servant who had the nerve to suggest Ariel should wear a dress.

As for her partner (and as the only other member of her crew, by default, first mate), Nancy Hwran had worn a dress. It was not, however, from the list of fashionable stores Welby had hinted would be appropriate for the occasion. Nancy had purposely chosen the shortest, most low cut- and frankly, sluttiest- dress she had in her wardrobe. The former pleasure droid looked stunning, if a little out of place, and Ariel smirked as she could see Welby battling his instinct to ogle her attractive partner.

Nancy just smiled innocently at him. Unblinkingly. That was one of the things that, once you realised what was missing, you couldn't not notice about droids. They didn't blink. Didn't breathe. Didn't cough, or clear their throat, or crack their neck, or do the million and one other little things that you didn't notice humans (or most aliens) doing until they weren't there. Plenty of people found it unsettling; Ariel certainly wasn't one of them.

Welby stared at Nancy suspiciously for a moment. Finally, he turned back to Ariel. "The ambassador has asked to see you after your speech, to arrange the first part of your agreed upon payment; it is felt that your presence at a few of the meetings- for the holographers and so forth- before the trade treaty is signed would be fitting. And of course, we will expect you at the signing ceremony tomorrow evening as well. At which point your… duties will be complete." Welby may as well have added, *and you'll get the rest of the money promised.*

Nodding absently, Ariel said, "Yes, yes, of course. I'm sure that won't be- wait, I'm sorry. What speech?"

Eyes widening, Welby said, "Your speech? In-" he glanced at his chronometer- "around 4 minutes time. It was in my notes to you, and in the itinerary I provided." Welby sounded a little reproachful. "You tell your side of first contact, and then Commander Steja will do the same for the Tipani."

Ariel looked desperately at Nancy, who simply grinned back, noting, "You're the one who said you couldn't be bothered to read all the 'legalese claptrap' once you made sure the payment terms were correct and ironclad, captain."

"Thank you, dear, that's extremely helpful as always." Ariel looked hopefully at Welby. "Uh, look Mr Welby, can we-"

"Skip it? Make your speech after the Tipani? No, and no." He sighed. "Why does no one ever read my notes… look, you only have to talk for a few minutes for form's sake." Welby rubbed his forehead, screwing his eyes shut for a moment, then added tiredly, "Just… just try not to swear, and simply tell everyone what happened- briefly. You get the applause, job done. Easy, right?"

"Um." Ariel thought about that, and tried not to look at Nancy, who she just knew would be smirking at her. "Right. Easy…"

***

1 year ago

"Damn it!" Ariel swore as the Selkie shuddered again from a near miss, and she flicked the controls, sending the ship spinning away on a different course. "That was too close! Have you got a course plotted yet?"

"Negative, captain." Nancy's eyes were flickering across her console. "They've blocked both of the gates out of the system with their cutters, and the commander of that patrol ship appears to be rather good. And very persistent."

"Hell's bells, I'm not heaving to for these sods!" At least not with our hold full of what that customs patrol would consider contraband.

The irony was, Ariel had always been very careful with what she smuggled on her small freighter. No drugs, weapons, or slaves. Or droids- at least not since she had met Nancy. Her lover had very firm opinions on that matter. The odd bit of artwork, looted technology, raw materials, even cooking spices- all had provided a lucrative sideline depending on where she was going.

This time, the hold of the Selkie was filled with nothing more valuable than sacks of grain. Completely legal under galactic law- except when one was trying to take that grain to the human settlers on Telos IV, settlers who were involved in a rather messy trade dispute with the neighbouring Seren system. It was the Seren navy that had blockaded Telos IV- and had intercepted (and were rather doggedly pursuing) the Selkie.

Ariel had assumed that, once they had driven her away from the Telos system, the Seren cruiser would have broken off pursuit. Instead, the cruiser had jumped through the warp gate after them, deployed its cutters to block both gates in this system immediately upon arrival, and were now in hot pursuit of the Selkie.

Another laser blast flashed perilously close, and Ariel cursed as she shot off on another vector, the Seren ship still close behind. She glanced at her scanners, hoping for something that might give her an edge. It didn't help; this star system was little more than a waypoint between the 2 warp gates in the system, contained nothing more than a single, uninhabited ice planet- and the heavily armed cutters were resolutely blocking both warp gates out of the system. The odds of her freighter being able to slip through either gate under their guns was slim to none.

For lack of a better plan, Ariel began weaving towards the ice planet. "Warm up the sublight drive," she ordered sharply. "Begin plotting us a course… anywhere. Away from the gates, away from Seren and Telos. Let's see if they are willing to follow us into deep space."

Raising a perfectly shaped eyebrow, Nancy simply noted, "As you wish, captain." A moment later- "Done. Bearing on your console now."

A quick look at the coordinates, and then Ariel spun the Selkie wildly, momentarily taking them out of the Seren cruisers fire arcs. She quickly settled onto the course Nancy had calculated, then slammed her fist onto the red button that triggered the sublight drives. The Selkie shuddered, and for a horrible second Ariel thought the drives had been damaged.

Then the stars outside disappeared into a burst of light, and Ariel slumped back in relief. "Are they following?" Nancy tapped a few buttons. "Negative, captain. No sign of pursuit."

"Ha. Suckers." Ariel grinned at Nancy. "Didn't I say I always came out on top?"

Her partner shook her head. "No. I have firsthand evidence that you do not, in fact, always come out on top." Nancy smiled at her, and then very slowly gave a very big wink. Ariel burst out laughing. "Oh, my word, when did you learn to wink?"

Cocking her head, Nancy noted proudly, "I have been practising."

Still chuckling, Ariel checked her console. "So… how long do we need to stay in sublight for?"

"Seven hours will take us to the nearest uncharted system. We can then take some bearings and calculate how to get back to the nearest warp gate." Nancy paused, then amended, "The nearest other warp gate. I calculate, however, that it is likely to take several days, at least. I will be able to assess the position more accurately when we arrive."

Nodding, Ariel stood from her chair and stretched. She had expected as much. The sublight drives were really only designed for short hauls between warp gates, but in this case she had gambled; the cutters the Seren ship had deployed didn't have sublight capability, nor the ability to traverse the warp gates, and as she had hoped the commander of the cruiser hadn't dared leave them behind.

She sniffed, wrinkling her nose at the smell of burnt wiring somewhere within the ship. Sighing, Ariel took a wistful look at Nancy. "There's plenty of better things I'd much rather be doing, but I suppose we had better see what the damage is. Some of those shots were too damn close."

Nancy was already retrieving some of her tools from one of the many pockets in her utility suit. "Yes, captain. I can detect a minor coolant leak in the main cargo bay which we should prioritise." Nancy paused as she passed Ariel to grab her hand, tugging her away from the cockpit. Then she gave that very obvious wink again. "I'm sure it won't take us seven hours, though. Captain." She purred this last word before dragging a flushed Ariel away.

***

Now

"-and that was when we stumbled across the Tipani ship." Ariel concluded her- highly sanitised- story. "We didn't know, of course, what to make of the strange ship- a type not in any of our databases- but after I dusted off the first contact protocols, and after a few false starts, we were finally able to speak to them. Or at least, my first officer was." There were a few chuckles at that, as Ariel shot a mock glare at Nancy.

They had lucked out in fact; apart from Galactic Common, Ariel only spoke conversational Xendi and Welsh (and that was because they were both common trade languages), and could just about understand Unitarian Standard- although she had never been able to get the tongue clicks right as far as pronunciation went.

Nancy, on the other hand, had been programmed with a full language suite, and was quickly chattering away in Old Formal Galactic to the Tapani ship.

Eventually, they had parted ways, to return word of the existence of the other to their respective governments. All of which had, eventually, led to this conference which would conclude with the signing of the first trade treaty between the Grisellian Republic and the Tapani Commonwealth.

Smiling, Ariel noted, "So now, I'll turn things over to my Tapani counterpart- who I suspect was a little more prepared than the captain of a tramp freighter."

Ariel was gratified to hear a few laughs, along with some lukewarm applause, as she leaned across to shake the hand of the Tapani captain. The Tapani were humanoid, fortunately, so the grey skinned Tapani hesitated only a moment before shaking her hand a little awkwardly with its own clawed, scaly hand.

As Ariel sat, relieved, she looked around the room. Half of the assorted dignitaries were talking amongst themselves as the Tapani captain began speaking. And Ariel felt her own eyes glazing over as she tried to look interested in what he was saying- despite the speech being in Old Formal Galactic, and thus completely indecipherable to her.

Nonetheless, Ariel jumped when she heard a whisper in her ear. "He's lying." Forcing herself to relax, Ariel leaned back slightly and murmured to Nancy, "What do you mean?"

Moving closer again, Nancy said softly. "The Tapani. He's lying, at least about something." Ariel didn't bother asking whether her partner was sure- pleasure droids could pick up minute clues in words and body language to detect any deception in anyone, after just a few minutes of observing them. Which, Ariel had to admit, was occasionally infuriating, but more often was very, very useful. Although when Nancy had, after first catching Ariel in a lie, explained why she was programmed to do so ('to most accurately meet our clients needs'- said in a chillingly calm voice, even for her), Ariel had been as horrified as she was disgusted. But she had never doubted Nancy's abilities since.

Watching her Tapani counterpart, and trying to block out his droning words, Ariel narrowed her eyes. This reception was the first time she had seen Tapani close up since first contact, so she was hardly an expert in the species. They were tall, grey, scaly, and looked a lot like rather blunt nosed lizards. But after a few minutes, she couldn't help but notice that the Tapani was flicking his tail back and forth rapidly, and she thought-maybe?- his speech was a little…stilted. It actually helped that Ariel didn't understand, as she could concentrate on his speech patterns and flow of words. Finally, the tail flicking stopped and the speech settled somewhat. Had he just been nervous?

Startled, the applause when he finished snapped Ariel out of her reverie and she hurriedly joined in. She politely excused herself, with a meaningful look at Nancy, who swiftly followed her off the stage.

Unfortunately, before they could actually find a discrete corner to talk about it, Welby was next to them. He actually gave Ariel a grudging nod. "That was… reasonably done, captain. You can clearly think on your feet. Now- as I mentioned beforehand, the ambassador would like a word. If you wouldn't mind…?"

Smiling politely, Welby led them away through the crowds. Even though they skirted the edge of the room, Ariel was still stopped twice - once to have her hand shaken by a cheerful alien military officer in a uniform she didn't recognise, and the second time to be rather crudely propositioned by a drunk Lomarkian. Ariel firmly, if politely, declined, and she felt Nancy take her hand a little possessively after that.

"Damn his eyes, Representative Krelbrn is a drunken sot, practically an insult sending him to this meeting…" Welby was still muttering under his breath angrily when they finally reached the back of the room.

Knocking politely, Welby led them in. It was clearly a study of some sort; data cards lined the walls, along with a number of computer monitors and desks. "Ambassador Sir Francis Howe, Captain Ariel Kaltenbach, Commander Nancy Hwran." Following the introductions, Welby stood to one side.

Nodding politely (she wasn't sure whether she should bow), Ariel murmured, "Pleased to meet you, sir."

Ambassador Howe didn't stand up from behind his desk; Ariel wondered whether he even could, unaided. He smiled, red faced and huffing, apparently struggling to even sit up a little straighter, his huge belly barely contained by his jacket and a very tight, straining golden sash. For a moment, Ariel wondered if he was even human, he was so large.

Finally, though he had barely moved, Howe panted, "Ah… yes, yes, captain, so… hn… so glad to meet you." He rubbed a stained handkerchief across his forehead. Howe reached for something on his desk, groaning in effort for a moment, before collapsing back into what Ariel couldn't help but note must have been a very, very sturdy chair.

"Mr Welby… hn… if you… wouldn't mind." He gestured Welby forward, and pointed at something. Welby nodded. "Of course, my lord." He picked up a sheaf of official looking papers from the desk, along with a credit chip, and then turned towards Ariel and Nancy. After a moment of hesitation, although Nancy was closer, he offered the papers to Ariel.

"Your…" Howe subsided into a fit of coughing, before continuing, "Your papers, captain. As… hn… as agreed. Clearing up any… hn… any outstanding issues surrounding ownership of your pleasure droid." Howe beamed up at them. "It's very pretty, you know. I… hn… don't blame you for… hn… stealing it." He chuckled.

Glaring at him, Ariel took the papers, and the chip. "I didn't steal her," she said coldly. "I freed her." Ariel flicked through the papers to check everything was in order, then handed them to Nancy. "There you are, dear. As promised."

Nancy seemed to freeze for a moment as she took the papers, then turned her gleaming eyes onto Ariel. Her voice was very quiet when she spoke, unusually so. "Thank you." Nancy clutched the papers possessively against her chest.

Ariel returned her attention to the ambassador as she tucked the credit chip into her pocket. "Unless you have any further business, sir, I understand I am to go and… mingle." Ariel barely managed to keep the disgust from her voice.

"One… hn… one moment, captain. I wonder… hn… if you would be interested in a little… investment opportunity. As… hn… as you were responsible for it." Howe gasped the words, but Welby looked uncomfortable.

"My lord, that information is-"

"About to become very public when we… hn… we sign that treaty!" Howe thundered. "Now, tell… hn… tell them!"

Sighing, Welby said, "Part of the treaty includes the handing over of the mining rights on one of the Tapani moons, to a consortium of buyers, backed by the Grisellian government. We… are still selling shares in these mines, which are expected to yield incredible profits."

Apparently seeing Ariel's disbelief, a grinning Howe interrupted, "The… hn… the idiots don't realise what they have! They think the mines… hn… mines there are nearly tapped out, so they are… hn… are selling cheaply, trying to… flog us an empty moon. But they… hn… they apparently don't use Ligerian crystals in their ships. Our… hn… our first official visit… we saw crystals the size of my thumb just… hn… just lying there, on the ground! Ready to be scooped up. I-" He coughed again, and Welby smoothly continued.

"As the ambassador has said, the Tapani apparently either don't use Ligerian crystals in their engines, or didn't see what we saw, just lying on the ground. I've heard their eyesight isn't very good. But once they sign that treaty, we get the rights to billions of credits worth of crystals for just a fraction of the profit we will make." Welby smiled smugly.

Raising a disbelieving eyebrow, Ariel exchanged a look with Nancy. Her partner was grinning at her. Ariel had to force herself to turn her laughter into a cough. "Um… if I may, ambassador… have you had a full survey done on the moon? By accredited geologists, or mining experts?"

Howe snorted piggishly. "And… hn… and tip the Tapani off as to how valuable the moon really is? No… hn… no, I trust my eyes, captain. One of my… hn… advisors managed to grab one of the… hn… the crystals for testing. Quite… hn… genuine. And we still have a few shares left in the consortium, you… hn… you know. Under… hn… the circumstances, perhaps you would… hn… want to invest." He waved a pudgy hand airily. "We… hn… could even offer a discount. It.. hn… it wouldn't have been possible without you, after all. Without your… hn… fortuitous run in with one of their scout ships."

Trying to stay as composed as possible, Ariel noted, "Well, that's… that's very generous of you, sir."

"It almost seems too good to be true," Nancy noted innocently.

Howe nodded enthusiastically, but Welby had narrowed his eyes. He had either picked up something in Nancy's voice or was a lot smarter than his master as he asked, "Wait a moment- what are you suggesting?"

Finally, Ariel broke into laughter. "Oh come on, really- the both of you! It's one of the oldest tricks in the book, the Alpha Centauri shuffle! I even worked it a few times myse- that is, I have heard it used a few times myself."

Blinking in puzzlement, Howe asked, "I… hn… I am unfamiliar with that… hn… that term, captain. The… Alpha Centauri shuffle?"

Pacing casually back and forth, Ariel rubbed her chin as she tried to recall where the term originated. "I think it's from the early days of colonisation, maybe even Old Earth itself." Ariel explained. At the continued blank looks from both men, Ariel snapped, "It's a con, gentleman! A very old one, at that."

"A con?" Welby repeated. While Ambassador Howe seemed puzzled, the younger man was clearly thinking furiously. "You mean…" Welby trailed off, suddenly looking pale.

"That's right." Ariel smiled sweetly at him. "Because I just bet you're overpaying handsomely for what you would pay for a tapped out mining planet. Heck, I bet you didn't even haggle over the price. You see, you think you have spotted the trick- the Tapani are trying to sell you a set of old, empty mines. Indeed, you think that you are tricking them and will be getting a moon full of valuable crystals for almost nothing."

Nancy added, "But you have done no surveys, no exploration. Did you even gather up a few more sample crystals to analyse? From different areas of the moon?"

Welby looked embarrassed, but Howe was still frowning, confused. "No, of… hn… course not. I said, they might have noticed us… hn… picking them up and rethought the sale, if they thought that we thought the crystals were worth something."

"The beauty of the Alpha Centauri Shuffle, folks." Ariel was shaking her head, still pacing back and forth as she explained. "You think that you spotted the trick, and are even conning them and coming out ahead. But you only saw what they wanted you to see. Picked up on the con they wanted you to. I bet they just threw a few handfuls of genuine Ligerian crystals on the ground in one of the mines, showed you that, then counted on your own dishonesty and greed to pay through the nose for what will, undoubtedly, prove to be a genuinely tapped out moon."

Shaking her head ruefully, Ariel said thoughtfully, "I can't help but admire the sheer ambition though. Conning an entire government, that takes guts. How much do you really know about the Tapani Commonwealth, ambassador? I wonder if we really did 'accidentally' stumble across that Tapani ship? I mean, what are the odds? Maybe that was what their captain was lying about…"

Howe had, apparently, finally caught on. "No, that's… hn… that can't be true! They… hn… they're just dumb… hn… dumb lizards, not… hn… not smart like us!"

With a bitter laugh at that, Nancy just shook her head.

"Oh, ambassador, I assure you," Ariel said, leaning over the desk. "Aliens can be every bit as cunning, dishonest, and downright sneaky as any human. Perhaps even more so. After all, deception really is the great equaliser."

To one side, Welby was already at a computer, tapping furiously at the keypad. "Welby… hn… Welby! This… hn… this can't be true, can it?" Howe looked even redder in the face now, and distinctly panicked. "Our backers… hn… all that money-"

"Won't be fully cleared until the treaty is signed, so we might still be able to get out of this," snapped Welby impatiently, before adding a second later as an afterthought, "My lord." He was already muttering into a personal comlink, and a minute later another pair of neatly dressed civil servants hurried in. Ignoring the spluttering ambassador, they moved across to Welby and they all began conversing in low, urgent tones.

Shaking her head, Ariel took Nancy's arm, nodding to the paperwork her partner was still holding onto tightly. "Well, gentlemen, it's been a pleasure, but I believe our business is more or less concluded. So we will bid you good evening."

Everyone ignored her.

"Come on," Ariel muttered to Nancy. "I think we need to get back to the Selkie, and get her warmed up- just in case. I don't think anyone- on either side- is going to thank us for our little intervention here." Nancy tugged Ariel's arm, pulling her back, caught her eye, and then opened her mouth wide. Ariel, wincing and knowing what was coming, barely managed to get her hands up to cover her ears in time.

The undulating cry of a Kavok Dragon tore through the room, and everyone, grimacing in pain, stared at the droid.

"Remember," Nancy noted smugly to the room at large. "Humans don't have a monopoly on cunning. And if it seems too good to be true, it probably is."

Then Nancy smiled at Ariel. "Now we can go… captain."

Ariel was already guiding Nancy towards the door, with an embarrassed smile and muttered apologies. Taking in the furious glares of the others in the room, Nancy added quietly to Ariel, "Maybe we should ask spaceport control for departure approval on the way back to the ship. Something tells me if we wait, they might come up with a reason to stop us leaving."

Shaking her head grimly, Ariel just muttered, "You know what? If we ever make first contact with an alien race again, I'm keeping quiet about it."

Born in Wiltshire in the UK, **Matt Wells** currently lives in South Wales with his cat, Jess, and spends his time reading, writing and playing a large variety of board games!

Three Bullets for a Glass of Chardonnay
By Mathew Austin

Jake put a 9mm on the table and clicked his fingers for service. The barman wandered over, looked down at the bullet and shook his head. "One 9 isn't going to get you drunk today."

"Since when?"

"Since Michaelson opened his munitions factory and started producing 9s by the barrel load."

"But this ain't no Michaelson trash, this is Luger's finest."

"It might very well be, but people aren't too picky these days, so give me half a chamber of 9s or you're walking out of here dry."

Jake scratched the back of his head and looked at the barman with one eye closed. "Thought we were friends, Barry."

"Friendship can't fight inflation." The barman held out his hand.

Biting his bottom lip Jake reached into his ammo pouch and pulled out two more rounds. He slapped them into the barman's hand and received a glass of chardonnay. He poured himself half a mug of water from the pitcher and swilled it around his mouth, cleaning the dust and grime of a hard day's labour from his gums and launching it into the spittoon.

The chardonnay was as good as one would find on Luna. It was terrible: warm, sweet and heavy on the anti-freeze; its only virtue was that it got one drunk fast. Jake leaned on the bar and took in the surroundings. The post-work rush was just beginning, men in hard hats and dirty overalls took their seats at tables and began counting out their hollow points. A man could expect to make at least three clips a day hauling rock, but if Michaelson carried on as he was no one would move for less than a handful of 12s. "Bad times are coming, Barry. Lunar ain't how it was when I first got here, the titanrush is over, there are no new prospectors, just opportunists."

"You must have saved yourself a small armoury." The barman polished a glass and placed it back in the rack. "Been here longer than any."

"I've done alright." Jake thought about the 50 cals sitting in his strong box and felt warm inside. "Still I hoped to have a few more good years. You ever thought about going back down?"

"Never." The barman surveyed his inn with a smile on his face. "Darkside will still be here when the banks arrive and maybe that ain't such a bad thing."

"Currency over calibre?" Jake swigged down the last of his wine and felt it in his knees. "Just don't sound right." He reached into his pouch and pulled out three more rounds. "I'm off for a smoke, let a glass of red breath for me would you?"

***

Outback the recycler hummed, stuttered and then hummed again as Jake pulled a pack of Bullington's from his pocket. He lit up, inhaled and blew a cloud upwards just in time to see the last of the sun disappear. For six years he'd had fortnights of light and dark, he couldn't imagine what it would be like to go back to a day/night cycle. Earth was calling, the ringtone was loud and clear, but a part of him didn't want to pick up the receiver. No man could haul rock forever, he'd already done double the duration of any who came before him, continued mining whilst other went down to get fat with wives. There was pride in hearing others say that 'pickmen came and went but Jake the Hammer kept on digging.'

He pulled more smoke into his lungs at the same time he heard trouble approaching. Metal heels clanged on the concrete as Mick 'the Slug' Johnson approached, his leather jacket and acid-washed jeans the uniform of a man who made his living off of the backs of others. "If it ain't Jake the Hammer."

"What do you want, Slug?"

"Now now, no need for that hostility. I've just come to talk."

"Sure you have." Jake took one last drag and then stamped out the cigarette. "Say your piece."

"Seen your brother lately?"

"You know Ringo's gone earthbound." It had been three months since his brother had bid Lunar a unfond farewell, jumping on the last shuttle with little more than a handful of bullet credit to his name and a line-up of sharks just waiting to take a bite. Having missed out on a feeding frenzy, Jake knew it would only be a matter of time before they came swimming around looking for fresh meat. "What's your game?"

"Your brother was three 50s and a handful of 10s deep. He signed a contract in blood. Well, the way I see it, your blood is his blood and you owe me a powder keg."

Jake leaned forward and spat on the floor by the Slug's boot, spittle staining the nickel plated heels that let everyone know just who was coming their way. "Ringo's business is his business and his alone. There's no one this side of the hemisphere who didn't know that Ringo walked around with holes in his pockets, God knows I turned his hand away more times than I can count. If you got stiffed by him then you got no one to blame but yourself. So let sleeping dogs lie or get yourself earthside, because this old pickman has nothing for you but disdain."

Jake walked back into the heat and hubbub of Darkside. There was not a spare seat to be had, but jaws stopped moving and laughter left the room as soon as the door slammed behind him. He heard the distinctive sound of a cocking of a gun and turned to find himself face to face with a 44 colt. The only thing the Slug loved more than spending bullets was shooting them and he was willing to pay more than most made in a month just to make a point. "You going to put me down in Barry's fine establishment?"

"You're not leaving much choice, Hammer."

"Seems a waste if you ask me."

"Oh yeah."

"Yeah. The way I see it is if you pull that trigger, you're out another 44 and have no way of getting any of that precious lead back."

"And what would you suggest?"

"Well, how about-" Jake grabbed the barrel and lifted. The blast filled the room and a bottle of the barman's finest exploded in a shower of glass and bubbles. Slug fought but was no match for the hands of man who had pounded rock for more than half a decade. Jake ripped the gun from his grasp and pushed him back against the doors. He pulled out his Saturday Night Special and sent a 22 between Mick Johnsons eyes. The body slid down the doors leaving a red streak as it went.

"What the hell, Jake." Jake turned and saw the barman with his hands on his head pulling at what remained of his hair.

"Cool your boots, Barry." He smiled and held up the 44 colt. "Drinks are on me."

***

The black baggers left as the barman sprayed the doors with bleach. "I have half a mind to ban you for a month." He wiped down the dark wood lacquer and his white cloth came away red. "There's a perfectly good slab of concrete out back that you could have painted."

"Needed a witness, don't want word spreading that I'm a stone-colder." Jake stood up and the room rotated. He put his hand on the bar to steady himself and fought down the nausea. He had drunk at least two bottles and bought the house three rounds of Lunarshine; that night everyone had been his friend. He threw the barman one of his two remaining 44s and put the other in his pocket. "Night, Barry."

"Yeah yeah," the barman said and went back to cleaning the door.

The cold air of the dark set his mind straight, even if his legs still wobbled. He could feel his head start to throb, the wine got you drunk quick, but left just as fast. He took the scenic route to get the last of it out of his system. He passed the old brothel and that was now a halfway house for glue sniffers. Once upon a time it had been a place of soft furnishings and soft women. The madam Betsy prided herself on satisfied customers, but dry plots made for mean customers and she had uprooted north where supposedly men still had manners.

Somewhere in the distance a pair of fools were wasting their money, as fireworks with no light echoed up against the dome that kept everyone breathing. Jake came to a pause outside of Michaelson Munitions. It wasn't much to look at, just a square building of brick and steel, surrounded by walls of concrete topped with razor wire and an iron gate that barred any hope of an uninvited entrance. Word had it that Michaelson had partners on Earth with deep pockets. They imported nickel and lead without care of the cost. The banks would be there soon, no doubt about it; the days of buying both a life and a meal with the same coin were limited.

The concierge of The Happy Sleeper looked bleary eyed, as Jake came across the threshold, his bed calling to him with a siren song. "Heard you got into some trouble with Slug Johnson."

"Oh yeah."

"Also heard you left him as food for the black baggers."

"News travels fast."

"Now why would you go and do a stupid thing like that?" The concierge rested his elbow on the reception desk and his chin in his palm. "You've been here as long as any and never said boo to the gaggle of geese that have run these parts."

"The man rubbed me wrong. Anyway, he pulled first, just ask around."

"First or second won't matter when acquaintances come calling. You know the types Slug ran with. They may not have thought much of him, but they won't accept it being open season on their profession."

"You want me out, Sam, is that it?"

"Your rounds are still good here, Hammer, but at the first sign of trouble you either get yourself up north, or a shuttle back home."

"This is my home."

"That it may be, but you'll be hanging your hat in the incinerator if you don't get off that high horse." The concierge came out from behind the front desk and barred the front door. "You did the world a favour by offing the Slug, but no good deed goes unpunished."

***

Jake collected his pick from the tool-locker. The handle was moulded to the shape of his fingers; holding it just felt right.

"Good luck today, Hammer," the foreman said and Jake gave him a point and a wink, before stepping into the elevator and descending into the bowels of the moon. The elevator smelled of cologne, but come closing time it would be replaced by the sweet smell of dust and sweat. Six men stood shoulder to shoulder as the metal cage creaked downwards.

"Heard you shot Slug," a voice behind him said. "Good man, about time someone did it."

"I was just defending myself."

"I don't care if you put one in his back from the shadows. You've done us all a favour." There was the sound of assent from the rest of the pickmen.

"Perhaps you lot don't repay me in kind. Half a bottle of white down at Darkside, will do just fine." The elevator came to a halt and the door opened. "Goodluck today, fellas. Strike it rich."

"Strike it rich." They said, the mantra of all those who still had hope.

Jake walked down the small incline of Plot 13D. It had cost him five 10s and a 45, half the price of his first plot. The demand was low, as each day more men shuttled back than shuttled in. He leaned the pick against the wall and pulled the sounding fork from his belt. An outcrop jutted from the ceiling nearest the southernmost support. He reached up and hit the fork against it and held it by his ear. It hummed a tune, but not one that was music to his ears. He repeated the process, until he hit pay dirt in the far eastern corner as the fork's ring resonated an octave lower. Jake grabbed the pick and heated the tip, until it shone red. He shot from the hip, boring a crescent shape into the wall, then setting the pick to hammer until rock began to shower.

The red light flashed and Jake set the pick to cool, before shovelling the rubble into the collector. When it was full to the brim, he sealed the lid and pushed it up the metal rampway and into the analyser. The screen told him to please wait. He wiped sweat from his brow leaving a grey streak across his forehead. A ping! He looked down and saw the word that made a pickman blush: Titanium.

***

"Any luck?" Jake dried his face with a grey towel that had once been white. The dark water in the basin disappeared and was replaced with a liquid that management assured him was pure but smelled of sulphur. "I could hear you digging for three hours straight."

Conrad smiled showing all the teeth he had left. "A chamber of 12s and half a clip of 10s."

Jake whistled. "That's a good haul right there."

"How about you, Hammer?"

"Enough to get me drunk tonight." Jake didn't want to kill Conrad's good time. The man had more calibre than most would earn in a month, but Jake had a fistful of 45s coming his way and that was par for the course. Some would call him lucky, but those were the sorts who went home empty handed. Jake the Hammer could turn a dry plot into a fountain, he had a sixth sense for metal and enough saved up to live comfy even if it never stopped raining. "How'd you do, Sweeny?"

Sweeny slammed his locker and rested his head against the metal. "Nothing but buckshot."

"Bad luck, but I'm sure tomorrow's your day."

"I don't think so, Hammer. Think I have had just about enough of this fool's errand."

"What you saying?"

"I've hauled enough rock for one lifetime. I'm hanging up my pick, already got my shuttle booked for tomorrow."

"Well…" Sweeny had been there for close to two years, he'd started off hot but then the cold had set in. He'd lost his hope and when the hope was gone, there was no point in hanging around. "Let's hit Darkside, Conrad here can buy you a drink."

"How's tricks?" The barman flicked his eyes to the back of the room where a loan figure sat sipping a glass of red. Jake eyed him and raised a brow. "What the hell's he doing here?"

"Beats me." The barman poured a glass of rosé and Jake raised it to Conrad. "Came in here an hour ago, been nursing that glass ever since."

Jake tapped his fingers on the bar and ran his tongue over an incisor. "Back in a bit," he said and walked over with his glass before anyone could object. Michaelson looked up as he approached. The man had a long beard and small brown eyes. "Mind if I join you?" Jake sat down before he had a chance to answer.

"Who do have I the pleasure of drinking with?"

"The name's Jake Leroux."

"Ah, the legendary Hammer."

"Some would call me that. And, if I am not mistaken, you are the famed Oliver Michaelson."

"That I am." Michaelson sipped from his glass and winced.

"Not your drink?"

"The wine here leaves a lot to be desired." Jake took a big swig and felt his head tingle. "So, Mr Hammer. How can I help you?"

"I know everyone in this town, been here to see them all come and all go, but you are an enigma. I hear of you, I feel you, but I never see you. Couldn't pass up this chance to get acquainted."

"How very neighbourly of you."

"We've got to look out for each other."

"Just like you looked out for Mick Johnson?"

"You knew the Slug?"

"By reputation, I don't tend to associate myself with Lunar-South's less desirable elements."

"Wouldn't want to get those hands dirty." Jake scratched at his chin with black fingernails.

"Do you always toss around mud when trying to get acquainted. Can we cut to the chase?"

"Fine, let's talk shop."

"Shop? Mr Hammer you are a miner and I am a manufacturer. I hardly see how we have business to talk about. Now if you don't mind…" Michaelson indicated to the open bar, but Jake didn't budge.

"The way I see it, your business goes hand in hand with everyone's, but I'm not here to talk facts and figures just to slake some curiosity. Permit me a question or two and I let you sip that wine in peace?" Michaelson gestured for him to continue. "You've been pumping out 9s like there's a war going on."

"What on earth is strange about a munitions factory making bullets?"

"Not a thing, if this was Earth, but it ain't. Don't act like you paid for that glass with cash, a bullet is meant for more than a chamber."

"Just what are you accusing me of?"

"No accusations just observations. The 9 millimetre has been the bedrock of this economy, its value had been the same since the dome went up. Now here you come making the money in my pocket worth a fraction of what it once was; you're turning bullets into copper coins. People ain't shooting each other more than they usually do, so it makes me think why does Lunar need so many bullets? That my first observation. My second, well, maybe you can help me with that one. See, we can't even get a drink here that doesn't take a year off your life." Jake took a swig and grimaced. "Anything that comes up costs more than its worth, yet there is only one way to get lead and that's off a shipment. I'm no businessman, but to make this many 9s must be costing you an arm and a leg in import. No one ever made bullets up here because it just wasn't profitable and no one comes to Lunar if they ain't interested in making money. So that gets me thinking and I hope you don't mind if I carry on thinking, a man like me doesn't get to do much of it. It makes me think that you have a reason for being up here other than making bullets. You mind telling me what that is?"

Michaelson pulled at his beard and challenged Jake to blink. "A lot of imagination you got for a titanium miner. This is a land of life and death, where a man has to think about whether he wants to eat or shoot. Well maybe he can have both with enough lead in his pocket. It's just 9s."

"Today its 9s, but sometime soon it'll be 10s and 12s, until eventually every Tom and Dick has got a 50 cal falling out of his back pocket. And then maybe when he doesn't have to think about shooting or eating, he ends up deciding to shoot a lot more."

"This is already a land of violence, don't delude yourself that Lunar is anything other than anarchy. You shot and killed a man just yesterday and not an eye lid was battered or a wink of sleep lost. My bullets are just a means and an end until this place gets what it needs."

"And what would that be?"

"Law and order."

"Bingo! Now you see, that doesn't make sense to me. Shooting means business for you, that is the nature of supply and demand. So why would a man who makes his living through violence want law and order, not natural to want to put yourself out of business, unless bullets aren't actually your business. I love this place. Sure it's rough round the edges, but the moon belongs to everyone. No country or government can lay claim to this ball of rock. The wine might be terrible, but I can drink it a free man." Jake downed the rest of his glass and breathed deep through his nose. "I know a good thing can't last forever, but I don't care for some carpetbagger trying to speed up nature."

"Of course, I am free to do whatever I want."

"That you are."

"And even if what you said was true, that I was some interloper with an agenda, what is a simple pickman like you going to do about it. You going to splatter my brains like you did Slug Johnson? That's the way you do things around here ain't it."

"I'm just making observations. But as you say, I'm just a simple pickman and you're free to do what you want." Jake stood up. "I'm not going to kill you, Michaelson, you ain't worth the price. That factory is going to keep making bullets until the banks arrive, whether you're dead or alive. I can't stop the moon from turning, but I like to go around with my eyes open wide. I thank you for your time." Jake walked over to the bar and emptied his ammo onto the counter.

"What can I get you?" the bar man asked.

"Anything, Barry. Just take all my bullets before I put each one of them into that bastard over there."

***

Jake lay on his bed holding a 10mm between his fingers. He turned it back and forth analysing it under the light of his bed lamp. It felt somehow wrong, a fraction too short or a touch light, something indistinguishable to the eye but evident to intuition. Nine days had passed since his tête-à-tête with Michaelson and already new 10s were pouring onto the market. He tried to calculate how long it would take before the change occurred, but couldn't, all he knew was that it was coming, maybe not tomorrow, but soon. He threw the bullet into air the and caught it in his fist, then loaded it into a clip and locked it away into his strong box.

Back in bed, he rested his head on his pillow and clapped the lights out, only for the peace to be broken by the ring of his telephone. "Hello?"

"Hammer?"

"Barry that you?"

"Yeah." Jake could hear the noise and regretted his bi-monthly day of abstinence. "I don't want to worry you, but think you've got trouble headed your way."

Jake sat up, his free hand instinctively moving to gun beneath his pillow. "What sort of trouble?"

"Got a man here and he's been asking a lot of questions about you."

"That man got a name?"

"Yeah. Harold Johnson… " Jake held the back of the receiver against his forehead and bit down hard on his lip. "You still there, Hammer?"

"Yeah, I'm listening. He say what he wants?"

"Just said business, but it don't take a mind reader to know what that means."

"You got a description?"

"About half a head shorter than yourself, salt-and-pepper moustache, suede jacket and denim slacks. He's as fresh off the shuttle as they get, you'll see him coming."

"Thanks for the heads up, Barry."

"Anytime."

***

Jake looked at the rubble as the black baggers carried Sweeney into the elevator. Dark red stained the floor, but his eyes were drawn to the green shine of titanium littered among the rock. "I'm not a quitter," he had said and talked of one last big score. Jake felt a hand on his shoulder and found Conrad staring at him, the water of his eyes shimmering in the light.

"It's early closing, Hammer, you know the drill." They rode up listening to the black baggers talk about where they would get drunk that night. Their kind never went to Darkside, they knew not to mix with the men they collected.

Sweeny had never been chatty but his absence was deafening as they fetched their belongings in silence. There was a knock on the door and the foreman stood there, his shirt buttons undone and his tie hanging loose. "Surveyors in now. Should be back up and running tomorrow. The boys are doing a whip around, trying to get enough credit together to send Sweeney home in style."

"He can have my haul." Jake said and Conrad seconded the motion.

"Thanks, boys. Got to take care of our own."

They walked out with only drink on their minds, yet Jake's eye was drawn to a man standing by the entrance. He wore a suede jacket and a sun tan. He had a thick moustache and a 44 colt strapped to his hip. "I'll catch you up," Jake said and no one spoke until Conrad was out of sight. "I hear you've been looking for me."

"Word travels fast here."

"It's a small town. Jake Leroux."

"Harold Johnson."

"You here to make my life difficult, Harold?"

"I'm afraid so."

"I don't suppose it would make a difference if I told you he started it?"

"Knowing Mick I'm almost certain he did, but family is family."

"All of your family in the business of killing?"

"We do what we have to do."

"Yeah well Slug did too much."

"Don't call him that!"

"He liked the name. He liked being despised. Slug just pushed his luck a little too far."

"I said don't call him that!" The man's hand brushed against the handle of his gun.

"Alright. Let's not get twitchy. You say your piece."

"You killed my brother. Facts are what they are. Can't let that go, got to have punishment."

"So you going to shoot me here?"

The moustache raised either side of Harold's face. "I said he's my brother, I didn't say we were alike. I'm not inclined to shooting an unarmed man."

"Me neither."

"Then what say you go and get yourself a gun and we solve this the old fashioned way?"

"There's no negotiating is there?" Harold shook his head. "Then give me a day to get myself right. We can do it down in front of the Darkside at seven tomorrow, have ourselves an audience."

"Don't you dream of running."

"Do I seem like a man who runs?"

"No, not really."

"Well, I'll be seeing you then." Jake walked and did not look back. He turned the corner, put his hands on his knees and threw up.

***

"You could have been on that shuttle." Conrad said as they watched Sweetney fade into the distance. The small group that had gathered near the launch centre began to thin and until only the two remained.

"Where would I go? This is my home, I've got nothing on the green and blue." They set off towards the Eldorado where dreams were made and died, their feet moving on auto-pilot. "If it doesn't go my way, I don't want a shuttle ride, put me beneath the rock."

The foreman greeted Jake with both hand and eyebrow raised. "Working today?"

"I'm not going to change just because someone wants to put a bullet in me. Why, Garry, you bored of paying me?"

"You're swapping a ton of titanium for a handful of nickel and lead; if all my pickmen were as chicken headed as you, Hammer, I'd have gone back earthside long ago." A ringing phone turned the foreman's attention. "Strike it rich, boys."

***

It felt like Jake couldn't miss. Every hit of the fork played a sweet melody, as container after container was filled and analysed. The result was always the same: Titanium. The analyser's incessant chiming drew a crowd, until only Jake's pick rumbled and hacked, the others content to watch a master at work. He felt the energy sap from his arms, but kept on hammering deeper into the moon's core. The container broke and he had to crawl and scramble up the slope to the metal ramp, rock carried in a leather sack that threatened to pull his spine out of shape. The analyser pinged one last time as the klaxon sounded and Jake stood staring down his plot, drawn to it with a mothlike obsession.

"Jesus, Hammer." The foreman stood in the doorway of the breakroom holding the counter sheets. "Would have sworn it was an error if half the pit weren't talking about it."

Jake noticed the man was sweating. "Aircon a little low, Garry?"

"I'm just the caretaker here, I do what I'm told and give what I'm given."

"Lay it out flat."

"You're owed more 50s than there are in all of Lunar. I've got an ammo dump coming my way tomorrow, but there won't be enough calibre to keep you loaded."

"How about we make deal." Jake stood up and stretched, the room filled with the sound of cracking bones. "If I walk back through those doors tomorrow we can work out a payment scheme, if not well then share it with the boys. I come out ahead either way I see it."

He walked back to The Happy Sleeper with weak knees. Passers-by stopped to say hello, wished him luck and said they would be there cheering on. There was still time to catch the last shuttle, but he didn't miss a step as he passed the launch centre. A man left nothing behind but a legacy. It came in many shapes and forms, but Jake did not have children, all he had was a name and the Hammer kept on hammering.

In his room he took a shower, ridding himself of dust and grime, shaved the stubble from his cheeks, then changed into his best outfit. The shirt and jacket were tight around the arms and chest. They were the clothes he had worn when he arrived at Lunar-South, a wide-eyed kid looking for a fortune. He'd had no reason to wear them, Lunar didn't have parties, restaurants or romance. There was only work and wine, neither of which had a dress code.

He put the Foreman's IOU in the strong box, took out his insurance policy and loaded it with six rounds of the .357 Magnums he received as a Christmas bonus. The gun had been the first indulgence that didn't end up with a headache. It had cost him four clips of 10s, but years later the stainless steel shone without a sign of a fingerprint. It felt heavy at his side as he attached the holster to his belt, but the great weight of tiredness began to fade.

***

There was no sport on Lunar, people worked, drank and shot at each other, there was little time for alternative recreation. As Jake approached the courtyard of the Darkside it felt like entering a stadium. A great circle of bodies had formed, as people jostled for position and climbed onto roof tops and balconies to get a better view. Heads turned as he was spotted, a cheer rose up and people parted patting him on the back as he walked through. In the clearing at the midst of the crowd, Harold Johnson stood impassive his jacket slung over a shoulder his other hand resting on the handle of his 44. Jake stopped twenty foot away with hands in his coat pockets. He withdrew one and brushed his hair from his eyes, then dragged the flap of his coat away from his hip showing off his gun.

"That's a nice piece you got there. What is it, Smith and Western Model 19?"

"It's a 66."

Harold whistled. "That's some pricey hardware."

"Figured this was as good a time as any to use it. So how are we doing this?"

Harold walked over to a nearby spectator and handed him his coat. He walked back to the centre of the clearing with slow steps, turning square on to face Jake with his legs spread wide. "We draw, I shoot, you die." The crowed moved from behind each man, flanking them in columns. "It's that simple."

"Is this really necessary?"

"Blood for blood, that's the way the world works."

"This ain't the world, my man."

"It turns just like it though. Shall we quit the yapping and get this over and done with?"

"You got a shuttle to catch?"

"Something like that."

Harold's hand went down to his waist and hovered over the handle of his gun. Jake could hear the crowd draw breath as he set his own hand in position, casually leaning left, but his eyes not moving from the man in front of him. The oxygen recyclers hummed and there was a rumble in the air as the last shuttle left for earth. Harold's shoulder twitched, thunder struck and cry of pain echoed off of the glass dome. Eyes turned to Jake whose gun remained in its holster, but whose jacket pocket had been torn open. The white of Harold's shirt began to turn a shade of red, as he staggered backwards the colour draining from his cheeks. His hand reached for his 44, but Jake already had his arm extended, the snub-nosed barrel of the Saturday Night Special pointed at the man's chest. "Don't." He said, but his target wasn't listening, so he shot once more and Harold hit the ground.

The old pickman walked over, his finger never moving from the trigger. Harold managed to free his gun, but Jake kicked it from his hand and it skidded off into the spectators. "You…" his breath had become short and erratic, the words came out with a smattering of blood. "You cheated."

"This is Lunar, Earthling. Think I was going to waste my hard earned money on the likes of you?" Jake walked to the Darkside but stopped at the door. "Get him to a doctor whilst he's still got enough of that precious blood of his." He pushed the door open and went inside whilst the word 'hammer' reverberated around the town.

***

The sun returned and Lunar-South faced a new dawn. The banks had come and with it law and order. Jake turned the corner on to Embassy Row, where the flags of nations hung unmoving. Somewhere amid the throngs of colourful stripes was the country of his birth, but he was a man of the moon through and through and would be till he died. "Sheriff." A lady said as she walked past and he nodded to her with a smile. It was still strange to see women walking the streets whose company had to be earned not bought. It was refreshing and the recycled air had a hint of perfume.

He saw two figures scatter as his metal heels hit the concrete. 'The Hammer' had switched from cracking rocks to skulls; it had been better to swim with the tide than fight the current. Not a day went by when he didn't miss the smell of dust or the analyser's ping, but the pride he felt pinning on his silver-plated badge was a feeling bullets couldn't buy. He turned the corner and came upon the square building of brick and steel that had once been Michaelson Munitions. Now the moon and star logo of Celestial Securities was etched onto the wall and it was fitting that the building that had once built bullets now worked to get them off the streets. Jake could hear the hubbub of drills as the new recruits were put through their paces. He swiped his card, the metal gate swung open, the watchman in his parapet threw him a salute and young patrolmen's backs straightening as he passed. Through the front doors of HQ he stopped to take messages from Carol at the front desk, then entered his office, hung his gun and belt on the coat rack and then collapsed into his chair. He pulled two aspirin from his desk drawer and swallowed. His head was still sore from The Darkside poker night, cards and chardonnay a dangerous combination for both his mind and wallet. He had barely closed his eyes when there was a knock at the door.

"Enter." The deputy walked in, deep bags beneath his eyes and a scowl on his face; he had lost more Lunar bucks than anyone, but something else appeared to be irking him. "What's up, Conrad?"

"We got a problem, Hammer."

"We do?"

"It's the Johnson Gang. They hit the credit depot last night."

"You sure it's them?"

"Looks that way, forensics' still pulling 44s out of the walls and the security detail."

Jake puffed out his cheeks and pushed himself upright. "Guess, we got to get to the bottom of this one." He strapped the model 66 back to his thigh and pushed his hat down on his head. "Let's pay my old pal Harold a visit." Lawmen came and went, but Jake the Hammer kept on digging.

Mathew Austin has a Master's degree in Creative Writing from Kingston University. He previously worked for a media trust contributing to the production of environmental films broadcast on BBC World. Mathew now hang art exhibitions and spend my time writing in London.

The Pied Pipers
By Petina Strohmer

The city of London was up in arms.
Vermin.
Everywhere.

Shops, hotels and restaurants were being hit particularly hard but tourist attractions, offices and even private residences were also suffering. It seemed that everyone, everywhere was affected.

The desperate mayor turned to the scientists for a solution, promising a huge financial reward to whoever could solve the problem. Many tried and failed but finally, one appeared to be up to the colossal challenge.

At last the besieged city council had something to offer its voters and a public meeting was announced. Industry leaders and community chiefs filled the biggest venue available and outside broadcasts fed the news to everybody else.

Met with boos and jeers, it took the mayor several minutes to calm the crowd before she could speak. "Ladies and gentlemen," she began, "I appreciate that you are angry --"

"Bloody furious!" someone called and the crowd descended into chaos again.

The mayor signalled to the sound crew to turn up the volume on her microphone. "Let me speak," she commanded.

The rabble was shocked into silence. She may not be popular at that moment but she was still the formidable figure that they had elected in the first place.

"Thank you," she said firmly. "Pestilence is a common but complex problem. Every city has its share of feral scavengers; foxes, pigeons, rats and the like."

"I would say it was more than our fair share now, wouldn't you?" Another voice was raised. "The whole city has become a mire of upended rubbish bins and animal shit!"

"Young man," the mayor chided him, "London survived the bubonic plague. I think we can handle a little vermin in this day and age."

A few rumbles rippled across the crowd but people were keen to hear of a solution to the problem that was destroying both their lives and their livelihoods. The mayor must have an answer or the long-awaited meeting wouldn't have finally been called.

"As our population intensifies and expands," the mayor explained, "we have become victims of our own success. The loss of natural habitat plus the abundance of food and shelter means that the animal population has increased alongside us."

The Green contingent grumbled but, sadly, they were too small to make themselves heard.

"There must be a balance," the mayor went on, "but, in recent times, it has tipped too far. As a result, property is being damaged and people, especially the tourists, are being driven away. There are no easy answers." She paused, almost daring the crowd to interrupt but she had their full attention now. "Obviously we can't use solutions that could damage people as well as animals so…" The audience watched the giant screen flicker into life. "I give you the BioExterm25 -- otherwise known as the Pied Piper."

The crowd stared at the image that materialized in front of them. Resembling a Jurassic Park raptor, it stood on piston legs, balanced by a strong tail. All four limbs brandished sabre-sharp

The Pied Pipers   Petina Strohmer

claws complimented by a set of razor teeth. Its 'eyes' were computerised blue optics with 'ears' like small radar dishes and an air vent acting as the 'nose.'

"The Pied Piper is a fully automated, self sufficient unit that has been programmed to recognise and exterminate undesirable life forms. It can run, climb, swim and fly." The image opened panels on its back and extended jet-propelled wings. "This enables it to pursue any form of prey over any terrain, allowing the swift and silent termination and disposal of a wide range of vermin."

The crowd began to buzz but were reduced to silence again as a parade of Pied Pipers marched onstage, their metal claws clacking on the checker plate floor. Once assembled, they turned to the audience, heads cocked like birds as they scanned the room through bright blue eyes.

The people became agitated under the sharp scrutiny.

Seeming to confer, several suddenly sprouted wings and took to the air while the others leapt from the stage and raced up and down the aisles.

The whole place erupted into shouts and screams, people scrambling over each other to escape this formidable threat.

However, the hunt was over almost as soon as it had started. The machines returned to the stage in unison and powered down, folding their wings away and squatting on their haunches. Eyes dimmed and ears became still.

It took a while longer to settle the crowd, many of whom eyed the machines fearfully, even in their 'resting' state.

"Impressive, eh?" The mayor smiled. "However, there is no need to be alarmed. You have just had a practical demonstration of not only their efficiency but also their safety. They are lethal to vermin." At this point, two of the machines opened their jaws and the bloody bodies of a rat and a pigeon fell onto the stage. "But they are completely harmless to human beings. Was anybody here injured?"

The people had to admit that, although terrified, no one had actually been hurt.

"I realise that the Pied Pipers will take a bit of getting used to," the mayor conceded, "but they will soon become as familiar as the refuse lorries that they are helping to keep the city clean. I have commissioned ten thousand units who can be patrolling the streets tomorrow."

***

The mayor was right; on both counts. People were initially fearful of these computerised killing machines and tourism dropped to an all-time low for the first few months. It was understandable; although The Pied Pipers remained true to the mayor's promise of animal attacks only, as they strutted the city streets, these metal monsters were as intimidating as hell. Rumours rumbled -- the fact that they didn't attack people with their sharp steel teeth and claws, didn't mean that they wouldn't -- ever. The locals had to learn to live with this, tourists didn't. Observing London's 'experiment' on the global stage, foreign visitors wisely decided to wait and see before they returned.

Just as beleaguered businesses were starting to despair, it became apparent that the Pied Pipers were working. The number of vermin had fallen steadily but no human had been harmed by these fearful 'creatures'. They had demonstrated their adaptability by recognising a rare swarm of wasps that descended upon the city as undesirable and eliminated them without harming other beneficial insects. The pigeon population was decimated but the ravens at the Tower of London and the native and migratory birds, were ignored. Rats were being eradicated but no cat was ever touched. Foxes disappeared but dogs remained safe. The corpses of the vermin were dumped into automated incinerators, leaving the city safe and clean. Adults, children and their pets seemed of no interest to the Pied Pipers at all.

It wasn't long before visitors returned to the city. In fact, the army of Pied Pipers became a tourist attraction in itself.

***

The Chief Commissioner at Scotland Yard was surprised by the figures before her. Pleased, but still surprised.

"Look," she told her officers, "the Met crime rate has fallen for the third month running -- and I've no idea why. I'd like to say that that there have been more arrests and successful prosecutions but those figures have remained the same. What's going on?"

"It's the same story in Vice," one officer replied. "We haven't picked up any more girls or their pimps lately yet there are definitely fewer on the street."

"Drug dealers too," a third officer joined in. "Even on the roughest estates. Local hospitals are reporting a significant increase in addicts being treated for sudden withdrawal."

The Chief Commissioner sighed. "In times of social unrest, perhaps we have a sudden rash of vigilantes on our hands. It happens. Sure, it helps keep the scum off the streets but we still can't allow mob rule."

"True." The officers agreed. "Sad, but true."

***

It had been noticed at street level too.

In the light of the recent unexplained disappearances, drug dealers upped their armoury and the prostitutes stopped working alone. Loose lips whispered about possible turf wars; starting with the loss of a few individuals, but possibly escalating into full-scale battles. The prospect of gang violence caused an increase in personal protection, but not everyone was afforded such security.

Charlie had been homeless for years. He knew how life on the streets worked and he had learned how to survive. There was safety in numbers but he hadn't seen some of his fellow 'hobos' for weeks. Rough sleepers went missing all the time and nobody noticed, much less cared, but Charlie's friends were as experienced as him and had been on the streets for as long.

Still, he had his own body and soul to keep together, a task that had become considerably easier now that there were so few animals scavenging alongside him in the bins. If anything changed on the streets, Charlie was the first to know and he, too, had regarded the arrival of the Pied Pipers with great suspicion. However, they hadn't harmed him, just reduced his competition. He was happy with that.

The bins at the back of the Grand Hotel often had the best pickings and tonight was no exception. Without needing to chase out the rats any more, Charlie had just climbed into one of the dumpsters when he heard noises outside. A fox possibly… but he knew what they sounded like, plus hadn't seen one of those for ages. Kitchen staff coming to chase him away again? It didn't sound like them either. Instead, it was a clacking, whirring, almost mechanical noise that he had never heard here before. But he had heard it somewhere. He was trying to remember where, when the inside of the bin was suddenly lit up by blue light and sharp metal claws clanged against the metal.

***

In the hallowed halls of Westminster, Sir Gregory Gallows M.P. was preparing to leave what he called 'work.' It had been yet another long, dull day, bearable only because of his plans for the evening.

Lucy, his oh-so-discreet P.A. appeared with the usual package.

"The usual I trust?" he grinned.

She smiled. "Of course; toiletries, a change of clothes and a little something special."

"You're an angel," he told her. "Where would I be without you?"

"In a lot of trouble, I imagine, sir."

He studied the young woman with a predatory leer. It's a shame she was quite so youthful. Oh, he knew plenty of colleagues who liked 'young girls' but he preferred a little more maturity than that. Still, it had been many years since he'd seen such perky boobs and a pert bottom...

The thought of his saggy wife reminded him to check. "What about-"

"I've already rung her and explained that you will be working late," Lucy replied. "Have fun."

"Oh, I will!" He slipped into the Gents to freshen up and then Sir Gregory was ready to go.

The wine bar wasn't far and the evening was warm so he decided to walk along the embankment rather than hail a cab. The moon gave the grey river Thames a silvery glint and as Sir Gregory walked, he could hear the phone in his pocket clinking against the key.

He and Sophie had been lovers for nearly a year now but recently, she seemed to be cooling off. His mistress was a classy lady – a world away from the dirty girls on dirty street corners – and he intended to re-ignite her flame with the key to their own little love nest. His wife would never know and he could always write the place off as a tax loss. After all, what else were his excessive expenses for?

There was a noise behind him and he turned.

Nothing.

There weren't many people out and about that evening, not even the ladies who lurked in the shadows. In fact, he hadn't seen any of them for weeks.

He shrugged and walked on.

Crossing the road, there were no signs of the drunks and druggies that used to dwell in the dark either.

No pigeons, no prostitutes, no pissheads.

No pests at all.

Perfect.

The only person he missed was the beggar in the alleyway by the side of the wine bar. The filthy old man, dressed in tatters, had a military tattoo on his forearm.

Sir Gregory's career in the Armed Forces was brief and boring – sitting safely behind a desk with some of his old friends from Oxford, but he had just enough soul left in him to feel a twinge of guilt whenever he passed this man without throwing a little loose change at him. The beggar was so pathetically and publicly grateful that Sir Gregory had got used to the sanctimonious satisfaction of "doing his bit," especially when there was someone else around to see him do it.

Tonight, there were quite a few people drinking at the tables outside the bar to witness his generosity – but the beggar had disappeared.

Sir Gregory knew Sophie would be late. Sophie was always late, so he reckoned he had time to find the military man, walk him back to the top of the alley and then make a big display of giving him a note or two. He was prepared to dig deep for a good audience.

He set off in the gloom. As the wine bar didn't serve food, the alley never stank of rotting organic waste – apart from the beggar, of course. Where was he?

In the distance, he could see a figure laying face down on the cobbles. Had the man been downing what was left in the discarded bottles and then passed out? Just when Sir Gregory wanted to use him for a little P.R How inconsiderate! Sir Gregory Gallows, M.P. believed that he was due some bang for his buck.

Behind him, bottles clinked but he assumed it was just more empties being thrown out.

He kicked the prone figure. "Come on, soldier. Up and at 'em. There's a good chap."

There was no response.

Sir Gregory kicked him harder. "Get up, man. You're missing a golden opp—oh!"

Dark fluid ran from beneath the body, too viscous to be wine.

Suddenly, everything was bathed in blue light and metal teeth slid over each other like the sound of sharpening knives.

Sir Gregory was too shocked, too swiftly, to scream.

***

London fell.

Nobody noticed when the low life and destitute disappeared. C.E.O.s, bankers and politicians were another matter. That's when the contents of the incinerators were examined and human remains found.

Having watched and learned, the Pied Pipers evolved and adapted, just as they were programmed to do. So their makers had no control over them when they concluded that humans were, in fact, the only undesirable species in the city.

The people have all gone now but the city is far from deserted. Nature has gleefully reclaimed the space and all kinds of flora and fauna proliferate. The 'vermin' that were once persecuted are now protected by the very machines that were designed to destroy them. It is rumoured that the Pied Pipers have even learned to laugh. Who said that computers would never understand irony?

Petina Strohmer is a traditionally published novelist who has also had thirty stories published in different anthologies. One was a #1 Amazon bestseller in October 2024. She lives in the magical Welsh mountains, U.K. with a raggle-taggle assortment of rescued animals. For more information, go to www.petinastrohmer.com.

For a Few $ollars More

By Anthony Boulanger

Samantha « Sam » Spade, human, wanted in five systems, 3,000 $ollars
Ace of Spade, AI and spaceship, wanted in three systems, 500 $ollars

The ship unfolded and left string space in the regulatory zone of its destination solar system, seeming to emerge from nothing in the skip of a heartbeat. This was almost what happened: the phenomenon was in fact instantaneous. Immediately, the onboard AI reoriented the ship for the comfort of its passengers and aligned itself with the nearby asteroid belt. New Nevada, the yellow dwarf, illuminated its hull with a white light, harsh and terrible despite the distance separating the ship and the star. Tiny black spots were still discernible, like so many warnings for all those who crossed this cyclopean gaze. In this system, you had to be strong and tough.

No sooner had the ship completed its rotation on itself than it deployed around it a hundred drones, which surrounded it and flew alongside. The ship was a heavy metal assembly, a black cobblestone with a shoddy, unwieldy appearance, a far cry from the ships streamlined to penetrate planetary atmospheres. On board, according to the registers, second-class merchandise has been stored in a hurry, passengers who couldn't afford anything better crammed into vermin-infested dormitories, under the guidance of a crew reduced to a minimum and the protection of a most dubious mercenary. With a three-day beard, a wide-brimmed hat pulled down his back, a synthetic wool poncho over his shoulders and an antique Smith & Wesson around his waist, the man in question had all the makings of a space cowboy in search of adventure.

— Welcome to Far Space," commented the ship's captain, analysing the information being transmitted to him by the enslaved Artificial Intelligence. "From now on, we've got three days' flying time before we reach our destination. We have it on our good side that Hangmen Planet is currently on the other side of its star..."

— Three days?" suddenly worried the passenger representative. "But that's not at all what was planned! Do you realise what can happen in that time? We're right in Laura Della Rose's zone of action!"

— She won't be a problem, tenderfoot...," intervened the space cowboy. "She was arrested three reference-months ago in the Cherokee system and hanged along with her men."

With his feet up on one of the side consoles, the man lit a cigarette, despite the unkind glance from the captain.

— I told you when you hired me," he continued. "With Jesse James on board, no one will dare take you on. Not Sundance Kid or Doc Holliday or whoever."

Jesse James laughed out loud and casually touched his gun at his side.

— You've got the sharpest trigger in the Outer Rim and its drones. That's why you pay such a high price to get where you're going.

***

Hidden away from her target's electronic sensors, Samantha Spade watched the transporter fly at cruising speed along the asteroid belt. Everything matched the information the outlaw had gathered. The model of the ship, its time of arrival, the deployment of the drones betraying the presence of Jesse James... For the rest, she had to trust her instincts. Spade was convinced that in the metal bowels lay much more than a few tons of seed, fertiliser and farm machinery. Farmers exiling themselves from New Arkansas to come and lose themselves in this area would hardly have been able to afford a trip through the space of strings and such an escort as James was asking for with the proceeds from their farms. Settlers would have travelled in convoys, by slower and more conventional means. It was perhaps the booty of the century that was flying before her eyes, and she was the only one on the spot. The other outlaws scouring this part of the galaxy had other things to worry about than a supposedly small transport of farmers.

— Ace, it's time to make Jesse James and his drones dance," said the woman to her onboard AI. "Have you adjusted your calculations according to their speed?"

— Who do you think I am?" replied a synthetic voice. "You've forgotten who I am, you little organic runt! I'm going to take you back to your backwater and herd cows if you keep this up!"

Samantha Spade allowed herself a wry smile. She loved teasing the Artificial Intelligence on her ship and it was always quick to react to her jabs and remarks.

— So, let's go, let's get this tub over with," she ordered.

Immediately, tiny stars appeared in the Spades' field of vision. They lit up in the asteroid belt, silent deflagrations and white explosions against a black background, knocking stray rocks out of their orbits. In a matter of seconds, a shower of meteorites rained down on the massive ship, which took evasive action as a matter of urgency. Several drones broke away from the group to avoid being hit by the mineral behemoths. Just as Sam Spade and Ace had planned. A second series of explosions dazzled the belt, a second shower of stone joined by the first fragments, projected again by the calculated deflagrations towards the outlaw's target. The rocks met at full speed and pulverised, generating new shards, smaller, less detectable and more dangerous. A veritable three-dimensional spider's web in which the prey was engulfed, attracting the lightest rocks with its own mass. A horror for the ship captains who could no longer navigate on their own, a horror for the artificial intelligences who couldn't calculate so many trajectories and couldn't anticipate new explosions. And when they could no longer trust physics and logic, there was only one thing they could do. Rely on human failure.

***

— Sir," said one of the crew. "The AI has just given up on us. It's looped into its probability calculations."

The ship's main organ had just abandoned its captain, and he was watching the fractions of asteroids pass in front of the observation bay in silence, slumped in his armchair. He was a small carrier, not one to be attacked. He was armed, but what could he do to fight his way through this mineral magma? A dull thump, soon followed by a second, made him sit up. He thought he saw the vibrations spread over his head and take over the whole cabin, like a death knell to him. At this rate, the hull wasn't going to hold. If it took one of the larger rocks head-on, they would all end up scalded by the depressurisation and frozen by the vacuum of space.

— We're abandoning ship," he heard himself say in disbelief.

— No, you're not. You're not doing anything. That's exactly what your guy wants you to do.

Jesse James rose from his seat. He had clipped a control panel onto his left arm and was sliding the fingers of his right hand over it.

— This is what I was hired for, so I'm going to sort it out. We're dealing with a clever one. He's made you deaf and blind by messing with your AI and he's got you locked up. I don't know if he wants to come and plunder you while you're still alive or wait for the meteorites to destroy this stagecoach, but I'm not going to be taken for a ride.

In front of the transporter, James's drones had assembled to form a shield against which the rocks were bouncing. Others, isolated from the structure, landed on the largest fragments and diverted them from their trajectory by activating their reactors.

— Step on it, we're getting out of here. Head for the sun, it's probably hidden in the asteroid belt.

Submitting willingly to the mercenary's orders, the crew regained control of the ship and launched the heavy craft forward. Streams of red light shot out from the drones, striking the larger asteroids around the transporter. Jesse James expected his attacker to appear from behind one of the rocks and hoped to surprise him and cut him in half. On his control panel, he controlled the lasers with one finger and held the shield in place with the other. Mute shocks deformed the wall as it picked up speed and swung like a prow against the rocks, but it held firm. Other impacts punctuated the hull and the ship's captain monitored the pressures in the outer compartments, ready to isolate any leaks if they were detected.

— Don't move," a female voice suddenly declared with authority.

The order was punctuated by the pressure of a cannon on James's back and he immediately found himself relieved of his revolver. Turning slowly despite the threat, the space cowboy discovered a tall, young woman with brown hair tucked under a hat. She herself took two steps back, keeping him at gunpoint. Beneath her blue eyes, the figure of the spade from the playing cards was tattooed.

— Samantha Spade," commented the mercenary.

— Jesse James," greeted the woman in return. "I don't believe we've been introduced before, so it's a surprise and an honour that you know my name."

— And if you know mine, kid, you should know better than to mess with me… I'm going to skin you and save it for wiping my boots.

— That's an interesting programme. I'd love to chat with you about the details, but I've got a ship to plunder, you see.

Spade hissed and a metal spider the size of a large hand appeared from the passageway. The silver patina of its body was engraved with the same symbol as the one on the outlaw's cheek. The robot nimbly scaled James's trousers and reached the drone control panel. Two of its legs became wires that connected to the peripheral.

— It's OK, Sam, I've taken control of the little ones. I'll get them to open the cargo hold.

— You're not going to get away with this, you know?" James announced with a predatory grin, without moving despite the robotic presence on his arm. "No one infiltrates a ship I'm guarding, no one uses my own drones, no one tricks me and, above all, no one threatens me with my gun."

— And yet I've managed to do all four in so few minutes.

Scanning the deck, Spade watched for the slightest suspicious movement. She had disarmed the most dangerous adversary of the lot, but that didn't mean that someone else wasn't armed. Whether it was the captain or the man she guessed was a passenger, someone would act, even if it meant killing Jesse James.

In their eyes, it was a small loss anyway. Out of zeal rather than real necessity, she fired a single shot near the hand of an officer who tended to get a little too close to one of the consoles.

— It can be done without bloodshed," said Samantha. "Or I could just as easily riddle everyone and save myself a lot of unnecessary stress..."

— And that's it," said Ace, indifferent to what was happening around him, "I've got their AI under surveillance. It's locked in its calculations for several more days, I've injected new parameters. Extraction of the cargo bay contents is underway. Eighteen per cent empty, so far."

— I have to admit that the asteroid trick was a good one," says Jesse James. "But how did you get on this tub? I had the belt under my eyes the whole time."

— You were looking the wrong way," replied Spade with a shrug. "We were hidden just in front of a sunspot, in the chromosphere, undetectable, but we had you in our sights. We just arrived on the side that you weren't watching. There's nothing easier afterwards for an AI like Ace to take over a ship by balancing the pressure with my own building... Ace, how far have you got?"

— Thirty-five percent, ongoing.

Samantha Spade sheathed her Colt and kept only her opposite number's Smith & Wesson in her hand. She found it incredibly light compared to her weapon and wondered for a moment if she wasn't going to make it her own. It would undoubtedly be the ultimate humiliation for Jesse James, and she would make him her lifelong adversary. But, on the other hand, with such a weapon at her side, she was sure to draw faster than anyone else. With a flick of her wrist, she shooed the ship's captain away and took her place on the seat, still with James at the end of her gun, and put her feet up on the console facing him.

— You have no idea what you're stealing," said the farmer.

The man's intervention reinforced Samantha's position. His tone was too calm, too cold to be that of a man of the land seeing his livelihood disappear. The words were more of a threat than a plea.

— The passengers have started to show up," Ace commented. "I've welded the doors shut, but they'll be breaking them in soon."

— Estimate?

— Two minutes and eighteen seconds.

— Divert a line of carbon dioxide to the corridors and rooms they're occupying, it'll knock them out.

Without taking her eyes off her new interlocutor, without lowering the revolver, Spade stood up and reversed towards the passageway she had used to reach the bridge. Through the observation bay, she watched the cracks appear in the drone wall as the flying machines hijacked by Ace left the area after loading into the cargo bay.

— You tried to be discreet with your little manoeuvre, but it worked against you. You're not a military man, you wouldn't have been afraid to play hardball. You're not very familiar with local customs and weapons, otherwise you wouldn't have hired a mercenary. I suppose I'll have to guess who you really are when I open the containers.

A second and then a third spider joined the woman.

— Pipe rerouted," said one of them. "Seventy-eight per cent of ship's cargo recovered."

— Superb. Scarping now. Ace, restart the engines, send a distress signal to Hangmen Planet for our guests and, well, it was a pleasure to cross your path. See you all again!

With that last tirade, the outlaw left the hostages' field of vision. Jesse James immediately ripped the spider from his arm and sent it across the room, but it simply gave an unnatural laugh as it clung to a wall. The ace of spades on its body began to glow and, as Samantha Spade's ship passed in front of the one she had just looted, it exploded in an electromagnetic discharge which fried the nearest circuits.

Update in progress
Samantha « Sam » Spade, human, wanted in (five) systems, (3,000) $ollars
Ace of Spade, AI and spaceship, wanted in (three) systems, (500) $ollars

It was only as she prepared to withdraw her ship into the space of the strings that Sam Spade allowed herself a breath. As she pressed the controls, she felt her muscles go weak, the adrenalin that had sustained her until then disappearing from her system. Jesse James would be a threat the next time they met, but the man wouldn't be able to follow her until he was out of the powdery pile she'd trapped him in, at which point he'd have to choose between his livelihood as a mercenary and the manhunt. The reward for her capture was not yet one that attracted bounty hunters.

The ship reappeared a handful of light years from the position it had occupied just a few seconds ago, close to a tiny spheroid that the Spades had taken over. For the moment, it was the ideal hiding place. A mass of silica vitrified by an ancient space battle, without interesting raw materials, apart from the booty it held, and no atmosphere. It was far from any point of interest, and close to a pulsar that jammed any equipment that wasn't compatible with its radiation frequency. No one, not even other outlaws cruising in this corner of the galaxy, had yet manoeuvred close to it. A miners' tracking probe had explored the area for a while but failed to find the entrance to the labyrinth in the glass structure.

Around the pulsar's satellite, the transport modules, extracted from the ship, orbited. Two metal spiders, larger than previous incarnations of Ace of Spade and equipped with jet engines, manoeuvred and swooped into the hideout at regular intervals to protect the loot from any unwelcome onlookers.

— I've started a summary analysis of our catch," began Ace. "They all have the same mass, the same volume. I've taken the initiative of storing them in the same atmosphere as the ship's holds."

— Was it a special atmosphere?" the woman wondered.

— Reference dry human atmosphere, twenty-one percent oxygen, seventy-eight percent nitrogen.

Samantha didn't react immediately. With her hands on the controls, she had switched to manual piloting, although Ace was in a position to bring her safely to her destination. Flying through the maze of dark glass she was approaching was a constant pleasure for her and gave her a few moments to think. Had she removed biological material? Perhaps collector's items for a reserve of rare specimens? Or, more ironically, had she plundered colleagues on their way to an organ dealer?

As she approached the string of laser-cut bends in the amorphous mass, Samantha Spade allowed herself a smile. She loved irony.

— I hope the short passage through the void didn't affect anything in this case. Have one of these containers brought to the hangar, I want to see what's inside as soon as we land.

***

Once the ship had come to a halt, Samantha and several spiders gathered around the dull grey module on the floor. The only decoration on it was an inscription: DOPPEL 0328. She drew her Colt and Smith & Wesson, more to give herself composure than out of any real need. In the event of danger, Ace would analyse it and react much more quickly than any human. The artificial intelligence had enough copies of himself to sacrifice a few to save the human he had bonded with.

— Open this, Ace," ordered Samantha. "Let's see what we've got."

One of the spiders approached the module's control panel. It was rudimentary, but it still took cracking a password for the lock to groove and begin to open with a hiss. Nobody was moving around the mass. It unfolded its walls like a macabre metal flower, releasing a chill that the hangar ventilation gradually dissipated. On the floor, a humanoid figure lay in a foetal position. The creature was the size of a three- or four-year-old Earthling, but its body was covered in a film of mercury. This reproduced the surroundings, and the images distorted by the curvature of the limbs multiplied with the reflections. The face was an equally smooth surface, devoid of mouth, nose or eyes. It was a bald oval, with no lines, no eyebrows, no distinctive features.

After several long seconds of waiting, Sam decided to approach the creature. With the barrel of her Colt, she tried to push the body, but the epidermis deformed like an elastic membrane, and the revolver sank into it. The outlaw immediately drew her weapon again, without the body seeming the least bit affected.

— What is this stuff?" she declared aloud.

— According to my analyses, which are rudimentary when it comes to biology, but it wouldn't hurt if you spent a few dollars on it," the AI said, "it's alive."

Sam Spade waited for the rest, but nothing came.

— Is that it? You've got to be kidding me. No idea what it is?

— A hunch. As far as I'm concerned. Because I'm just an Artificial Intelligence, O lady of Organic Intelligence.

With little taste for her team-mate's scathing remark, Spade crouched down next to whatever was holding the creature's face when it opened one eye. Or rather, when an eye appeared. Or to be more precise, when the reflection of Samantha's eye stopped following the movements of the original eye. It was the second eye's turn to give in to the same phenomenon, and soon the nose and mouth followed. Spade's features froze on mercury's face, which gradually grew cheekbones and eye sockets, lips and nostrils. The humanoid stood and, in the center of a circle of onlookers, woman and spider drones, which widened as it receded, adorned itself with the reflections of the woman's clothes, then began to swell and distort until it reached Spade's height. In its hand, like the original, the being of mercury held a Colt and a Smith & Wesson, conjured out of thin air but looking very real. They shone in the same way, seemed to weigh in their owner's hand in the same way. Samantha was looking at her exact replica.

— Bloody hell..." she murmured.

She saw the creature's lips move, catching a fleeting glimpse of a mouth of darkness, devoid of tongue or teeth. She immediately emptied both her weapons into the body facing her. Twelve bullets perforated the head and trunk, exited and struck the walls of the hangar. There was no bleeding, no apparent wounds apart from the projectile entrances that cut neat holes in the creature. The creature seemed unaffected and lowered what was left of its head towards what was left of its body. It took another step, unaware of the gas escaping from its wounds or the crumbling that its body was undergoing every second. Spade hastily grabbed her cartridges from her shoulder strap, reloaded her Colt and held the thing at gunpoint.

— Not another step!" she shouted.

A certain hysteria, far from her usual calm and cynicism, was perceptible in her tone and words. Her hand trembled at this disintegrating monster, this double of herself she had shot at point-blank range, but which was still advancing, more and more slowly, until it crumbled into dust at her feet. Samantha fell to her knees. Her hands clenched and unclenched beyond her control, her fingers brushing the triggers. She was barely aware of Ace's incarnations, putting away the weapons, then lifting her up and taking her to her quarters. She fell asleep and, in her restless sleep, that smooth face kept coming back to take over her features and, in the voice of Jesse James, predict her certain death.

Update complete
Samantha « Sam » Spade, human, wanted in seven systems, 12,000 $ollars
Ace of Spade, AI and spaceship, wanted in five systems, 2,500 $ollars

In the shadow of her human companion's bedroom, Ace of Spade kept watch. The Artificial Intelligence had spent time on the virtual networks that his fellow creatures had woven since their appearance, under the very noses of humans. It was aware of the danger and knew that an AI that was too curious, in the service of Spade's victims or a bounty hunter, might try to trace its origins, but it had multiplied the relays and decoys on its virtual route. In exchange for some information on the movements of sheriffs in the systems he knew, he obtained details of a platinum mine to be built on a moon of a nearby gas giant, information which he sold to a new chemical AI in exchange for analysis of the results he had collected from the creature's dusty corpse. He already had a cluster of converging intuitions in place, drawn from galactic urban legends, between the name DOPPEL that each module bore, and the appearance and abilities of the beings trapped inside, but when his interlocutor revealed that the properties of the powder matched those of stabilised ununennium, he knew he'd been right. What he and Sam had recovered was far more valuable than it looked. Ace plunged into more dangerous layers of information, monitored by government and police AI, and grazed the networks he was interested in.

—What on Earth have we got ourselves into?
— What are you mumbling about?" asked Sam.
— Aren't you supposed to be asleep?

— Little computer on legs, you think it's simple after what I've seen? Tell me what you've found out instead of playing the mother hen card.

— I think for once we've seen too much. If my sources are correct, and believe me, I've come across them several times... Let me start at the beginning... Do you know the Iroquois?

— I know the Iroquois system, but I've never been there. It's a few dozen light years from here, I think.

— Fifty-eight to be exact. They're at the cutting edge of atomic and quantum research. They have been involved in exploiting string space for space travel, for example. They have succeeded in synthesising a number of artificial atoms that were reputed to be completely unstable. And there's a rumour going round the networks about the Doppelgänger project.

Samantha rose from her bunk and faced the AI.

— Originally," Ace continued, "the Iroquois wanted to create bodies capable of housing their spirits once their original envelope had become too old. One thing leading to another, they would have created hollow shells capable of imitating any form of life by gradually metamorphosing on contact with the original and absorbing its spirit, its memories and its personality."

— And you think that's what we got?

— I'm sure of it. It all matches up. What we witnessed, the names of the modules, and I ran a facial ID on the passengers. Most of them are scientists from the Six Nations of the Iroquois. I think they were on their way to Hangmen Planet for the Doppelgängers to take over the local planetary leaders. They're all due to meet in a week's time. Can you imagine an army of subservient doppelgängers? They would have controlled the politics of the region in no time.

Spade approached the large opening in the glass of the asteroid. It opened directly onto the hangar where her ship was awaiting her will and where incarnations of Ace were busy with handling and maintenance. She could imagine the scene perfectly, having witnessed the metamorphosis of one of the doppelgängers. She could almost see lines of Samantha Spade within range of her ship, scouring the region, filling the asteroid in an uninterrupted stream with the proceeds of their plunder. A gang of double-crossers with a single objective: to enrich their original.

— My dear Ace, we're going to be rich in no time.

Samantha « Sam » Spade, human, wanted in twelve systems, 345,000 $ollars
Ace of Spade, AI and spaceship, wanted in nine systems, 57,500 $ollars

Hovering over the farm, Ace watched the doppelgängers deploy. They were all armed with the same revolvers as Samantha, all wore red scarves around their mouths and differed only in the numbers on their hats, replicas of the module numbers that Ace used to coordinate the attacks.

— Eighteen and three hundred and twelve, look out, a shooter on the roof of the barn.

Immediately, the creature reacted by throwing a stun grenade in the direction of the threat and continued their advance. Their target was a load of phosphate and raw materials that had arrived earlier and, naturally, the gang wanted to seize them to sell to the highest bidder. The farmers - real farmers this time - had put up some resistance, which was quickly quelled by the skill with which the creatures handled their weapons. Whether it was this attack or the dozens of previous ones, there had never been a single human casualty. Samantha was very clear about this. Killing civilians was pointless as long as she wasn't in danger herself. Disabling them was enough. On this subject, Ace would have imagined that his companion would have sheathed her six-shooter, with her new recruits able to carry out everything for her, but she was too addicted to the adrenalin and thrills of raids to stay and monitor operations. In fact, she was ready to break down a door, the AI noted, with her hat visibly blank of any numbers.

Leaving the monitoring of the operation to an automatic subroutine, Ace of Spade connected to his own cybernetic copies to assess the situation in the various systems where they were in action. There, a space convoy assault was going well near Rope Planet, while a diamond mine was under full-scale siege in the Tannen system. A bank raid on a moon was coming to an end, and the Doppelgängers were leaving the building with bags full of the local currency. A few light years away, Ace was hanging on to a crystal cable linking two moons and blocking the path of a space lift. The AI realised that his association with Sam had been taken to a new level, a level never reached by any other outlaw. The level where a multiplied AI worked with a human duplicated in several hundred copies too. The company's secret didn't seem to have been uncovered, and the two originals made up one of the most renowned duos in Far Space, living up to the reputation of Billy the Kid and Calamity Jane.

The main incarnation of Ace was suddenly summoned to a particular location and it temporarily supplanted the copy in the heavy ship there. A very specific face had been identified among the opponents of the Doppelgänger looting a train. Jesse James. The space cowboy was pouring bullets into the rock behind which the creature had taken refuge, swearing at the top of his voice. The man was attacking without a drone this time, having obviously learnt his lesson from his first encounter with the Spades. What was Ace to do in such a situation? The AI calculated the various possibilities, ranking them in order of feasibility and interest. From his position, he could lodge a projectile behind the man's ear, retrieve the double, retreat into the space between the strings and call for reinforcements, but there was one parameter he could hardly estimate: what was the real Samantha going to do about Jesse James? Before he could find a satisfactory answer, he saw the Doppelgänger do a somersault and, with a shot of frightening precision, put a paralysing bullet right through the heart of his opponent. The creature then went on to loot the train.

Ace immediately left the supervision of operations to return to the one in which the real Sam was taking part. In the short space of time, his group had made off with the phosphate and the materials they were looking for. Spiders were loading the ship, which had landed on autopilot. The AI transferred to one of the small robots and crawled over to the human, who was busy rolling a cigarette on a haystack, gazing approvingly at her booty which was piling up in the hold.

— We've got an imponderable that I'd like to leave you in charge of," says Ace.

— Come on..., the last time you told me that was when one of the Doppelgängers got shot. Didn't you manage to make the body disappear this time?

— No, that's a different kind of problem. I've got a visual on Jesse James, paralysed on the ground by one of your doubles. How do you want to dispose of him?

Samantha didn't answer immediately. She tapped her cigarette to pack the tobacco at the bottom of the rolled leaf, raised it to her lips and then took a match from a box. She scraped the stick against her sole and took a long puff, which she breathed out through her nose.

— Let's leave him a message. In the ground, if possible. He'll be tracking us, now that he's seen me. Meet him in three months' time on Hangmen Planet for a duel. He won't be able to refuse that kind of offer. And make sure the doppelganger takes his gun, that'll annoy him even more.

— OK. But why three months? Why not in two hours, when the sedative wears off? It's not like you need to prepare yourself, is it?

— Because we're about to reach a milestone. In three months' time, the rewards on our heads will be nothing like they are now.

— If only mine could catch up with yours, with everything I'm doing. That's discrimination against AIs, lady!

Samantha « Sam » Spade, human, wanted in sixty-eight systems, 950,000 $ollars
Ace of Spade, AI and spaceship, wanted in forty-four systems, 300,000 $ollars

It was pain that woke Jesse James. An intense burning that radiated through his body like pulsating waves from his heart to the ends of his limbs. For a moment, he wondered if he was dead. The thought terrified him. His head ached from the impact of Spade's bullet and he couldn't move. If he was dead and condemned to retain the use of his senses, then he would prefer to be sent into a sun to put a radical and definitive end to his torment. The space cowboy tried to speak, but his tongue wouldn't respond. He concentrated on his senses, but heard nothing, smelt nothing, felt no heat. Only a regular heartbeat that reassured him somewhat. It had to be his heart, the organ had escaped paralysis.

Above him, the sun of this world continued its slow course, indifferent to what was happening on the ground of the planets it showered with its rays. Fortunately, his eyes were in the shade and did not suffer the direct burns that the sun might otherwise have inflicted. It took several more hours before he could bat his eyelids on his burning eyes, then a handful more before tingling spread through his fingers. He was able to move fully the next morning, after a night with a parched throat, weeping dry eyes and constant sensations of pain. When he struggled to his feet, he immediately put his hand to his side and spat out his frustration. Spade's minx had stolen his gun again. She should have killed him rather than let him live again. As he picked up his hat, he discovered the message left for him. Three months... That would be just enough time for him to recover. He had to find enough money to buy a proper gun and travel to Hangmen Planet. After this new humiliation, this new blot on his record, he was going to find it hard to get hired anywhere. Spade was going to pay for that too.

Samantha « Sam » Spade, human, wanted in three hundred and twelve systems, 3,000,000 $ollars, dead or alive
Ace of Spade, AI and spaceship, wanted in two hundred and twenty-eight systems, 2,000,000 $ollars, activated or not

When Ace first flew over the village where Spade and James were due to meet, he scanned the area and found no human presence. It was with a pang of relief running through his circuits that he deposited his human in the alleyway with all the containers she had asked to bring. She had chosen to come alone, without sending a Doppelgänger to fight in her place, without a single one of her copies posted to watch the area and protect her if necessary. Alone in a village haunted by wind and dust.

***

When the AI had asked her about this, about her reasons for acting in this way, Sam had just smiled sadly. She put her hand on the spike that adorned the spider, then spoke in a slow voice.

— Put it down to the irrational impulses that still differentiate organic from artificial intelligence. Or doubles," she added.

Ace then turned his sensors all around him, on the hundreds of doppelgängers who were busy taking stock of the human's wealth, discussing strategies for future attacks and repairing the ships of all sizes in which he was duplicated.

— You are looking at a hive of which I am the queen," Samantha continued. "But I'm not an insect. I've given enough of my time and myself to make these creatures as complete as we needed them to be. Now the Queen has to remember that she is alive too and why she embarked on this lawless career. I can hardly remember..."

— And what reason is that?

— The thrill, Ace, the thrill. To be a hunted loner, to live by your wits without knowing what tomorrow will bring. Discovering new stars, new worlds, flying free. Insidiously, I've chained myself to this asteroid that I no longer recognise, to richness that I've blinded myself with and don't know what to do with.

— You could buy yourself immortality. An eternity of thrills.

The AI analysed that it was losing its companion. She had never said anything like that before and her tone was filled with echoes of grief.

— What's the point? The thrill is putting your life on the line. Take care of that money. Use it to help the less fortunate, defend causes that are just. You have the resources and the intelligence to know what to do with it. You have billions of potential $ollars. Deliver a doppelgänger to a sheriff, and you'll get three million more every time.

When the time for the duel approached, Ace withdrew at Spade's request into the lower layers of the atmosphere. Using his sensors, he followed the human's preparations. She had taken out containers and strapped several revolvers to her waist, legs and trunk. There was her trusty Colt, Jesse James's two Smith & Wessons and other models gleaned from her wanderings. She wasn't preparing for simple hand-to-hand combat.

Ace realised this when he saw the fleet of spaceships passing him by. He recognised the models, the fingerprints on the network of AIs that accompanied most of the bandits and bounty hunters in the galaxy. There was Jesse James leading the fleet, then Calamity Jane, Doc Holliday, Soapy Smith, Butch Cassidy, Masterson, the Youngers... Samantha Spade hadn't just warned the space cowboy she'd trapped twice, she'd let him talk about this meeting with the woman who was now worth three million dollars to the whole galaxy. She had waited three months to increase her bounty and give everyone time to regroup. To become the target. And the galaxy had answered her call.

In a matter of seconds, Ace gained altitude and turned his sensors away from the village and the planet's surface. He folded in on himself in the space of the strings and disappeared from this system as the first shots were fired below.

— Goodbye..., my friend...," he murmured.

***

Epilogue
Queen of Heart, human, wanted in two systems, 200 $ollars
Ace of Heart, AI and spaceship, wanted in one system, 100 $ollars

After the third attack on mining ships, Queen contemplated the booty piling up in the hold of her tiny ship. A spider, its thorax stamped with the heart symbol, climbed her shoulder and came to nestle in her neck, drawing a discreet laugh from her.

— I've got an idea how we can make a lot of money at once," said the woman. Get richer and richer, and set up a gang worthy of the name! With a fleet of at least a hundred ships. I've spotted a suspicious transfer of equipment, and I'm willing to bet you there's something fishy going on. They're going to pass close to an asteroid belt that we could blow up and trap them in the debris. That would render their engines and weapons useless, and all we'd have to do is open the cargo holds like a tin can. Can you calculate all that for me?

Ace looked at the profile of the human he was perched on. He'd spent Sam's entire fortune cloning her body, a true human body, and accelerating its growth, multiplying specimens until he found the exact size of his friend, the same hair colour, the same blue pupils, the same freckles and beauty spots on her nose and cheeks... To find the same personality, the same ambition. The same faults and qualities. He remembered a similar discussion a few years ago, the one that had led to his meeting Jesse James.

— No..." said the spider. "Being rich? We don't need that. You don't need that. What you want is the thrill, right?"

Born in the Rouen area of France, **Anthony Boulanger** now lives in the Norman countryside in the company of his muse and their three children. He works on short stories, novels, and scripts for role-playing games and comics in the fantasy and science-fiction genres. His favorite subjects are birds, golems, and world mythologies.

The Last Actor
By Matthew McKiernan

Oliver Tipps never imagined that the last movie he'd star in would be about his life. Then again, it made sense that the final film featuring a human actor should be about that actor. Fat raindrops bounced off Oliver's ebony trench coat as he strutted over the fine streets of New York City to Studio 51. Oliver wondered if this was what the last of the bards had felt like. The doors to the studio slid open. The lobby was no different from that of a dentist's office. It smelled the same as well. Oliver checked in at the front desk terminal, and the door in the back unlocked.

No one else was here. Oliver couldn't remember the last time there had been. He put his coat on a rack, flipped his holophone, and hit record. "Today is December 19th, 2097. I just arrived at the studio. I could have done this at home, but I wanted to do it here. I think it will mean more that way. It's the easiest thing in the world for an actor to play himself, but then again, I always thought my life was boring. That's why I became an actor in the first place."

Oliver found himself choking back tears. "Becoming an actor allowed me to live hundreds of thrilling lives and have unforgettable experiences. I mean, I got to go to the Moon and Mars! My fans, I couldn't have done this without your support for almost sixty years. Now that it's all over, I don't know what I'm going to do."

Oliver ended his vlog and posted it on All Space. He wiped his eyes. He would make a follow-up vlog post once filming concluded and another when it went streaming. Afterwards, that might be it. Would his five hundred million followers want to keep following the mundane life of a retired seventy-three-year-old man? Well, it was never too late to get into drugs, especially since, as of last week, all of them were now legal. He could try a new drug every day and post about his experiences.

Oliver proceeded down the hall, pausing at the supercomputer room. He didn't have the access card required to enter, but he could gaze through an indestructible window. That's where his costars resided, where the set was located, and where the scripts were often composed. Deep Fakes and AI had led to the creation of artificial actors who only existed inside computers.

Artificial actors could be modeled after any actor or actress or have a unique appearance. AI actors didn't need to be paid or pampered. They never argued with the directors or showed up inebriated. No scandals or scheduling conflicts. Their ages could easily be changed along with their weight, muscle mass, skin, and gender. They never died. Unpopular ones were put into storage or demoted to extras. Most importantly though, AI actors believed they were whatever characters they were assigned.

It wasn't even acting, but maybe that was the point. Real emotions from fake people would always strike harder than fake emotions from real people. Oliver tapped the glass and sighed. An entire profession was dead because of a bunch of ones and zeros. There was always the theater, but Oliver never acted on stage. The eyes of the audience would devour him. He had spent most of his life being other people. How was he going to handle just being himself?

Oliver continued to the VR room. It was the coldest room in the building, not that he cared. All that stood in the room was a solitary leather chair with a virtual reality headset attached to its top. It would allow Oliver to go inside the "movie" and interact with the artificial actors who would be cast as people he had known throughout his life. No, it would be more than that. They would be perfect facsimiles of those who had played a role in sculpting Oliver into the man he was today.

This saunter down memory lane would have plenty of pitfalls. Well, at least he had no ex-wives waiting there since marriage had never been his bag. No resentful brats either, although he regretted that. There would be a lot of angry women, though, who hated him for the stuff he did and the stuff he didn't do. Oliver would have to re-experience his parent's divorce, his brother's suicide, and getting shot in the back by a crazed hooker in Germany.

Oliver scratched his stubble and chuckled darkly. He knew you couldn't make a biopic without all the juicy bits. But this was going to destroy his wholesome image. Who was he kidding? He never had a wholesome image. Although Oliver wasn't looking forward to receiving a bullet to the back again.

Not that he would feel any pain. When real actors got into an AI film, they felt no unpleasant sensations. The AI in charge of this film had not written a script. Instead, it would toss Oliver into the highlights of his life and edit them into a coherent narrative. Oliver sat in the comfortable chair and put the headset on. By turning the headset on, his body was instantly immobilized so he would remain in the chair no matter what he experienced. The room vanished in a surge of dazzling light. Oliver was in his old studio apartment with the synthetic polar bear fur carpets. God, this place was smaller than his eighth bathroom. His ex-costar, Fatima, stood frozen, waiting for the scene to begin.

A prompt appeared with scene directions along with a timer showing he had five minutes till the AI director called action. Oliver quickly rushed to the mirror by the waterbed and checked himself out. He was twenty with a mane of long brown hair instead of the white buzz cut he had now. He looked like an Abercrombie & Fitch model, which he was at that time. He'd also been starring in General Hospital, America's last remaining soap opera, until this day, when he left it and ended things with Fatima.

Oliver stood on the highlighted space, and the timer hit zero. A robotic voice called. "Action!"

Fatima sprang to life. "Do you really want to drop everything so you can spend eight months in Morocco for a three-minute scene that probably won't make it into the film!"

The AI had captured the raw frustration perfectly. Fatima looked so stunning when she was mad. "Babe, it's a remake of Casablanca. Even if they cut out my scene, I'd rather be involved with that than this shitty soap opera!"

Fatima took a step back. She'd acted on General Hospital since she was six, while Oliver had only been on the show for six months. That had been six months too long. "This shitty soap opera is my life, Oliver!"

"Well, it isn't mine. Look, I don't feel like doing a long-distance thing, so why don't we end things now."

"What...no..."

Fatima looked like a wounded deer with agony in her eyes and hurt in her voice. The AI had to be adding it in for dramatic effect. It could not have been that bad, right? A part of Oliver wanted to save their relationship. But he couldn't because that's not what happened. "Look, we're just fuck friends, after all. Our time together meant nothing, so don't get your thong in a thorn bush."

Loathing consumed Fatima like fire, and her left hand twitched. Yes, that had happened. To this day, Oliver didn't know if she was thinking about hitting him. If she had, he would have happily hit her back. Instead, like in real life, Fatima took a deep breath and crossed her arms. "I thought we could be more. But clearly, you're not man enough for that."

The scene changed. Oliver was in his old Miami mansion wearing a tie-dye robe. He was cutting a lime for his tequila on the kitchen cutting board. Oliver patted his head and face. Sure enough, he had a mustache and a mullet. He knew he was forty-six now, at the height of his popularity, currently filming the fifth Space Badger film. Those movies had been stupid as shit, but they made him a shit ton of money. He put that all at risk when he slept with the wife of the franchise's director, Doug Dome. When the timer hit zero, Oliver knew Doug would be pounding at his door, ready to confront him. In real life, Oliver had tried to deny the whole affair. However, Doug had seen through his bullshit and gave him a good kick in the crotch. This time though, Oliver was going to own it. The outcome would still be the same anyway.

The timer clocked down to zero, and the AI director called out, "Action."

Furious knocking resounded from the front door. "Oliver, I know you're in there! Open the damn door!"

Oliver took a sip of his tequila and answered the door. Doug barged in. He had been dead for decades but stood before Oliver very much alive. Oliver guessed he was like that now, a sad old, pudgy man. Except for the pudgy part, he was currently as fit as a falcon. Spit flew from Doug's mouth as he yelled loud enough to wake up everyone in China. "I know you've been fucking my wife, Oliver. The best boy told me everything!"

It was time to do this the way he should have. Oliver twirled his glass and took another sip. "Well, what goes around comes around. After all, you cheated on all your former wives."

"We both know I never cheated on her!"

Oliver grinned. "Yeah, but it was easy for me to make her think you were."

Doug's fist slammed against Oliver's face. Crushing pain pulsed through him as blood gushed from his nose. Pain, no! He shouldn't be feeling anything. Oliver hit the floor as Doug came at him like a rabid boar. Oliver had too much adrenaline to think of logging out. Instead, he dashed back to the kitchen, snatched a knife, and held it out. "Stay back!"

"Fuck you!"

Doug lunged at Oliver, grappling for his knife. Oliver jabbed it into his sternum. Still, Doug clawed at him, so Oliver stabbed him once more. This time much deeper. Doug fell like a demolished skyscraper. Oliver was far from finished. He kept stabbing Doug long after he was dead and only stopped when his arm grew tired. Oliver tossed the bloody blade aside.

The AI director shouted out. "Retake!"

Everything reset, and this time Oliver stuck to the accurate depiction of events. Still, he should not have felt that punch. It had to be a glitch or something. The scene changed, and Oliver awoke in his childhood bedroom wearing his Star Wars pajamas. His toys and video games were strewn around the floor, and the notebook on his desk was splayed open with a freshly colored page. Oliver flipped through it. In reality, there had been many drawings in it, but the AI had only selected one since it was all that was necessary for the scene. Oliver spoke in a voice that hadn't hit puberty. "When is this?"

A date popped up next to the timer: July 14th, 2035. Oliver's heart raged, and his entire body quivered. Fresh tears streaked down his cheeks. Oliver knew what was going to happen when the timer hit zero. When Oliver was eleven, his parents attended a weeklong therapy session to save their marriage. So, they called Uncle Dan to babysit him and his little brother Anthony. Uncle Dan was the cool uncle who lived in a van and sold meth. Oliver and Anthony loved having him around. On this night, though, he entered Oliver's room and violated him.

When finished, he went to Anthony's room and subjected him to the same evil. However, it lasted a lot longer. Oliver heard everything, and he just laid on the floor and did nothing, even though his cell phone was on his desk. Dan had been too high to notice. Dan said he would kill them if they told anyone. They never did, even after Dan OD'd the following summer. Thirty years later, when Anthony jumped in front of a bullet train, his daughter asked Oliver why he did that, and Oliver couldn't say anything. The AI could not have found this information online, so how did it know? The timer was ticking away. When it hit zero, Dan would be coming through that door. The scene would cut out, of course, before anything happened. Maybe cutting away to his brother's funeral. Oliver couldn't go through with this. He couldn't see Dan again. He shouldn't have to. "Skip to the next scene! Skip to the next scene!"

Nothing happened. "Log me out! Log me out!"

Still, nothing. There had to be some severe glitch in the computer for it not to release him. The timer was at five seconds. "Pause the countdown. I need more time to rehearse!"

The timer stopped at one second. "I want to access the manual fail-safe."

A screen popped up with the icon for the emergency logout. Hopefully, it still worked. Otherwise, Oliver would have to try to contact the IT department. But they were all AIs, too; if this was a virus, it could also affect them. Oliver muttered a prayer and pressed on the logout tab. He woke up in the chair and tumbled onto the floor. When his vision cleared, he saw a dozen studio executives standing around him in fine Italian suits. The film's executive producer, Jonathan Bowman, led the pack. "You're not done filming yet, Mr. Tipps."

Oliver blinked in confusion. "How did the computer know… I didn't ever tell anyone about that night!"

Mr. Bowman sighed. "The AI we selected composes scenes not based on the information gathered online but on your memories. Now, are you going to get back in? We want to be streaming tonight."

Oliver shook his head. "No, no, that's not happening. I'm done!"

"That's not wise, Mr. Tipps."

"I said I'm done!"

Mr. Bowman pulled a beretta from his belt and pressed it against Oliver's skull. "Either you finish the film, or I'm finishing your life."

Oliver laughed. This couldn't be real. He still had to be inside the computer. It would make sense for Mr. Bowman to threaten to sue him for a breach of contract. But threatening to kill him was beyond extreme. "Redo the scene from the beginning!"

Nothing happened, except Mr. Bowman looked more pissed. Did that mean this was real, or was the computer malfunctioning severely? Either way, he did not want Jonathan to pull the trigger. "Fine, let's just skip over that part. It will turn audiences off."

Mr. Bowman replied, "No, it's the only way they will sympathize with you."

Sadly, he was right. Oliver got up, sat back in the chair, put the helmet on, and logged back in. Instead of appearing in his childhood home, he was back in the VR room. Only he wasn't sitting in the chair but standing next to it. Mr. Bowman and his goons were standing like wax dolls. "Hey! Hey!"

Oliver clapped his hands in front of Mr. Bowman's face. No response. He punched his groin with as much strength as he could muster, but still got no reaction. "Start the scene!" Oliver shouted. Everything remained still. Oliver ran his hands through his thin hair. "Grant me access to the manual fail-safe."

This time nothing happened. Oliver tried to contact the IT department but couldn't get through. He stomped his feet against the ground. "What the hell is going on?"

This confirmed that the computer was indeed malfunctioning. Now it wouldn't even let Oliver leave. He had to think of something. There had to be a way out. He didn't trust Mr. Bowman to free him, that's if his encounter with him had even been real. Oliver sat on the floor, drumming his knuckles against his knees. He had to think of something. Well, he was still in the film. What if he rewound it to the very beginning? Would that allow him to log out? Probably not, but it was better than doing nothing. "Go back to the first scene."

Oliver found himself standing back outside Studio 51. The fat raindrops were falling on him again and were just as frigid. No, the first scene in the film was him and Fatima in their old apartment. Why was the computer selecting his arrival at Studio 51 as the film's first scene? "Pause," Oliver shouted.

The barrage of icy raindrops froze in place. Although, now Oliver felt a far more profound kind of cold. How had he arrived at Studio 51? Had he walked or driven? Was he having some senior moment? He'd never had lapsed memory issues before. "Show me scene select."

Small card-sized screens popped up all around him. Showing him thousands of moments from his entire life. Oliver found himself glued to one screen that showed him climbing a cliff on Mars. Oliver clicked on the screen and found himself standing in a blue space suit atop the ridge. He appeared to be in his mid-thirties. He had no memory of this, then suddenly he did, and it was as vivid as anything else that had ever happened in his life. How could anyone forget something like that? What if the computer had created this memory?

What if he was just an artificial actor who only believed himself to be real? Perhaps the reason for all these glitches was that the computer didn't know how to make a film about an artificial actor and was overwhelmed. Oliver's outrageous and depressing life did seem almost like something more fitting a screenplay than reality. After all, who has a meth dealer babysit their kids?

What was the point of anything if his whole life was just a simulation? All the misery, all the pain, the fame, the pleasure, and the excitement would be meaningless. Oliver sank to his knees. There had to be some way to prove that he was real. Wait, he could ask the AI director, "What is the title of this film?"

The AI director responded. "The Last Actor."

"What's the genre?"

"A biopic."

That gave Oliver a degree of relief. "Am I the real Oliver Tipps? Or just an AI who's programmed to believe that I am him?"

"You're the star of this production."

"What kind of answer is that?"

Silence. No matter how many times Oliver asked, or how many ways he worded his question, it refused to give him a straight answer. Eventually, Oliver gave up. He didn't know whether he was the genuine Oliver Tipps or a replicant. Either way, he was trapped in this broken film, and he didn't know when the computer would fix whatever this glitch was. All Oliver knew was that he didn't want to be alone on Mars anymore.

He accessed the scene selection and clicked on his breakup scene with Fatima. When he looked back on everything, whether it was his life or not, his relationship with Fatima had been the closest thing he ever had to love. Going against the actual events would make the AI director restart the scene again and again. But Oliver didn't want to stick to the truth of what occurred anymore. He wanted to revisit all the bad decisions he'd made in his life and find out, even if for only a moment, what would have happened if he'd made the right ones.

Matthew McKiernan was born in Cranford New Jersey in 1990 and moved to Yardley Pennsylvania in 1994. He graduated from LaSalle University in 2013 with a BA in English and History. He received his MFA in Creative writing at Rosemont College in May 2016. He has published over nineteen short stories in various genres, most of which are available on Amazon.

Thank you…

Thank you for taking the time to read our collection. We enjoyed all the stories contained within and hope you found at least a few to enjoy yourself. If you did, we'd be honored if you would leave a review on Amazon, Goodreads, and anywhere else reviews are posted.

You can also subscribe to our email list via our website,
Https://www.cloakedpress.com

Follow us on Facebook
http://www.facebook.com/Cloakedpress

Tweet to us https://twitter.com/CloakedPress

We are also on Instagram
http://www.instagram.com/Cloakedpress

Join us on TikTok @Cloakedpressllc

If you'd like to check out our other publications, you can find them on our website above. Click the "Our Books" button on the homepage for more great collections and novels from the Cloaked Press Family.